add color to my Sunset Sky

A NOVEL

add color to my Sunset Sky

A NOVEL

BAHORA SAITOVA

ADD COLOR TO MY SUNSET SKY

Editor Jessica Powers
Cover design by Caitlin B. Alexander
Book design by Annemieke Beemster Leverenz

ISBN: 978-1-7778974-2-0

First Edition 2022

10 9 8 7 6 5 4 3 2 1

To my mom,
for her unconditional love
&
To my little sister,
for being one of a kind

CHAPTER ONE

HAYDEN

"Come on, Hayden, jump already!" Hayden's physical education teacher sounded as impatient as he looked.

Hayden suppressed a sigh and focused on the swimming pool beneath him, trying to focus on his breathing. *Come on, Hayden, you can do it. It's just water. Suck it up and do it already.*

His hands dampened as he squeezed them to prevent them from shaking. He could feel his classmates eyeing him curiously, some mockingly.

First day of school. First class of the year and it had to be the swimming class.

Closing his eyes, Hayden dived into the pool and found himself submerged in water, the world deafening around him.

He couldn't see anything. Couldn't hear anything. He tried to breathe and realized his mistake a split second too late before the chlorine water filled his nostrils and he felt the burning sensation all the way to his brain.

He tried to make his way upwards but realized he had lost his sense of direction. Where was the surface? Panic submerged him as the water closed down on him, pushing him further down. *That's it, I'm going to die.*

As he tried to push against the water, battling with the heavy mass surrounding him, he felt someone grab him and drag him to the surface.

As soon as he felt the pool border, he grabbed the cold marble and broke above the water, gulping the air greedily. Never had oxygen seemed so sweet before.

He coughed and sputtered and tried to regain his senses.

"You alright, mate?" asked Kane, keeping himself above water, his dark eyes filled with concern, his straight, black hair plastered to the forehead.

"Yeah, better now," said Hayden before coughing some more. He hated chlorine. He hated pools and he hated swimming.

"Hayden," called his teacher as he approached him.

"You still alive?" he asked gruffly, but Hayden could see he was worried.

"Yes, sir. Just had a bad cramp," he lied, hoping he sounded convincing and feeling embarrassed by all his classmates' eyes on him.

"If you can't do the laps today, you can sit it out," said

Mr. Roy as he made his way to the other students. "Come on, guys, let's start those laps already!"

"Thank you, Kane," said Hayden once the teacher left, turning to his best friend.

"You scared the shit out of me," Kane said, a relieved smile on his face.

"Sorry, my foot started cramping when I got in the water," said Hayden, avoiding his piercing eyes.

"Kane Lee, you don't have all day. I want you to swim already," yelled their teacher, a frown on his face as he watched them from the other side of the pool.

"Have fun doing those laps," said Hayden with a smile to let his friend know he was okay, even if his heart was still beating so fast he was afraid it would hammer through his chest. He got out of the pool and went to the benches where he grabbed his towel. The floor was freezing under his naked feet, and he hated the feeling of being wet. *One semester. You can do it for one semester.*

He sighed, already feeling that the four months until the end of December would be long indeed.

His high school's curriculum made swimming classes mandatory in Grade 11, and unless he came up with some extraordinary reason, he had no choice but to take it.

Thank God he at least knew how to swim.

His father was always adamant he learned how to swim, and Hayden winced as he remembered the horrible swimming lessons he had with various instructors who taught the scared boy how as best as they could.

Hayden could never understand his fear of drowning or even where it came from, but for as long as he could remember, he had had this irrational fear.

He had even asked his father if he had had a bad experience when he was small, but his father had told him to stop being ridiculous.

You need to overcome your fear of swimming by learning how to swim, his father said.

Hayden knew he was not afraid of water, but for some reason, whenever he thought of getting in a body of water like a pool or a beach, it made him queasy.

The day flew by, and Hayden couldn't have been more grateful.

"Only the first day of school, and so much work already," Kane groaned as they made their way to the lockers.

Olivia, his other best friend, was already waiting for them. She smiled when she saw them approach.

"Hey guys, want to go to Timmies and grab an iced coffee?" Olivia pulled the straps of her bag higher on her shoulder.

"I can't," said Hayden. "I have soccer practice, and I better hurry. Coach Franck will have my head if I'm even one minute late."

"We can wait for you," said Olivia.

"Yeah, I was planning to go to the library to work on my project, anyway," said Kane.

"Me, too, I'll work on my history homework," said Olivia.

"Great. I'll meet you in one hour, then," said Hayden.

He loved soccer, but their coach could be ruthless, always pushing them to work harder, be better, and while it made them a very good team, the end of each practice session felt like his whole body had been pulverized a thousand times over.

Since his little accident in the pool, he had felt lethargic most of the day, and after the grueling workout, his muscles were screaming for mercy. It was too much for one day.

He thought he'd weep with joy when practice ended and he ran to the lockers.

"Where's the fire, Hemingway?" asked Kurt Anderson, the captain of the team, looking at Hayden with a raised eyebrow.

"Nothing, Kane and Liv are waiting for me. Man, I'm so glad the day is done," he sighed as he put his stuff in his soccer bag. He felt droplets of water run down his neck where his hair was still wet. He had taken a shower in record speed.

"Gotta go, see you," said Hayden as he waved a quick goodbye, not waiting for his friend's reply.

Hayden went to meet his friends who were already waiting for him outside of school. After ordering iced coffee—a welcome refreshment in the heat of the first day of September—and a box of TimBits, Hayden, Kane and Olivia headed to the park in front of the school.

The park was crowded with families and teenagers alike. They sat on a bench, enjoying their drinks and the warmth of the day.

"Look at that cute dog," said Olivia, pointing to an adorable white Lab fetching a ball for his owner, a small boy with a green cap.

Hayden watched the boy throw the ball again, but this time, the ball went too far and landed behind Hayden, in the bushes.

He knew the pup wouldn't be able to find it, so he got up and went to retrieve it.

Not wanting to hurt the little boy by throwing the ball at him, he approached him to give him the ball.

"Thank you, young man," said the boy's grandmother, approaching behind her grandson.

Her smile turned to elated surprise as she took a closer look at him.

"Hayden, is that you?" she exclaimed happily.

Hayden looked at the older woman, unsure of what to say, as for the life of him he couldn't remember ever seeing her.

"Yes," he said finally, "it's me."

"I knew it! I'd recognize those eyes anywhere. So similar to your mom's," said the woman with a big smile.

Hayden felt his insides twist painfully at the mention of his mom.

"How is she?"

Before Hayden could reply, the elderly lady continued talking, "I heard about your grandmother passing away. She used to dote on you whenever you came to this park with her and your mom."

"I'm sorry?" Hayden was getting more and more confused.

"It's been a very long time. You probably don't even remember me. I used to live here and that's how I met your grandmother and mother. I came to visit my grandkids."

"I think you're mistaken," said Hayden. The woman must have mistaken him for another Hayden.

"What?" The stranger woman looked puzzled at his words.

"My mom passed away when she gave birth to me," replied Hayden, feeling the familiar guilt assuage the pit of his stomach.

"When she gave birth to you?" repeated the woman, blinking her eyes, and now she looked as confused as Hayden felt. "But, my dear, that's impossible, since she often came to this same park with you when you were a toddler. I might be getting older, but I'm still able to recognize Aviannah's son." Her tone left no room for argument.

Hayden felt queasy, hearing his mom's name. Before he could say anything and make the woman realize her mistake, Kane joined him. "Sorry to interrupt, but we need to go, ma'am," Kane said politely, pushing Hayden gently on the shoulder when he saw his best friend wasn't moving. "Hayden, let's go," he said.

Hayden saw the older woman look at him with concern and had a hard time taking his eyes away from her. When they were a few feet away and out of earshot, Kane put a hand on his shoulder. "You alright, mate?"

Hayden nodded, too numb for words.

"Don't pay attention to that lady. Obviously, she mistook you for some other Hayden from her past and got confused."

Hayden shrugged, frowning, trying to understand why the woman said those things.

"You think she was mistaken, Kane?" asked Hayden quietly, afraid to speak loudly.

"Of course. Her story doesn't make sense at all," replied Kane. He was watching Hayden closely, looking concerned.

"Hey guys, who was that?" asked Olivia as they approached the bench where she was sitting with their drinks.

Hayden followed her gaze. The old woman kept looking at him as her grandson was pulling her arm. The child wanted to go on the slides.

Hayden turned away.

"No one, just some lady who mistook Hayden for someone else," Kane said when Hayden kept quiet. But Hayden could see he kept stealing worried glances at him. Not wanting to make his friends worry, he shrugged and nodded. "Yeah, she thought I was someone she knew," he said.

He wondered if he should mention it to his father but knew he wouldn't be able to. Anytime he had tried to bring up the topic of his mother, his dad's face would contort in pain, and Hayden, feeling guilty, would drop the subject.

Later, as he drove home, he tried to put the old woman out of his mind.

Instead, he focused on the feeling of driving his car, an old dark blue Audi A3 his dad had helped him buy by adding to the money he had saved from his salary working as a dishwasher at Ben's Cozy Home. He had been working there since he was fifteen and the owner Ben took a liking to Hayden as he was a fast worker. He did break his share of dishes, but he made up for it later, learning quickly and being diligent.

With school starting, he would only be working on the weekends again, an arrangement that Ben had agreed upon last year.

The car had been a lucky find. The owner of the car, an old man, took great care of it so it looked almost brand new, and most importantly, he hadn't had to make any repairs yet. Granted, it had been only one month, but he had a good feeling this car would serve him a long time.

His dad's car, a mocha Mercedes, was already in the driveway.

"Dad?" he called as he went inside the kitchen but found it empty.

He poured himself orange juice. He was starving, and his nose picked up the mouth-watering smell of chicken pie in the oven.

Hearing voices in his father's study, he went down the corridor to find his dad. *Was he on a call with someone?*

As he got closer, he saw that the wooden door was slightly ajar, and he could hear his dad say: "Mom, I don't know if it's a good idea." He sounded tired.

His grandmother was here. That explained the baking.

"Hey Dad, hi Grandma." Hayden kissed his grandmother on the cheek.

"Hayden, how are you?" His grandmother greeted him with a warm smile, her golden-white hair done in an elegant updo as always.

"Good, I can't wait to try that amazing pie baking in the oven," he replied, grinning. He turned toward his father. "You alright, Dad?"

"Yes, yes," his father replied, giving him a strange look. "How was school? Did you arrive a long time ago?"

"No, just now," said Hayden, noticing his dad's expression. "Dad, you should stop working so hard, you look really tired."

"That's what I've been telling Liam before you came in," said his grandmother, giving her son a look Hayden couldn't decipher.

"Yes, I probably should." His dad passed his hand through his thick, blond hair.

Hayden saw his temples had started graying. When did that happen? It felt weird realizing his dad was getting old. And scary. His dad was all he had.

"Dad," Hayden put a hand on his father's shoulder. "Let's go eat."

His dad's pale blue eyes seemed to refocus on him, and he smiled.

"Good idea," he said.

Just then, his phone rang, and Liam froze when he looked at the caller display.

"You won't answer the call?" asked Hayden, perplexed.

"No," he said brusquely. "Enough work for the day," he said and declined the call, shutting it off.

"That seems like a wonderful idea," said Hayden, chuckling as they went to join his grandmother in the kitchen.

CHAPTER TWO

Leah

As Leah looked at all the boxes that were still left to unpack, she wanted to throw her arms up in frustration.

One box at a time. You can do it, Leah Driscoll.

She pulled up her sleeves and went to work. She could hear her father in the living room as he moved the sofa and the TV around.

She opened a box and her eyes fell on a framed picture of her mom. As always, her heart gave a painful squeeze and she tried to breathe calmly to keep the tears at bay.

She was told it gets easier with time. It had been almost two years and the pain still felt as raw as the first day.

Sighing, she picked up the golden frame and looked into her mother's laughing eyes, her curly hair, beautiful and glossy. The picture was taken when she was still healthy and as she looked at her happy face, Leah saw an image of her mom during her last days, frail and pale, trying to smile despite the pain.

A tear fell on the glass, and Leah wiped her tears, not wanting her dad to see her sadness. He was trying so hard to bring some semblance of normalcy into their life. They were like actors on stage, pretending to be happy, smiling at each other while stifling their sobs at night.

"Hey, pumpkin, need some help?" asked her dad, appearing in the doorway of her bedroom.

"No, thank you, Dad, I'm almost done," she replied with a smile. "Well, mostly," she added as she looked around her. She was nowhere near done.

"Okay, then, I'm gonna make us dinner." He gave her a small smile and went away.

She looked at her backpack on the chair and sighed. Tomorrow would be her first day of school, and she dreaded having to start Grade 11 in a new school where she knew no one, and to make it worse, she was already one day behind.

Her eyes fell on the necklace her best friend Anaya gave her on her last day in Montreal.

It was an infinity symbol with both their names engraved on it. Leah and Anaya.

Her dad had laughed. "You girls are acting as if you're moving planets apart. It's only a different city. You'll see each other often enough," he had added with a gentle smile.

The girls had looked at each other, trying not to cry.

After all, they weren't children anymore.

She missed Anaya already. She wanted to be back in her old house so bad. Her old school. Her old life.

Her phone rang and she saw with delight it was her best friend.

"Hi Anaya!"

"Leah, today was horrible without you," announced her friend dramatically. "I kept looking over my shoulder, wanting to tell you something, but I would see that annoying Jason instead."

"I miss you, too," said Leah.

She could picture her friend ruffling her black hair as she glared at the wall where posters of different anime were displayed. Right now, her best friend was obsessed with Hunter x Hunter, or more precisely, the character of Kurapika.

Leah had tried to watch the anime with her, but could never get into it, and soon gave up.

Give her *Lord of the Rings* any time, and she'd rewatch it for the hundredth time with as much enthusiasm as the first time.

"Are you done unpacking?"

"Kinda," answered Leah, trying not to get discouraged by the view in front of her. She went to sit on the bed.

"I'm dreading tomorrow," she said, closing her eyes, trying to keep her voice steady.

"I know how you feel," said Anaya, her voice quiet. After all, she knew how much of an introvert Leah was and that it took her a long time to get close to people.

After the loss of her mom, she had withdrawn and only Anaya had stayed by her side.

"I wish your grandfather could have moved to Montreal instead of you having to move all the way to Bellevue," said Anaya.

"I know, but Dad's brother and his family are all here, and I knew it would do my dad good," said Leah, thinking of how tired her dad had been trying to run the house, look after his sick wife and take care of his teenage daughter.

"It's okay, we'll visit each other many times," said Anaya.

"Didi, dinner is ready!" Leah heard Anaya's little brother, Ishan, say on the other side of the line.

"How many times did I tell you to knock?" sighed Anaya, annoyed.

"Sorry, Di, but Ma told me to call you," the little boy replied.

Leah smiled, remembering the bright boy who was already extremely smart for his ten years.

"I have to go eat, Leah, I'll talk to you tomorrow, okay?"

"Okay, *bon appétit*," said Leah.

"*Bonne chance pour demain!*" said her friend, wishing her good luck for tomorrow as if she was going on some battlefield.

"Thanks, I feel like I'll need it."

She hung up and already felt nostalgic. She remembered the countless dinners at the Patel house, the delicious meals Mrs. Patel always made.

Her smile faded as she remembered how Mrs. Patel had held her when they came back from the hospital the day her mom died. She had hugged her so tight Leah had wished she would never let her go. She felt she would crumble without her strong grasp.

"It's going to be alright, *beti*," Mrs. Patel had said as she kissed her head. *Beti* meant daughter in Hindi, and Leah had realized she would never be able to hold her mom like this. Nor would she ever feel her arms around her anymore.

She thought she would never stop crying then. It felt beyond impossible to ever feel normal again. Happiness was out of the question.

Through her blurred vision, she saw Anaya stand beside her, silent tears rolling down her cheeks.

"Leah, dinner is ready!" called her dad and snapped her back to the present.

You need to be strong, Leah. For Dad.

She went to the bathroom and splashed cold water on her face to lessen the puffiness of her eyes. If her dad noticed she had been crying, he didn't comment on it, and she was glad for it.

Their first dinner in the new house was quiet, the acute awareness that they were not in their house too strong for them to pretend everything was fine.

The first day in a new school and already she was running late. Leah had had a hard time falling asleep yesterday night and missed her alarm, waking up outrageously late and running around the house like a madwoman to get ready.

She borrowed her dad's car as he was working from home on Tuesdays, and she thanked God for the small grace as she would have completely missed the first period if she had had to take the bus.

She arrived in the parking lot of the school and saw one spot available. Thank God! She wouldn't need to waste time finding parking.

Just then, a dark blue car drove in from the opposite direction and stole her spot.

"Hey!"

Leah got her head out of the open window. "That was my spot!" she yelled to the blond guy who came out of the dark Audi as he walked past her.

"Really? I didn't see anybody's name on it," said the blond with a raised eyebrow, looking at her as if she was mad.

"I saw it first, I even got here first!" she said, glaring at him.

"Well, I parked it first. Better luck next time." He smirked and went away.

"Urgh, the jerk!" screamed Leah and hit her wheel. She wasted another ten minutes looking for a new place and it was all the way on the other side.

She wanted to cry as she realized she had to run across the parking lot to the entrance of the school, and she was already late for class.

As she got inside the school, she saw it was much smaller than her previous school, which should have made it less intimidating, but Leah felt she wouldn't be able to get used to the cold atmosphere. The blue walls and the dark blue lockers felt foreign. Uninviting.

Once she was in the reception area, she asked for her schedule and the secretary gave her a dirty look.

"You're fifteen minutes late, miss," she said as she gave her the schedule.

"I know, I'm sorry."

"Don't let it happen again," said the woman, looking at Leah above her glasses, her thin lips pinched in disapproval.

Nodding, Leah took the paper and left as quickly as possible. She could feel her cheeks burn.

She ran in the corridor, looking desperately for her class. Finally, she found the door she was looking for—D28—and opened the wooden door apprehensively.

"Good morning," she said timidly as she got in the class.

The teacher, who was in the middle of explaining the curriculum, stopped talking and looked at her. As did everyone in the class. Leah tried to keep her blush at bay. Without success.

"Yes?" said the teacher.

"I'm Leah. Leah Driscoll," she said, clearing her throat so the teacher could hear her.

"Oh, yes, the new student. Please come in… Leah, you said, right?"

She nodded and stood in front of the class, looking at the teacher, trying to ignore the stares of the teenagers in front of her. Her classmates.

"You can take a seat in front of Hayden," said the teacher, pointing to the last row near the windows.

She turned to where he was pointing and saw the blond jerk from the parking lot trying to hide behind his desk, avoiding her gaze.

The nerve! Had he not taken my spot, I would have avoided this embarrassing situation right now, thought Leah angrily.

She made her way to the desk and—sending daggers with her eyes toward Hayden—sat in front of him.

"So, as I was saying, this year, we'll start by reading two novels by John Steinbeck, *Of Mice and Men* as well as *The Grapes of Wrath,"* the teacher carried on as some students groaned in the back and others smiled happily.

Leah had read *Of Mice and Men* and had loved it. She was looking forward to her English class. Although she excelled in most of the subjects, English had always been her favorite class in school.

Soon, the class ended, and the students made their way out. Leah grabbed her stuff, and her pen rolled down the desk, falling on the floor.

Before she could take it, another hand appeared in front of her and picked up the pen for her.

"Hey, Leah, right?" said the blond jerk as he got up.

Leah remembered the teacher mentioning his name. Hayden.

"Yes?" she said, her voice cold.

"Sorry about this morning. I was in a rush," he said apologetically.

"So was I," she said before she could stop herself.

"I know," he chuckled nervously, his blue eyes contrite.

"It's okay," she relented, not wanting to start the new school year on bad terms.

"I can help you around if you need some help," he said, scratching his neck.

"Thank you, I'm good," said Leah, feeling her anger fade.

"Okay, then, I guess I'll be seeing you around," he said before nodding and leaving.

Leah hurried to her next class, realizing she had no idea where it was. *Maybe I should have accepted his help while he was offering,* she thought dejectedly. *Ah well, too late now.*

During her lunch break, Leah ate her sandwich quickly and went to the library. The only place she felt safe.

As she went through the aisle, looking for a good book, she stopped in front of the classics and perused through the titles.

She saw the book she was looking for, *Notes from the Underground* by Dostoevsky, and tried to reach it, but it was on the highest shelf and her fingers couldn't grasp it.

She searched for a step stool, but it was nowhere in sight.

"Which book are you trying to get?"

Looking on her right, she saw a boy she had seen in her math class.

"This one, *Notes from the Underground,*" she said, pointing to the novel with the white and black spine.

"There you go," he said as he reached the book easily and gave it to her.

"Thank you," she said, smiling to show her appreciation.

"I'm Riley," he said, extending his hand in a handshake. "I'm in your math class."

She took his hand. "I know, I remember you from this morning." She smiled. "I'm Leah."

"You like Dostoevsky?" he said.

"I do, I've read most of his books. And you?"

"I've read *Crime and Punishment*, it was interesting, hard to read, but very thought-provoking."

"You should read *The Brothers Karamazov*. I personally find that it's his best novel," she advised.

"I'll give it a try," he said, smiling, cute dimples showing.

Lunch went in a flash, and as Leah went to her next class, she realized with delight that she and Riley shared most of her classes.

He was super kind and she found it was easy to talk to him.

"You didn't miss much, but if ever you need help, I'm here," he said as he came to say goodbye at the end of the class.

Leah thanked him, feeling so grateful for his kindness

she kept smiling like a fool.

When she went home, she let out a sigh of relief. She had survived the first day of school.

"How was the first day, pumpkin?" asked her father as they sat to eat dinner.

"It was good," said Leah as she took a piece of her lasagna.

"How are your classmates and teachers?" Her dad's forehead creased.

"They're nice," said Leah, not wanting to make her father worry unnecessarily. She was a big girl. She could handle being in a new environment. No big deal.

"You'll see, before you know it, you'll get used to the new school," her dad comforted her.

Leah continued to chew her lasagna and nodded, thinking about Riley and realizing that for a first day, it had gone pretty well.

When she sat in bed, her laptop on her lap, she scrolled through the school's website. She had seen an announcement on the walls near the lockers where they were looking for a writer for the school's journal, and she had been excited at the prospect.

There it was. The link where she could postulate for the

position. They were asking for a sample of her writing, and she attached an article she had been working on and felt proud of.

She hesitated before pressing submit and took a deep breath. *You can do it, Leah. You want it.*

Before she could change her mind, she pressed the green button and closed her laptop.

Now, all she could do was wait.

Feeling tired, she went to bed. Lying on her bed, looking out of the window, she saw the moon, radiant and full, watching her with a twinkle in its glowing face.

She turned to her nightstand where the picture of her mom rested, her mom's laugh forever immortalized, and sent it a kiss.

"I love you, Mom," she said, finally managing to fall asleep.

CHAPTER THREE

Hayden

Hayden was sitting on the beach, playing with the sand, his chubby fingers strangely small, his feet like that of a toddler's. He was trying to build a castle and was failing miserably.

Other kids were playing while their parents watched over them.

He turned around and saw a woman sitting on the sand, looking sad. She was not paying attention to him, but Hayden knew he knew that woman. He just didn't know how or from where.

He wondered if he should go play in the water as the sand burned his naked feet, but he felt apprehension grab his heart.

He approached the woman, trying to get her attention, but her long, blond hair was like a veil between them. A wall.

As he turned toward the beach, he saw that they were

alone, everyone had disappeared, even the sun had left. A lone seagull was flying in the last of the sun's rays, and he could hear its distant squawking.

He couldn't understand the painful tugging at his heart, and why it started beating so fast.

The woman sat beside him, and he could see tears falling down her cheeks. The sight caused him pain, and he tried to speak, but his throat kept closing off.

He looked at the sky and saw that it had turned dark and lost its serene atmosphere. The ocean got angry, the waves crashing against the shore, and the seagull flew away, screeching.

He turned to the woman to tell her that they should head home, only to discover that he was alone.

"Mom!" he screamed, but his screams were taken away by the howling wind.

Hayden woke up, drenched in sweat, and breathing heavily. He looked at the clock on his nightstand and saw it was only 3:45 a.m.

His heart slowed down as he realized that it had been a nightmare.

Again. Always the same one. And each time he woke up with a sense of profound loss.

He knew that the woman in his dreams was his mom. He had seen her pictures. What he couldn't understand was why his mind kept imagining he was a toddler every time he was around her if she had died in childbirth.

He knew it was his brain's way of making up for the fact

that he never had to spend time with his mom, and his fear of swimming seemed stronger in those dreams. He was constantly near a body of water, whether a beach or a pool, whenever his mother was in the dream.

He never talked to his dad about his nightmares as his dad always got withdrawn whenever he tried to bring up the topic of his mother, so he had stopped talking about her altogether. All he was left with were unanswered questions.

What was she like? What kind of movies did she like? How did her laugh sound? What did she like to eat?

Small things like that would have meant the world to Hayden. He couldn't understand how he felt such acute loss when he had lost her before he even got the chance to know her.

He breathed and rubbed his face. He needed to fall asleep if he wanted to be awake in class and he had soccer practice. His coach would kill him if he didn't give his best as they had a match coming up soon.

Tossing and turning, he finally managed to fall asleep only to wake up even more exhausted the next morning.

As he dragged himself to the kitchen, he saw that his dad had already left for work as usual.

He yawned and resisted the urge to go back to bed.

I can already feel it will be a bloody fantastic day, thought Hayden with a sigh as he poured himself coffee. He didn't enjoy the bitter drink, but he knew that if he wanted to survive the day, he needed caffeine in his system.

He added cream and lots of sugar to try to sweeten his cup of coffee and grimaced when the bitterness still bit his tongue.

Eating quickly, he grabbed his stuff and drove to school.

As he made his way to his locker, he saw that Kane and Olivia were already there. Olivia was excited, showing Kane something on her phone.

“Hey guys, what’s up?” Hayden asked.

“Hayden, good morning,” said Olivia with a bright smile. “Hey mate, you look like shit,” said Kane, ever truthful. Olivia laughed.

“Thanks, Kane, you sure know how to make one feel better,” deadpanned Hayden.

“I aim to please,” replied Kane with a chuckle.

“Let’s go to class already,” said Hayden with a roll of his eyes, while fighting the smile that made his way to his face. Already, he felt better, having forgotten his bad night. Trust Kane to always put him in a good mood.

He approached the door to his English class and saw the new student, Leah, standing near the door and talking to someone who had his back to him but strangely familiar.

As he got close, he saw that it was none other than Riley Connors, and he felt his light mood evaporate. Trust the douche to prey on unsuspecting new girls.

Just then the other boy turned around and their eyes met. Hayden knew the same scowl was on his face as the one he was witnessing on Connors’s features.

His eyes fell on Leah who looked at him, perplexed. She had sensed the tension in the air. Even a blind person would.

He walked past. He had thought the girl was smart, but apparently, she wasn't if she had fallen for the likes of Connors, judging by her smitten smile.

As soon as he thought of Riley, he felt his blood boil and tried to distract himself by catching up on his reading.

Leah sat in front of him in silence and Hayden thought she would simply ignore him, but she turned to look at him, her expression almost shy.

"Hayden, right?"

He nodded, looking at her with a raised eyebrow.

"I heard you play soccer."

"I do," he said, wondering where she was going with this.

She put her bangs behind her ear and cleared her throat.

"I was actually asked to do an interview with you as you got the award for the best player of the season last year and I was wondering if we could meet up so I can ask you a few questions so the others can see how a student-athlete's life is."

He smiled, trying not to look too smug.

"Sure, when do you want to do it?" he asked.

"What about tomorrow?"

"I have soccer practice."

"Okay, then I guess we can meet on Saturday if you don't mind?" she asked.

"Sure, let's meet at the Tim's down the street, in front of

the pharmacy," said Hayden. All the students went to that Tim Horton to hang out after school as it was the biggest café in the area.

"Okay, sounds good. Will one o'clock do?

"Fine with me," said Hayden. "We actually have a match tomorrow night. You can come and watch if you want."

She nodded, and turning toward her desk, took a post-it and jotted down something on it before giving it to him.

"My phone number, just in case," she said.

He nodded and put it inside the cover of his notebook. She was about to say something else, but the teacher came in and she turned toward the front of the class.

The day seemed interminably long and hot, and Hayden wondered about skipping practice, but the irate face of Coach Franck dissuaded him quickly. Whenever the coach was angry, it wasn't a pretty sight. His thick neck got so red that even his short hair cut close to his scalp became pink.

No, better die than miss practice, Hayden decided, wisely.

After the practice ended, he drove home, his sore muscles protesting as he pressed the brake. He consoled himself with the knowledge that he'd be sleeping like a baby tonight.

He parked his car in the driveway and made his way inside.

His dad was in his office, walking to and fro, agitated.

"Dad?" He opened the door and the sight of his dad on the phone, pale and shaken, made Hayden speechless.

His dad squeezed the phone.

"Dad, what's going on?" asked Hayden, worried, as he took some steps toward him.

His father looked lost and stayed silent. "Dad, who are you talking to?" asked Hayden, apprehension making his blood pump.

"I'll call you later," said his dad abruptly as he disconnected the call. "It's nothing," he said, untying his tie and avoiding Hayden's eyes.

"You sure? It sure didn't look like nothing," said Hayden as he studied his father's face and saw how haggard he looked.

"It's just work stuff," said his dad, throwing the phone on the couch and rubbing his face.

"Can I do anything?" asked Hayden.

His dad's eyes got strangely bright. Hayden didn't like seeing his dad like that. His dad was always smooth and in control of everything. Who was that man in front of him who seemed almost scared?

"Don't worry about it, son," he finally said as he put a hand on his son's shoulder and squeezed it lightly.

"Okay," conceded Hayden, not wanting to upset his father further.

No more mention was made of the phone call as his dad went to make dinner, but Hayden wondered if maybe his dad was having financial problems with his company.

He'd try to find out from his grandma next time.

The next day, as Hayden put on his soccer uniform, he thought about Leah. She seemed like the type of girl who didn't enjoy sports. He doubted she would come to the game.

He wondered if his dad would have time to make it. He hoped he would. In the last game of last year, he was there, and Hayden had never played better. The whole season he had been good, but he simply killed the last game, scoring three goals—a personal achievement he was proud of.

He wondered if he had a chance to get a scholarship. He still had this year and the next to go before college, but his coach had mentioned the options. *If you keep working hard enough, you might be eligible,* said Coach Franck, proud and beaming.

When they got on the field, he saw that a lot of people had come.

"Hayden!" He turned toward the stands and saw his dad wave at him, Kane and Olivia beside him, smiling big. His face broke into a big grin, and he waved back. He felt pumped now.

"Come on, guys, let's play our best tonight," said Coach Franck as all the players got around him.

"Yes, Coach," they replied in unison. They were all ready to beat their opponents.

Kurt smiled at Hayden. They were thinking about the same thing.

Just then, Hayden's attention was caught by a lone silhouette making her way through the bleachers. Leah Driscoll had come to the game.

Look at that, who would have thought. Despite himself, he smiled.

"Hayden!" said his coach.

"Yes, coach?"

"Focus on the game," said the older man looking at him with his piercing eyes.

"Yes, coach." His coach never missed a thing.

He was going to play his best as he always did. He never let his team down.

CHAPTER FOUR

Leah

Leah made her way toward the bleachers and took a seat. The game was supposed to start soon. She saw with surprise that a lot of people had gathered to watch the match. Or maybe it was normal for such a game. She couldn't tell as it was her first.

However, she hadn't let her ignorance of the sport get in the way and had researched the basic rules of soccer in order to follow the game. All in all, the sport seemed pretty simple and easy to follow. She just hoped she wouldn't fall asleep out of boredom.

She sat beside some boy who smiled at her. She couldn't remember his name but knew he was in some of her classes.

"Have you seen them play before?" she asked.

He turned and looked at her critically. She became self-conscious. Should she have kept her novice status under wraps? "You're the newbie, right?"

"Yeah," she admitted, her smile embarrassed.

"Then you won't regret coming today," he exclaimed, breaking into a wide grin. "The Fierce Lions are the best! They won the regional high school tournament last year," he added, proudly.

"Yes, I heard. I'm supposed to write an article on one of the players—Hayden Hemingway."

"He's a very good player. They're all amazing. We have the strongest team," said the redhead, beaming like a proud papa sharing the exploits of his children.

Leah didn't know what to say after that. The redhead seemed a pretty fervent fan of the soccer team, indeed.

The excited redhead continued talking, and Leah thought he would never stop, until, finally, the game started, and the young man focused his whole attention on the field. "I'm sure we'll win," he said with pride.

Leah had to admit that her neighbor's enthusiasm was contagious. No more than a quarter of an hour into the game and their school team had already scored a goal. As the game progressed, Leah could see what the fuss was. She didn't know what she had been expecting, but certainly not this. She kept a close eye on Hayden and noticed how fast and graceful he was on the field.

As the game went on, Leah found herself more and more immersed. She held her breath as one of the players was maneuvering the ball for a goal and crossed her fingers for the goalie to prevent the rivals from scoring.

As the teams battled for victory, she wished fervently that their side would win. At that minute, she was among the Fierce Lions' most ardent fans. She no longer found the team's name ridiculous. Never had she thought that a soccer match could be so captivating. Had she known, she would have been coming to more games!

"Only two minutes are left in the game. Southampton Saints will need serious luck to tie with them in order to get a tiebreaker," said the redhead.

Leah could see from his confident air that he knew that victory was theirs. She turned to see that Hayden had gotten a pass from one of his teammates and was sprinting toward the opposite goalpost.

He took aim and shot the ball which went straight into the opposite team's goal and scored.

The referee whistled, indicating the end of the game.

"We won! What a splendid long-range goal!" exclaimed the redhead. "I told you we'd win."

The supporters of the winning team erupted in loud cries of joy and victory.

Leah smiled despite herself. She felt as elated as her classmate. She wondered if she should go see Hayden but felt awkward. After all, she hadn't come to see him specifically, but to get a better understanding of the game. He'd probably find it weird if she went to talk to him. She could simply mention she came to the game tomorrow afternoon.

She took one last glance at the field and saw that he was surrounded by the players, a big grin on his face, his hair sweaty and his cheeks red. She smiled and left the stands.

"Leah!" her best friend Anaya answered her phone.

Leah smiled. Her best friend was constantly bursting with energy. "How are you?"

"Forget about me, how were the first days? Did you meet any cute guys?"

Leah laughed. She wondered if Riley qualified as cute for Anaya who preferred boys with a wilder look.

"There's a guy in my math class who seems very nice," Leah answered.

"How nice? Boring nice or too hot to handle nice?" her friend teased.

"You're a fool," replied Leah but she had a big smile on her face. "Just normal nice. How's everyone at school? Anything interesting happened since I left?"

"I have so much to tell you. When Amanda and I went to the movies—"

"Amanda? Amanda Bouchard?" interrupted Leah. "Since when you two are friends?"

"Since always, duh," replied Anaya. "So, listen, we went

there, and you'll never guess—"

As Anaya continued to talk, Leah had a hard time shaking off the feeling of jealousy.

"Anaya, dinner's ready!" Leah could hear her best friend's mom call her and she missed Mrs. Patel's motherly hugs and her food more than ever.

"Oh, shoot, I have to go eat. You know how Mom gets whenever I don't come to the table immediately," sighed Anaya. "I'll call you later. Bye, Leah!"

As she put her phone on her night table and looked at her half-unpacked clothes, she felt so forlorn she wanted to cry. She missed her old life so much. But she promised herself she wouldn't cry anymore. She needed to be strong for her father.

"Hey pumpkin, you're not coming down to eat?" asked her father, appearing in the doorframe of her bedroom.

"Sorry, Dad, I have a lot of homework tonight," Leah lied, hoping he wouldn't notice her eyes.

He frowned. "Already?"

"Yeah, it's a new school. I'm trying to make sure I don't get behind on the workload."

Her dad smiled. "Do you want me to bring you something then? I made some pasta salad and salmon."

"No, thank you, I'll grab something later."

"Okay, pumpkin, don't stay up too late. Good night." When he left, Leah looked at her textbooks and sighed. It was going to be a long year.

CHAPTER FIVE

Hayden

On Saturday morning, Hayden was grateful for the opportunity to sleep in. He woke up to find the sun basking his room in warm light. He yawned as he stretched on the bed. It felt so good.

Yesterday's game had been fricking amazing.

He still remembered his dad's proud look.

"I'm proud of you, my son," he had said.

In all the commotion following their win, he had missed Leah's departure. He smiled as he wondered what she thought about his game.

"That was a perfect goal, my boy," his coach had said, his face red from excitement, and Hayden felt pleasure at the rare praise.

He got out of bed and went to take a shower. When

he was done, he made his way downstairs and went to the kitchen, whistling all the way. He was ravenous.

The kitchen was empty, and he found a post-it on the fridge. *In the office. Made pancakes. Love, Dad.*

Hayden shook his head. He wished his dad would stop working on Saturdays. Having only one day off a week wasn't healthy and already, the effects could be seen. His dad had been acting weird lately, always tense, always on edge.

He poured himself an orange juice and sat at the table with a plate of pancakes. The dangerously high stack was devoured in minutes and Hayden went to wash the dishes.

He looked at the clock and saw it was only 10 a.m. He had a couple of hours to work on his homework before he went to meet Leah.

As he worked on his assignments, someone rang the door. They rang again as he went down the stairs.

"Coming!" *Geez, who was that impatient?*

When he opened the door, the sight that greeted him made him stop short. His breath caught, and he thought he was hallucinating. It couldn't be. It simply wasn't possible. He was so dumbstruck he couldn't utter a word. The face that had haunted his dreams for so many years. The one he had cried for at night in his childhood.

He blinked but the woman was still there, looking real and solid. Not a dream. She looked exactly like he saw on his parents' wedding pictures, the only indication his mom had ever existed.

"Hayden," she whispered, and her eyes welled up with tears.

When he was able to speak, he let out a word he thought he would never be able to speak in his life. It escaped from his lips like a bird finally escaping its cage.

"Mom?"

"Oh, my Hayden," she said, taking a step toward him.

He felt everything around him spin. He was going to throw up, he was sure. "I don't understand," he wheezed. The emotions were assailing him, but he felt too numb to process them all.

"My baby, how you have grown," she exclaimed, extending her hands toward him.

"You can't be real," he exclaimed, feeling himself shaking, his knees getting weak.

"Is this a dream? Have I gone mad? Surely, you're a hallucination? It doesn't make sense," he whispered, desperate, grabbing his hair.

"No, Hayden, it's me. Your mom," said the woman gently.

He wasn't sure what he wanted to do: laugh or cry. "How come you're alive?" he blurted out stupidly. His question sounded so unreal. So far-fetched.

"I never died," replied his mom, looking him in the eyes.

"But how? Dad said—I don't get it…"

His knees were shaking so badly, he grabbed the door for support.

"No, no, it can't be." He could feel his heart pounding and felt his vision blurry.

She took a step toward him, and he looked at her incredulously and wished for things to make sense. "Where were you then?" he asked slowly. "All these years, where were you?"

He felt like he was looking at a stranger. And he was. This was not his mom standing here. His mom would never have left.

"I'm so sorry for leaving you, Hayden," she replied with a sob.

He looked at her sharply. Everything made sense now. That strange lady at the park was right. His mom had not died. Here she was, standing in front of him after all these years. What was she expecting?

He felt a horrible cold settle inside of him and he couldn't control his shaking. A white anger blinded him. The hate he felt must have been visible on his features, for she shrank back, and her face collapsed.

"Why did you come back?" he asked, his voice shaking. He dug his nails into his palms and welcomed the pain.

"I wanted to see you," she said, her chin trembling. He could see she was fighting tears.

If he had been in a rational state of mind, he would have realized he was hurt seeing her wounded. But as it was, all he could feel was his rage and an overwhelming desire to scream.

"I don't want to see you. I don't even know why you

assumed I would," he said, not caring how mean he sounded.

He was holding onto the door for dear life. The only solid thing that was grounding him in the present. That let him know all this was all too real.

"You left all those years ago and I… I always believed you died in childbirth, making me feel terribly guilty for causing your death, and now, you're telling me you want to see me? You gotta be kidding me."

He let out a nervous chuckle that veered toward a sob. Sweat dampened his back and his vision blurred.

"I didn't want to hurt you, I thought me leaving was for the best," she said with a small voice.

Hayden grabbed his hair. "Urgh, I want to wake up from this nightmare."

"You don't understand, Hayden," said his mom.

"I don't want to understand! You left! You never–" He stopped suddenly, trying to not cry. "I don't want to see you. Ever," he said, his voice shaking.

She started crying, hiding her face in her hands and her shoulders shaking.

Distantly, Hayden saw that she was lithe like him. But he was tall like his dad.

He winced at the feeling of betrayal that assailed him as his father crossed his mind. Why did his dad tell him such a lie? Because she asked him to? Because he wanted to protect him?

He didn't know, but he was going to find out.

The sound of his mom crying made him sick and he wanted her to leave. "Leave. Please," he choked. He wanted to beg her to stop the horrible noise.

Her face was stained with tears, and he felt something pierce his heart. No, he refused to feel remorse. He was not going to feel guilty for hurting his mom. She didn't care about him when she left, so why should he care now?

She turned and he watched as she walked away, feeling abandoned and completely alone. Closing the door hard, he fell on the floor, and bawled like a baby.

CHAPTER SIX

Leah

If there was one thing Leah absolutely abhorred, it was a lack of punctuality. She was sitting at the table, tapping her foot impatiently, surveying each person who entered the café in the hope that it was the one she was waiting for.

Leah looked at her watch for the tenth time and saw that it was already half past one. Hayden Hemingway was late, and he hadn't even had the decency to call and let her know.

She prayed he would show up, or she would be doomed. She was supposed to submit the article for Monday. She didn't want to lose her chance of writing for the school journal just because he forgot.

Why didn't I ask for his phone number? Stupid.

She took a sip of her mint tea and grimaced when she

realized it had already become cold.

"Leah?"

She looked up, expecting to see Hayden, but, instead, saw Riley.

"Riley, hi!" she said, happy to see a familiar face. Since they had so many classes together, they had started to hang out on breaks, and he had introduced her to some of his friends. She suspected he wanted to make sure she felt welcome, and she was really touched by his kindness.

"May I?" he asked, gesturing at the seat in front of her.

"Of course." She moved her notebook and book so he could have more space.

"So, what are you doing here? Besides drinking tea, that is," he added, with a smile.

"Waiting for someone who is quite late, unfortunately," she sighed, dejected, looking at her watch once again.

"Why don't you call that person? Maybe something came up."

"I wish I could, but I don't have his phone number."

At his questioning look, she explained how she had to write an article on soccer and had asked a classmate who played soccer for an interview.

"But, foolish me forgot to take his number."

"I see. And who's the player?"

"Hayden Hemingway," she said, watching his reaction as she had noticed the tension between the two the other day. Sure enough, she saw Riley grimace at the name.

"If you don't mind me asking, what happened between

you two? I can tell you two don't get along."

"It's a long story, but let's just say that because of some misunderstanding this summer, things just got worse between us, and we were never the best of friends, to be honest. So, I'm not the best person to tell you about him, as it'll be a highly biased opinion." His smile showed his cute dimples.

Leah liked Riley even more. He could have dissed Hayden, but he didn't. That showed good character.

"Well, to be honest, he didn't start with a good impression, and now he's just reinforcing my opinion of him," Leah said. "He's forty-five minutes late already. I wish I knew his address, so I could go and see him."

"I know where he lives. I can drive you."

"Oh, I don't want to waste your time."

"It's no problem. We live in the same neighborhood, and I'm heading home as it is."

As they drove to Hayden's house, Leah told him how she saw the posting for the school journal and how she hoped to get it.

"But now I might not even get it," she lamented.

Riley looked sympathetic. "I wish I was playing soccer and could help you out, but I'm not really into sports," he said.

"Books are so much better," said Leah with a big grin.

During class, they had discovered they had a very similar taste in books, especially when it came to classics, but while Leah loved high fantasy, Riley preferred science fiction.

"I couldn't agree more," Riley acquiesced, his gentle

brown eyes twinkling with pleasure. "Here we are," he said, stopping his car and indicating the light gray house.

The neighborhood was quaint and very green. Hayden's house had a beautiful lawn on the front and small hedges on each side of the sidewalk.

"I better go. I know Hemingway. He won't be pleased to see you in my company, and I want you to have the best chance possible for this."

"Thank you so much, Riley! I'm indebted to you! If ever you need anything, don't hesitate to ask," said Leah.

"Don't worry about it," he said. "You're in luck, he's home," he added.

"How do you know?" She turned toward the house.

"His car's in the driveway." He pointed to the dark blue Audi. "Good luck!"

"Thanks!" She waved as he drove away.

She turned toward the house, and breathed deeply, realizing she was nervous. "Get a grip, Leah. You want this position, remember?"

She rang the bell. No one came to the door. Not one to get discouraged easily, she rang again. Was he sleeping? *At 2 in the afternoon? The lazy sloth!*

Feeling spiteful, she kept ringing until finally she heard footsteps behind the door, and it was swung open by none other than Hayden Hemingway who was looking at her furiously. He seemed strangely disappointed when he saw it was her.

"What?" he said. He didn't even pretend to hide his annoyance.

She stood speechless for a few seconds, blinking, too stunned to speak. His anger ignited her own ire, and she decided to forego civility.

"Good afternoon to you, too." Her smile was devoid of all warmth, her tone frosty. She was trying hard not to glare at him, but she knew she was failing miserably. She didn't know what had caused him to change so much overnight, but she wasn't going to put up with his bratty attitude. "I think you forgot we were supposed to meet today at one o'clock."

She had intended to make it sound like a question, but it ended up like a statement. An accusatory one. Something flickered in his eyes as his dim brain registered the fact that he had missed their appointment. She was expecting an apology or an explanation, but instead he just scowled.

"I was busy. As a matter of fact, I'm still busy. So, if you don't mind, I'd appreciate it if we could do the interview another time."

He sounded tired and annoyed, and it irked her even more. He made it sound like she was inconveniencing him when he had agreed to this in the first place.

Trying to breathe calmly, she spoke clearly and slowly, watching his eyes turn into slits with each of her words. "As someone whose schedule is, I'm sure, constantly busy," she was sure he could detect the veiled sarcasm as clearly as if she had shouted it, “I think you would understand that I have only today to do the interview as I have to submit the article on Monday. And had you not been so busy before, we wouldn’t have this problem right now.”

His nostrils flared and she knew even before he opened his mouth that she had lost her case.

“I’m sure you can write the interview without my help, after all, we both know journalist *wannabes* aren’t reputed for their veracity. Now, excuse me, I have other important things to attend to.”

And with that, he shut the door in her face.

Not only was Leah stupefied, but the feeling of indignation and humiliation made her shake with rage.

She didn’t know what she had been expecting, but she certainly hadn’t expected Hayden Hemingway to look so angry. The last time she had seen him, he had been smiling and laid back. He had transformed from Dr. Jekyll to Mr. Hyde. What had she done to him to cause this change?

She turned to leave, but something made her stop. Why was she accepting his refusal so easily? But then again, did she really want to infuriate him even more when she had never liked conflict in the first place and had always strived to avoid it at any cost? But her feet wouldn’t move, and she decided that it was time to stand up for herself and let him know her piece of mind.

She turned and rang again. And again. Till he finally

opened the door.

"What the hell do you want? What part of 'I'm busy' didn't you get?" He was almost panting with anger, and she would have laughed had the situation been different.

She couldn't believe a person could be so condescending and mannerless. Not only did he not show up to their rendezvous, he didn't even have the decency to call to let her know he wasn't coming, and now he was throwing her out without an apology or even an explanation!

Praying to God to give her enough restraint not to slap the snobbish dimwit silly, she tried once more to get the message through his thick skull as calmly as she could. "As a reasonable person, I think you realize that it is important for one to keep your promises and engagements, and the least you could have done was apologize." She was having a hard time suppressing her irritation but knew it would be no good to lose her temper, or else her coming here would be for nothing. "I'm sure your mom taught you some basic manners," she added condescendingly before she could stop herself.

If he had been annoyed before, now he was definitely angry, Leah realized. He looked like he was trying to reduce her to ashes with his glare.

"I'd appreciate it if you keep your opinions to yourself, Miss Leah Driscoll. As it is, they're not welcome here. And no, my mom didn't teach me good manners, so I guess you're in bad luck, huh? Now you won't be able to write your article. How sad. Better luck next time."

And he closed the door in her face for the second time, leaving her seething. After some deep breaths, Leah was composed enough to think clearly. She was still going to write her article, with or without Hayden Hemingway. She could already see the headlines with her article on the front page of the newspaper: "The true face of Hayden Hemingway."

An almost savage feeling of triumph coursed through her as she imagined his expression upon seeing the student newspapers. She never knew she was this vindictive, but revenge was sweet indeed.

CHAPTER SEVEN

HAYDEN

Hayden paced his room, feeling like he was about to explode. He was still reeling from the shock of seeing his mom and was trying to assimilate this information when the door rang.

He had hoped it would be his dad. He had texted that he needed to talk urgently, but he hadn't received any response yet. Nor had his father picked up his calls.

But it turned out to be Leah Driscoll. He was annoyed at seeing her as she had chosen a really bad time to show up, and then she had reminded him about the interview. He was too irritated to do anything but snap.

The door opened and he heard his dad walk into the house. *Finally,* thought Hayden as his dad walked quickly to his bedroom. He found his feet were stuck to the floor and he couldn't move. His heart was pounding. Suddenly, he felt scared. He didn't know if he was ready to hear the truth from his father.

The door opened and his dad walked in, worried. "Hayden, what's wrong? I was in a meeting, and I couldn't take your calls. Is everything okay?"

Hayden found he couldn't speak. He was shaking so bad he could hardly focus.

"Hayden, son, are you sick?" asked his dad, approaching him quickly and taking him by the shoulders. His eyes were filled with worry and Hayden suddenly wanted to cry. His anger evaporated like a balloon, and he felt bone-weary.

"You lied to me," he whispered as he tried to keep his voice from trembling.

"What?" said his dad, frowning as worry was replaced by confusion.

"You lied to me!" yelled Hayden, pushing his dad away.

"Son, what are you talking about?" said Liam, his voice tense.

"She came to see me!" he said, looking at his dad with disgust as hate and hurt warred inside him. How could his dad lie to him about this? About his mom being *dead*?

His dad paled. He said nothing.

"Why? Why, Dad?! Why did you lie to me all this time?"

"Hayden, look, I can explain–"

"You had no right!" yelled Hayden. He didn't want to listen to an explanation.

"You need to listen to me, son," said Liam, trying to speak calmly even though Hayden could see he was shaken. His forehead was glistening with sweat, and he looked stricken, much older than his forty-three years.

Hayden laughed through his tears. "I didn't want to believe her, you know," he said. "I kept telling myself that it was impossible, that my mom was dead, even though she was standing right there in front me, real and ALIVE!"

His dad was pinching his lips, a nervous tick in his right eye.

"She told me that she had to leave," said Hayden. "Is it true?" He hated how his voice sounded so small, so scared. He was afraid of finding out the truth.

"I told her to leave, Hayden," said his dad quietly.

"You told her to leave?" repeated Hayden, feeling listless.

"You don't know the full story."

"Then tell me. Tell me what you were supposed to tell me all those years ago. Tell me the truth, Dad!"

His dad looked at him and he looked so pained, Hayden almost felt bad. But his anger consumed him whole, leaving no place for empathy.

The room was silent except for Hayden's heavy breathing, and he looked at his dad and waited.

"Your mom was not a good mom," said Liam at last. "She was not well. I got scared for your life, so I told her to leave."

"What do you mean, 'not well?'"

"She had always suffered from anxiety even when we were young. As we got older, it got worse. When her mom passed away, she fell into depression and started taking medication. I tried to help her get better, but I was already taking care of everything, and it was hard. One day, when she was giving you a bath, she fell asleep on the couch and—"

His dad stopped as if the memory was too painful to let him speak. He closed his eyes and when he reopened them, Hayden saw they were full of tears.

"You almost died that day, Hayden. I was never so scared in my life than when I found you in the bathtub, unresponsive. The doctors said it was a miracle you survived."

Hayden kept quiet, too shocked and numb to react, but so many questions were suddenly answered. His fear of drowning. His weird dreams, always surrounded by water, and his mom always sad, always unaware. It felt like some curtains he had never seen had suddenly fallen, revealing the scenery behind.

"I was so scared, so mad. We got into a huge fight. Then, she went away. I didn't know how to tell you the truth, I didn't want to hurt you with the truth, Hayden. I just let you assume she passed away."

Hayden looked at his dad and wondered if it was a nightmare. But he knew it was the reality, and that, instead, all his dreams had just been shattered. Finding out the truth had shattered all the illusions. "You never thought she would come back?"

Liam shook his head. "She left a letter before leaving. Saying she was leaving and to forget her. Those were her words." His voice sounded hollow.

Hayden was unsure what to say. His heart beat painfully and his head spun. *Breathe, Hayden. One breath at a time.* He wondered if he was going to be sick. He regretted eating all those pancakes now.

"Thank you for telling me the truth, Dad. I just wished you had told me from the beginning." He felt sick.

"Hayden–" his dad started to speak up, but Hayden didn't have the strength to listen anymore.

"No, don't," he said as he left the room and headed to the front door.

He needed to get out of the house before he suffocated.

As Hayden made his way downstairs on Monday morning, his dad appeared in the kitchen threshold.

"Hayden, can we talk please?" asked his dad as he reached the end of the stairs.

Hayden opened the door without a glance in his direction and slammed it behind him as he got out.

He could feel his blood boiling as he drove out of the driveway. He saw his dad standing at the door, his arms at his sides, looking smaller than he had remembered.

He pressed on the gas pedal with more force than

necessary and only when he reached the intersection, did he force himself to calm down.

His dad had come into his room on Sunday, asking if they could talk, but had given up when Hayden had continued to completely ignore him.

His head still couldn't comprehend the truth. He had woken up on Sunday with a sense of dread, wondering why he felt so awful. The memory of the previous day rushed in and he had felt a hole in his chest. A painful emptiness.

As he went inside the school, he wondered how he'd manage to pretend that everything was normal. Would it ever be normal again?

"Did you see the article in the journal today?" asked Carter, his classmate and one of the fellow soccer players on the team, as he approached his locker.

"No, why?" asked Hayden, perplexed.

"There, you should read it," said Carter, giving him a copy, looking at him strangely, almost unhappily.

Someone called Carter's name and the latter left to join his friends after giving Hayden one last weird look. *What was going on?*

He opened the newspaper and went through it quickly to get to the sports section. What he saw made him see red:

The Face Behind the Name: Hayden Hemingway Revealed

Those of you who are fans of soccer and our school team, the

Fierce Lions, probably know the name Hayden Hemingway. After all, he is considered by many as one of the most skillful players on the team. However, not many of you might know the real Hayden Hemingway. Today, I will reveal to you the face behind the name.

I saw the player play for the first time during the Fierce Lions' game against the Southampton Saints. Although not a great connoisseur of soccer, I noticed almost immediately that he was good. Really good. Amazing, even. His speed, his agility. The effortless way he maneuvered the ball left me in awe. Moreover, there was strategy behind his game, which spoke of intelligence and sharpness of mind. Needless to say, I was looking forward to the interview.

Unfortunately, this good impression shattered into a thousand pieces after I got to know the real Hayden Hemingway during our meeting.

We had already agreed to meet on Saturday for the interview at a place of his choosing.

On the said day, I came to the place of meeting, and saw that I had arrived first. I ordered a cup of tea and waited patiently for his arrival. Half an hour later, I was still waiting. I told myself that something probably came up, and he would show up any minute. Finally, a whole hour later and still no sign of Hayden Hemingway.

I was at a loss of what to do when a friend came to my rescue and dropped me at his house. I was determined to not let the journal team or the readers down, for I knew they would be waiting impatiently for the promised interview, and I, unlike some people, take my commitments and promises seriously.

After arriving at his place and waiting a whole five minutes—I knew he was home as his car was in the driveway—his Highness finally deigned to open the door. No, his first words were not "Oh, I'm so sorry, Leah, I couldn't come to the interview because I broke my leg." Not even "I'm so sorry, I was dumb enough to forget about the interview."

No, when he opened the door, he barked at me an annoyed, "What?" Talk about being civilized. Yet, I still kept my calm, and very politely reminded him that we were supposed to meet an hour and a half ago. His reply? "Well, I was busy. In fact, I still am. So, if you don't mind, I'd like to get back to my stuff."

Can you believe the nerve of that guy? Not only did he not show up after promising he would, nor did he even apologize, and worst of all, all this time, he had been at his house doing God knows what! And let me tell you, it wasn't a project to eradicate poverty on earth. Looking at his disheveled state, I am left to assume that Hayden Hemingway had been napping to catch up on his beauty sleep while I had wasted a whole two hours of my life.

Let me tell you that I was beyond seething with outrage at that point. Yet, miraculously, I still managed to keep my emotions under control—and the urge to twist some necks—and tried to make him understand how important the interview was as the deadline was on Monday.

Unfortunately for me, I was not dealing with a decent and compassionate co-student who understood the plight of meeting deadlines on time. He basically told me to get out because mister was not in the mood to give an interview. Basically, the world should stop turning and the sun rising because Hayden Hemingway was feeling under the weather. It pains me to say it, but, sadly, this is the real face of Hayden Hemingway: a conceited, self-centered, and extremely rude person who thinks he is allowed to behave like a jackass because he can kick a ball. I know many will be shocked, and some might not even believe me, for their admiration for the player might make them blind to the truth. Whether you want to believe me or not, it is up to you, dear readers. I did only my job: present you Hayden Hemingway.

Hayden tried to take deep breaths as his anger boiled inside him. *You so shouldn't have done that, Leah Driscoll.*

He was trying to decide what to do. Or to be more precise, how to get his revenge. He would not let her get away with this. A pesky voice inside his head kept telling him none of this would have happened had he shown up like he said he would, but he quelled the annoying voice quickly.

"Hayden!" He turned, and saw Kane approach him, a copy of the journal in his hand, and a perplexed look in his dark eyes as he was trying not to laugh.

"Mate, what have you done to that Leah Driscoll that she hates your guts so much?"

"I guess the poor girl was miffed I didn't give her any attention like she wanted. But that can be arranged. I will give her so much of my attention now, she will regret having ever crossed paths with me," said Hayden, scowling.

Kane shook his head and put a hand on his shoulder.

"Just forget it, Hayden. It's not like everyone believes her. She was probably just trying to get attention by writing what she thought was a sensational article. I'm just surprised they allowed her to publish such an article."

"Which is why I need to show that journal team to think twice before publishing such crap, and I have to teach her a lesson for messing up with me."

"Come on, mate, it was just a joke. What has gotten into you lately?"

Hayden pinched his lips, afraid the truth might escape. He hadn't been able to feel normal since *she* reappeared in his life. "Nothing, I'm just tired," he said, trying to deflect Kane's suspicions. The latter had always been too perceptive for his own good.

"Are you sure? I can clearly see something has been bothering you. Even Olivia said you didn't answer her text messages this weekend."

"Yeah," said Hayden, closing his locker loudly. He saw Olivia walking toward them. He pretended not to see her.

"I need to go to class. See ya," he told Kane.

He could feel Kane's and Olivia's eyes on his back as he walked away. He imagined his coach berating him tonight at practice and he had no excuse for why he had not come to the interview. Unless he told the truth.

Yeah, right, as if that was much better. He shook his head and prepared himself to come up with some lame excuse where he had been too sick to get out of bed, and Leah-Miss-Drama-Queen-Driscoll had made such a big deal out of it. That's all.

He considered just going home but knew he couldn't. His coach would eat him alive if he didn't show up to practice, especially after seeing the article.

He could already feel it was going to be a very long day.

CHAPTER EIGHT

Leah

As Leah sat in the principal's office, looking at the old, tired man in front of her, she regretted more than ever having written the article. It had felt like such a smart idea yesterday night when she sent it for publication. She had delayed it till the last minute to make sure they would simply print it without having the time to go over it. She had felt vindicated then.

Now, she just felt miserable and horrible. She hoped the principal didn't call her dad and ask him to come to school. *Oh my God, what if they suspend me? Or even expel me?*

She tried to swallow and gripped the chair tighter, her hands under her thighs, her shoulders hunched over.

"Leah, what pushed you to write such a degrading article? An article that goes against our school's motto?"

asked Principal Macey as he put the school logo in front of her where the words *Knowledge, Integrity,* and *Dedication* were printed out in bold letters.

"I'm sorry, I wasn't thinking. I was too blinded by my anger," admitted Leah, deciding that honesty was the best policy.

"You're not a child to act so impulsively. I have read your records. Your teachers from your last school all praised you as a diligent and responsible student."

Leah lowered her head in shame. The triumph she had felt when she sent the article tasted bitter now. She should have taken the higher road and asked the journal's editor for more time.

"I'm not like that usually," said Leah. "I will work hard to improve myself, but please don't say anything to my dad, he already has enough problems as it is," she pleaded.

The principal sighed. "I'll have to think about it. As for now, I guess you probably already know that you won't be writing for the journal anymore."

"Yes," she said. She felt it was a small price to pay if it meant she wouldn't be suspended, and her dad didn't find out.

"I also need to speak with Hayden, and then I'll let you know about your punishment. You may go for now."

Leah left the office and saw that she had missed her second class and it was time for lunch. *Thank God for small mercies.*

She went to her locker and put her textbooks inside. Someone tapped her on her shoulder, and she turned around to see Riley smiling at her.

"Hi, Riley," she said, trying to smile despite feeling so low.

"Hey Leah," he said. "I just read that article you wrote."

"I know, it was such—"

"It was brilliant," said Riley, laughing. Looking at her down-spirited expression, he calmed down. "I heard you were called into the principal's office," he said with sympathy.

"I just hope he doesn't suspend me," she said, biting her lip.

"Principal Macey is a nice guy. He'll try to be fair. And had Hemingway not been such an ass, none of this would have happened."

"Yeah, but I still wish I hadn't been so petty and sent that article. Now, I can't even write for the newspaper. Although I'll be super lucky if that's my only punishment. I deserved it."

"Anyone would have done the same, it's not your fault, it's Hemingway's. Don't think about it now, let's go eat," said Riley, offering her a kind smile.

As Leah and Riley made their way to the cafeteria, she noticed that a lot of students in the hallways were giving her weird looks, sometimes downright hostile. She knew it had to do with the article as many probably felt outraged that some newbie came and wrote such things about a guy that was well liked and a good soccer player on top of that.

She groaned inside. *Can I go back in time and erase my decision to write that article?*

Riley must have felt her discouragement for he whispered, "Don't worry, they'll get over it. They're just not used to someone having the guts to say the truth about their players."

She smiled. "Thank you, Riley, for always trying to make me feel better."

He winked and they went inside the class.

At the end of the day, the principal called her into his office, and as she sat down, she felt her palms were sweaty.

"After considering the situation and in light of the explanation Hayden provided me, I have decided not to take any further disciplinary action. Of course, you will no longer be part of the school journal, but Hayden told me you already apologized to him, and he told me how he missed the interview, prompting you to write this article. Since you already feel repentant and have acted maturely by trying to resolve the conflict, I won't be calling your dad this time."

Leah blinked, too stunned to be relieved. Since when had she apologized to Hayden? She couldn't believe he had lied to save her neck. Was the guy bipolar? That would explain his extreme mood swings and confusing behavior. She better stay away.

"You can leave, Leah," said her principal, not unkindly.

"Thank you, sir," she said.

"Leah," said the principal as she opened the door. "Let this be a lesson for you to not give in to your anger."

She nodded and closed the door behind her, thanking God for getting away with such a light punishment.

Riley was waiting outside, leaning on the wall, scrolling through his phone. He looked up when he heard her come out. "So how did it go?"

"He said he won't be taking any disciplinary action and won't be telling anything to my dad this time," said Leah, relief coursing through her.

"See, I told you Principal Macey is a nice guy," said Riley with a dimpled smile.

"He said he won't do anything because Hemingway told him I had already apologized to him," said Leah.

Riley raised his eyebrows in surprise. "You did?"

"That's the thing. I didn't. He lied for me," she said, still not believing what had happened.

"That's the least he could do, Leah. That still doesn't make him a chivalrous guy," said Riley with a small frown.

"No, of course not, I was just surprised."

"Let's go to Dairy Queen, my treat to you," said Riley with a big smile.

"You don't have to. If anything, I should be the one treating you for standing by me," said Leah, laughing.

"Another time. Today is on me," he said as they left the school.

"How was school, pumpkin?" asked Leah's dad as they were eating dinner.

"It was good," said Leah.

She still couldn't understand why Hayden hadn't sought retaliation, but she was so grateful she wasn't going to protest or confront him. Her gratitude quickly turned to annoyance as she remembered it had all been his fault to begin with.

"Did you make some friends?"

"I did, I went to have ice cream with a friend. Everyone has been really kind," said Leah.

"Of course, they'll be nice to my daughter, who is one of the kindest teenagers I know," her dad said with a warm smile and Leah felt guilt eating her guts.

She was so glad he hadn't been told about her blunder. He would have been so disappointed.

"Dad, I'm your daughter, of course you think I'm nice." Leah shook her head.

"No, I am a very good judge of character, if I can say so myself," said her dad.

"You think everyone is nice," said Leah with a roll of her eyes, smiling. "Grandpa always says that's your biggest weakness."

Her dad laughed. "You think it's a weakness? I don't think it's a bad thing."

Leah looked at her dad with affection. "No, that's a very good thing, indeed. I'm happy you're like that."

That night, Leah told her best friend everything that happened, complaining about starting on such a bad foot at the new school.

"I wish I could see that idiot Hemingway so I could give him a piece of my mind. No one messes with my bestie," said Anaya, outraged for her.

It felt good to hear her rant and vent for her.

"Just ignore the a-hole, he's not worth your time," said Anaya.

"You're right. Thank God we only have one class together."

She was dreading having to go to school tomorrow and cross paths with Hayden. With her luck, she'd be bumping into him first thing in the morning.

She checked her emails and grimaced when she saw some nasty emails from some students who were angry at her for daring to make assumptions about one of them when she was only a newbie.

She sighed and put her palms to her eyes. She had brought it upon herself, so she might as well just deal with it. She went to sit on her bed and took her mom's picture and looked at the lovely sight.

"I wish I was more patient, Mom," she said, sighing. "I got lucky today, so I guess it should serve as a lesson to me to be less vindictive next time."

She looked at her window and saw that the moon had started to wane. Feeling too tired to continue her homework, she decided to wake up early tomorrow morning to complete it instead.

As she made her way to classes the next morning, Leah wondered if she should just ignore Hayden or thank him for lying for her and apologize? But did he really deserve her apology when he was the cause of all this mess?

She had hardly slept, thinking the situation over in her head.

Wasn't morning supposed to be better than the evening? So how come I didn't come up with a solution this morning?

Her thoughts were interrupted as she approached her locker and saw that a redhead was already there.

She tried to get around her, but the girl spoke to her.

"Leah, right?"

"Yes?" she asked. The girl seemed familiar, but she couldn't place her. She was still getting used to her new classmates and the new teachers.

"I'm Olivia," said the girl, extending her hand in a short, but surprisingly strong, handshake.

"Hi, Olivia," said Leah, trying to smile. The girl was looking at her so seriously she was getting nervous.

Her long red hair was done up in a high ponytail and her piercing green eyes were set off by light freckles. She was a really pretty girl.

"I'm Hayden's friend," said Olivia as she continued to watch her.

Ahh, the cat got out of the bag. Was she trying to intimidate her, too?

"Are you going to reproach me for writing that article? Because he deserved that. He might be your friend, but he's a jerk," said Leah.

"You're wrong, he's a very nice person. I don't know what happened that day, I wasn't there, so I can't judge, but I can tell you it wasn't typical of him. That article was a bit too much."

"I know, trust me, I regret having written it a thousand times," said Leah, sighing as some girls passed them by and glared at Leah. So much for trying to make a good impression and make friends. Olivia watched the girls leaving and turned to Leah with a sympathetic look in her eyes.

"I'm sorry for you that you had such a bad start at a new school," she said. "But, it's never too late to make things better."

She offered her a smile and Leah smiled back.

Olivia looked over her shoulder and her smile disappeared. "Well, I better get to my class. Have a nice day, Leah," she said and left.

Confused at her brusque departure, Leah turned around and saw Riley coming her way, but he was watching Olivia leaving.

"Hey," she greeted him.

"Hey, I didn't know you knew Olivia," said Riley, looking at her with surprise.

"We just got acquainted," replied Leah, trying to discern

what he was thinking.

"I see," he said, nodding, but not quite meeting her eyes.

"Are you two friends?" she asked.

He grimaced. "No, not really." He chuckled but he didn't sound amused.

Leah didn't press him further. They might have become friends, but they weren't close enough for her to have the right to ask him anything.

CHAPTER NINE

Hayden

As soon as soccer practice was done, Hayden made his way to the lockers. He saw Tyler smirk at him as he took out his stuff. He had been smug all practice, enjoying every moment of Coach yelling at Hayden and his poor performance.

He ignored him as punching him would only bring him more trouble. He could never stand the guy and he was not going to give him the satisfaction to know that he was getting to him.

Kurt had tried to talk to him, but he had shut down all conversations. He was never going to let them find out the truth.

He decided he was simply going to pretend that Saturday hadn't happened.

As far as he was concerned, his mother was no longer a part of his life, and he was going to keep it that way. No point giving her a chance to hurt him again. To leave him again.

By the time he got home, he hoped his dad was still at work so he could get something to eat and shut himself in his room.

"Hayden?"

Crap.

Why did his father have to be home today of all days? He had a feeling he knew why.

His dad came out of the kitchen. "I made chicken and potatoes."

"I'm not hungry," grumbled Hayden as he went upstairs.

"Hayden, you can't just ignore me all the time," said his dad, following him.

Oh yeah, we'll see about that.

"Hayden, please listen to me, son," said his father as he reached his bedroom.

Hayden turned and saw his dad walk toward his door. He closed it hard.

"Hayden, please open the door," said his dad.

"I don't want to talk," said Hayden.

He heard his dad sigh and finally leave.

Hayden sat on his bed. He had homework to do, but he was hungry. He felt his irritation increase as he tried to ignore his grumbling stomach.

Sighing, he lay down on the bed and before he knew it, he fell asleep. When he woke up a couple of hours later, he knew he had to eat, or his empty stomach would keep him awake all night.

Hoping his dad was in his study, he quietly made his way downstairs and went into the kitchen.

He was waiting for the microwave to be done so he could bring his heated dish upstairs when his dad came in the kitchen.

"Hayden, we need to talk, son." He looked even more tired than Hayden.

"About the fact that you lied to me all my life?" asked Hayden, his voice brittle.

"I'm sorry, Hayden. I really wanted to tell you the truth, but I didn't know how," said his dad, rubbing his face.

"Do you even know how it made me feel?" asked Hayden, his voice cold. "Do you know how guilty I felt all this time, believing I was responsible for my mother's death?" His hands were shaking as he put them into tight fists. He wanted to break something.

"I'm really sorry, son. Believe me, had I known, I would have told you sooner."

"Are you sure? If she hadn't come back, would you still have told me?"

His father stayed quiet a second too long, enough to answer Hayden's question. The beep of the microwave was loud in the silence.

He snorted. "I thought so."

His voice was scornful as he felt anger burn inside him. It hurt to breathe.

"Hayden, I never wanted to hurt you," said his dad, his voice broken.

"Yeah, well you have a poor way of showing it," said Hayden as he passed by his father, his meal forgotten.

"Hayden, I was doing what I thought was best for you. I was trying to protect you, please understand that," said his father following him.

Hayden stopped at the stairs and turned back to look at his father.

"No, Dad, you didn't want to protect me. You were just too scared to tell me the truth. You didn't think I was too weak for the truth; you were the one too weak to tell me the truth."

His dad looked at him as if he had slapped him.

And in a way, he did. He had told him the truth his dad had been avoiding all these years and it was a hard blow.

Hayden held his dad's shocked stare before turning away and going to his bedroom, the fury inside of him threatening to wreak havoc.

Inside his room, he tried to calm down. He looked at his textbooks and sighed, remembering all the homework he needed to do.

As he sat at his desk, he swore when he remembered that he still had to write a reflection on anger and how to control your temper.

The principal had summoned him into his office and asked to explain why Leah Driscoll wrote such an article about him and if the accusations were true.

Hayden had lied how he had felt under the weather and snapped at her and might have been a tad rude.

The principal had sighed, a disappointed look on his face. To avoid making things worse, Hayden had told him she had already apologized, and they were good now.

He hoped the elder man believed his lie and was relieved when he told him that he wanted him to submit an essay on how destructive anger was and the steps one can implement to manage it.

Hayden had nodded, feeling he had escaped the worst of it. But now he felt annoyed that he had to do extra work just because Leah Driscoll had been offended and was petty enough to publish about it in the school's journal.

It wouldn't have happened if you had been nicer, Hayden, a pesky voice inside him whispered.

Whatever.

As far as he was concerned, he had done more than enough and saved her neck by saying she had apologized when she had done nothing of the sort.

He knew how their principal valued apologies and how it would lessen her punishment, if she had any.

He opened his laptop and wondered what he could write to make the principal happy. He was glad he hadn't been suspended from soccer—although his coach's ire had been punishment enough, if anyone were to ask him—and he wanted to make sure his principal would get off his back after he gave him the paper.

He almost wanted to laugh. Here he was, consumed by anger, and he was told to write about its effect. As if he wanted to feel this angry. He rubbed his face, feeling tired again. He could already feel it was going to be a fricking long year.

CHAPTER TEN

Leah

The day passed fairly quickly, and the English class she had been dreading so much since yesterday turned out very anticlimactic as Hayden had proceed to simply ignore her. She was almost wishing he'd say something, so she knew how to act around him. When he had come in, the students in the class looked at them, expecting what she wasn't sure, but she had tensed in anticipation. She wondered if he'd start yelling at her again or tell her she owed him since he had lied for her. But he simply walked by her and took his seat.

She had a hard time focusing in class and couldn't leave fast enough, and was annoyed to feel guilty for something that hadn't been her fault to begin with. The rest of the day went by quickly and she felt grateful when she was done.

"Do you want to go to Timmie's?" asked Riley as they got their backpacks from their lockers. His was not very far away from hers, Connors being close to Driscoll.

"Not today, I have a lot of things I need to catch up on, so I'm going to the library," said Leah.

"Okay, see you tomorrow, then," said Riley and they went their separate ways.

As she worked on her assignment, she looked through the library's tall windows and was surprised that the sky had darkened. She decided she had better get home before it started raining.

She took her phone to see what time it was, but the screen refused to open.

Urgh, just my luck, having the phone die on me. She packed her backpack and left the library. She saw that some students had remained to practice their musical instruments or to practice some play.

It had already begun raining and she ran to the bus stop.

Fifteen minutes later, she was still waiting for the bus. She had on her light cardigan and she was starting to feel cold while the rain seemed to take a perverse pleasure to pour harder. She wanted to call her dad but there was no one around from whom she could borrow a phone.

She sighed, resigning herself to the fact she would have to walk all the way back to school and ask someone for their phone.

As she gathered the courage to go into the rain, a dark

blue Audi stopped in front of her. *Just great. Is the whole universe conspiring against me today?*

The driver's window rolled down to show her the last person she wanted to see right now—correction, the last person she wanted to see ever.

"Leah Driscoll, what a pleasant surprise." She knew he was bipolar. First, he ignored her and now he acted all cordial.

She didn't even bother answering him. She prayed that if she continued to ignore him, Hayden Hemingway would eventually drive away.

"Get in, I'll drop you home," he said.

She continued to ignore him. She hoped he would get soaked through the window, but nature wouldn't allow her such small favors today, it seemed. In effect, the wind was sending the rain to the other side, so his seat and his clothes escaped most of it. She knew she was being immature, but it only made her that much more resentful.

"Oh, come on, don't be so childish. With that weather, the bus won't show up anytime soon–if at all. Do you really wanna stay here all night? That would be pretty foolish of you."

She remained stubbornly silent.

"Are you still angry about the interview?"

She scoffed. "I don't waste my time or anger on such petty things."

"Then why do you refuse to let me give you a lift?"

"Why do you keep asking me when my silence should

be answer enough?"

"Fulfilling my good deed of the day," he said, sounding annoyed.

"Very generous of you, but then, you better ask someone who really needs it."

"Actually, I was also doing it for myself. I would have the opportunity to enjoy your company." He flashed his smirk.

She rolled her eyes. "Your courting manners seriously need practice."

"Who said anything about courting?" he asked, his expression innocent.

She narrowed her eyes at him and was about to retort when the black sky seemed to explode as a thunderstorm broke. She startled, and her riposte died on her lips. She flushed when she realized Hayden had noticed her reaction.

She didn't like storms. Scratch that. She hated them. She used to love them, but the night her mom died, there had been a thunderstorm, too, and she had come to associate the weather with painful and bad memories. Soon, her fear of them grew worse. She realized with regret she had no choice but to get in the car or stay there and possibly have a heart attack.

She looked at Hayden and saw that he was watching her. However, he had the decency to keep quiet about her show of emotion. With a heavy sigh, she opened the back door, and got in.

The first minutes were spent in uncomfortable silence as he

drove to the main street. She could see his soccer uniform bag on the backseat beside her. The atmosphere was tense, but she refused to speak to him more than necessary. He cleared his throat. “Where do you live?”

“East side, Wentworth Avenue.”

A couple of minutes passed by, and she could feel his eyes on her through the rear-view mirror.

“Look, I’m sorry for what happened. I was in a really bad mood that day.”

“Yeah, well, you should learn how to control your temper,” she said snidely, instantly regretting it.

After all, he had lied to the principal that she had apologized to him. He had saved her neck without her asking it.

He chuckled. “Look who’s talking. I never saw such a mean article. About me nonetheless.”

Leah sighed. “I guess I should thank you for lying to Principal Macey, and for writing that article. It was mean, even if you did deserve it.”

He laughed. “You’re not the forgiving type, are you?”

“Depends on what needs forgiving.”

Another awkward silence followed. Not soon enough, they finally reached her neighborhood.

“Turn right here. The third house on the left is mine. You can let me out here.”

However, she was surprised to see that he drove all the way into the driveway so she wouldn’t be soaked by walking from the car to the house. She didn’t know what to make of such sudden consideration.

"Thank you for giving me a lift." She tried to sound nonchalant, but she couldn't wait to get out of the car.

He met her eyes in the mirror. "No problem. Good night."

She was surprised to notice he looked very tired.

Only when she got in her house, and closed the door behind her, did she hear him drive away. As she watched his car through the door window, she saw that it looked black in the rainy night. She leaned against the door and closed her eyes.

"Leah, is that you?" Her eyes flew open.

Her dad came out of the living room. "Are you okay, pumpkin? Why are you so late?"

"Yeah, Dad. Just got held up in the library, and my phone died, so I couldn't call you to let you know."

He nodded. "I made some chicken for dinner. It's on the stove."

She smiled. "Okay, I'll just go change, and will be back."

When she entered her room, she realized she was still feeling edgy. Shaking her head, she went to take a hot shower and changed her clothes.

She wondered what had possessed Hayden Hemingway to give her a lift tonight. Maybe as Olivia said, she had been wrong on his account? He had appeared so different. Subdued. Exhausted. For all she knew, he might be suffering from a split personality disorder. That was the most reasonable explanation for his behavior.

She didn't like how he made her feel: anxious and jittery. It was probably due to their bad beginning, but she felt automatically defensive in his presence. In short, he wasn't good for her mental health.

From now on, she'd keep away as much as possible.

Later that night, as she went to do her homework, she was still trying to process what had happened.

Had she imagined the whole thing?

Clearly, he had some extreme mood swings. She never knew which Hayden she'd meet. The happy-go-lucky one or the angry, moody one.

She put her chin in her palms and stared at her textbook, feeling morose. She had a feeling it would be a long year indeed.

Her phone rang and she saw that it was Anaya.

"Leah, guess what?" said Anaya as soon as Leah answered the phone.

She sounded breathless with excitement.

"What? Tell me," said Leah, smiling at her best friend's enthusiasm.

"Mom said she can drive me to Bellevue soon!" squealed Anaya.

"Really?" exclaimed Leah, grinning. "When?"

"In a couple of weeks. Is that okay with your dad if I spend the weekend at your place?"

"Of course! Oh, Anaya, I'm so happy! I can't wait to see

you. I really miss you," said Leah.

"I miss you, too," said Anaya. "But soon, we'll get to spend a whole weekend together. It'll be so much fun!"

"Like old times," said Leah, smiling.

After everything that had happened, she felt she deserved some good news.

She wondered if she should tell Anaya what had happened tonight, but as her best friend kept talking, she wasn't able to bring herself to bring it up.

She might just as well forget about Hayden Hemingway and pretend this week hadn't happened in her life. For her own sanity.

CHAPTER ELEVEN

HAYDEN

As Hayden drove home, he smiled despite himself as he remembered Leah's disgruntled expression when she saw him. She looked so cold out there, waiting in the freezing rain, that he took pity on her, and decided the decent thing to do was to propose a lift.

When she at first ignored him, he had felt somewhat insulted, but, at the same time, he was amused by her stubbornness and defiance. Then, the thunderstorm broke, and the poor girl had looked like a deer caught in the headlights. Her fear had been so palpable, he didn't even have the heart to taunt her. He wondered if she would have gotten in the car, if not for the thunder.

When he arrived home, he saw that his grandparents' car was already in the driveway.

"Grandma?" he called as he got inside.

"In here!"

He came into the kitchen and saw his grandmother setting the table.

"Hmm, smells good," he said, kissing her on the cheek. "You've been baking a lot these days."

"Are you complaining?" she asked with a tender smile.

"Not at all. If I can be the one to taste all your delicious pies," said Hayden. "Grandpa didn't come?"

"He should be in soon with your dad."

As Hayden helped his grandmother set the table, he saw she seemed preoccupied and tired.

"You okay?" he asked, worried.

"Yes, of course," replied his grandmother. Too quickly.

Hayden looked at his grandmother. "Are you sure?"

His grandmother looked at him and sighed. "Your mom called me yesterday."

Hayden froze. "What?"

"She told me she went to see you, but it didn't go very well, and you didn't want to listen to her."

Hayden tried to breathe calmly. "I don't want to talk about her." He was trying to not get angry at the fact that his grandma had known the truth all along and was still talking to his mother.

"Hayden, I think you should hear her out. And after that, you can decide whether you want to forgive her or not."

"Women's solidarity, right?" asked Hayden, hating how biting his voice was. Hating how he was taking his anger out on his grandmother when it was meant for someone else.

"I'm telling you as a mother. I wouldn't be able to bear it if my son refused to speak to me."

"This is different. You didn't do anything to deserve that. You didn't leave your son. You were always there for him, no matter what."

"She's only human, Hayden."

"Well, I'm human, too. What can I say? Can't find it in me to forgive her."

She approached him and put her hand on his cheek, watching him with her warm, gray eyes. "Life's too short for anger and resentment, my love."

"It's too short for betrayal, too. Besides, I have you. And Dad and Grandpa. I don't need anybody else."

His grandmother opened her mouth to say something, but the front door opened, and Hayden heard his dad and grandfather come in.

As they sat down for dinner, Hayden tried to pretend everything was fine. He tried to act as if nothing had changed. As if his world hadn't turned upside down last week. And his dad was trying to do the same.

"Hayden, son, have you thought about which university you'll be applying to?" asked his grandfather. He had always been highly ambitious and expected everyone in the family to be the same.

"Not yet, Grandpa, I still have two years before I need to decide."

"Less than two years since you already started Grade 11," said his grandfather.

"Vincent, Hayden still has time to decide," said his grandmother, smiling at her grandson. She knew he didn't like being pressured.

"Time can be wasted easily if one is not careful about it," said his grandfather.

"I'll be thinking about it soon," said Hayden to pacify his grandfather and change the topic.

While he was grateful his grandfather didn't try to bring up the topic of his mother, he was also surprised. It was like his mother didn't exist for him. Still, he saw the looks his grandparents kept exchanging between themselves and his father when they thought he wasn't looking.

He almost wanted to shout that he knew the truth and to stop pretending, but then wanted to kick himself for thinking about *her* again. Especially after he had promised himself he would erase that morning from his memory.

In the awkward silence, only the sound of their forks against their plates was heard.

Hayden helped his grandma clear the table and put the dishes in the dishwasher while his grandfather and dad went into his study.

"Hayden, please think about what I said," his grandmother said quietly, as if almost afraid of being heard.

If she didn't want his dad and grandfather to overhear them, why was she still asking him to give his mom a chance?

"Dad told me she told him to forget her. So, I don't know why she suddenly decided to come back now, and I don't *want* to know."

Images of his mother's hurt eyes flashed in his mind, and he shook his head. *Don't be a fool, Hayden. Are you going to forgive her just so she can hurt you when she decides to leave again?*

"What she did was wrong, but, Hayden, your mom was really sick. She went through a lot in her life, too, you know. Her dad left them when your mom was only twelve, her mom was her everything and then she died suddenly of a heart attack. It was a hard blow for your mom."

Hayden looked at his grandmother, his temple throbbing painfully. He could feel a headache coming. "I don't want to talk about it anymore," he said.

His grandma stayed quiet and looked at him with compassion.

"I need to do my homework," said Hayden, avoiding her gaze.

As he went to his room, he saw that the door to his dad's study was ajar, and he could hear his grandfather's voice. "Don't tell me you're considering forgiving her after everything she's done?" He sounded incredulous and angry.

He knew instantly who they were talking about and,

despite himself, stopped to listen in.

"No, Dad, of course not. I just don't want Hayden to suffer. I told you, he took it really badly when she came. I don't want him to be hurt again."

"She left, she made her choice. Now, do me a favor and be strong enough to not think about her again."

The finality in his grandfather's voice left no room for argument, and Hayden thought his dad would concede as he usually did with his father but was surprised when he heard his dad speak up again. "She told me that she wants to be involved in Hayden's life from now on and that I can't stop her as she is his mother."

"That horrible…" His grandfather's voice was too muffled for Hayden to make out what he said, but he got the gist of it and was surprised by his sudden anger.

Why was he angry at his grandfather for speaking ill of his mother? The shock made him step back.

Afraid they'd hear him, he left quietly to his room. His head was spinning. He sat on the bed, remembering how his mother's eyes welled up at seeing him. He remembered his terror.

How she had looked at him with such sadness.

He rubbed his face. He felt his heart beating against his ribcage. His palms were sweaty, and he had a hard time breathing.

He needed to get out of the house. He needed some fresh air.

Making sure no one could hear him, Hayden went downstairs, put on his running shoes, and went for a run until he felt he was going to collapse with fatigue. The rain had stopped, leaving the air damp and the soil glistening under the lamps.

He felt lightheaded and he welcomed it. He was not going to think about his mother again. He couldn't bear to think about her.

CHAPTER TWELVE

Leah

Leah looked at the clock and saw there were still ten minutes left before the end of the class.

The day had been unbearably long, and she couldn't wait to go home. A couple of desks ahead, Riley turned around and smiled. She returned his smile.

He had been so supportive since the whole article fiasco, and she debated whether to tell him about Hayden giving her a lift yesterday evening.

She still couldn't believe he had done that. In English class this morning, she had been even more shocked when he gave her a brief nod as he passed her by.

He hadn't smiled nor did he acknowledge her presence after that, but she still felt weird. He seemed so calm she felt she had almost imagined the furious Hayden.

But she still remembered his fury. His blazing eyes and his anger.

The bell rang, breaking her out of her reverie and, picking up her textbooks, she joined Riley.

"Thank God the day is over," he said with a smile.

"Yeah, same," said Leah as they walked in the corridor.

"Mr. Duncar gave us so much homework, I feel it should be illegal to burden students to this point," said Riley, annoyed.

"He's intense, I know. Even in my previous school, my teachers didn't load as much as him, and our school was pretty demanding," said Leah, putting her stuff in her school bag.

She saw Hayden walk by with his friends—Olivia among them—and turned away, not wanting to be caught staring. She couldn't help but notice he looked tired again.

She looked at Riley and saw that he was frowning. He, too, had seen them. She remembered how Olivia had reacted upon seeing him and wondered what happened between them.

Riley seemed to sense her gaze on him, for he looked at her and smiled.

"Let's get out of here," he said.

She nodded.

"Hey, do you wanna go to Tim's with me and my friends? We were planning to get some Iced Capp," he said.

She shook her head. "I can't today, but thank you for asking," she said.

After saying goodbye, she looked at her Google Maps to see where the closest flower shop was.

She wanted to buy flowers before she went to visit her mom.

She went to the bus stop that led to the opposite direction of her house, hoping she didn't have to wait too long.

"Hey," someone said behind her.

Turning around, she saw Olivia smiling at her.

"Hi," she said, smiling back. The redhead would smile at her in the corridors whenever their paths crossed since she had come to defend her friend a few days ago.

"I didn't know you took this bus," said Olivia, shielding her eyes against the bright sun, her emerald top making her eyes look greener.

"Not usually, no," said Leah.

In the awkward silence that followed, she debated whether to tell the truth.

"I'm looking for a flower shop," she said as the bus stopped in front of them.

"Oh, I know one, a couple of stops from here. Florist Bella, it's called, I think," said Olivia, getting on the bus with her. "I'll show you."

"Thank you," said Leah as they sat down.

Olivia smiled and Leah could tell she wanted to ask what the occasion was, but she was too polite to do so.

"I hope you like your new school," said Olivia.

"Yeah, it's alright, different, but not bad," said Leah.

She missed her old school, especially Anaya and her

friends, so much, but she knew she was still lucky. It could have been worse.

She thought about Hayden. Or maybe it could have been better.

"Oh, your stop is next," said Olivia, looking at the streets. "You won't be able to miss it. It has bright yellow windows."

After thanking her, Leah got off at the next stop and Olivia waved her goodbye through the open window.

She saw the florist immediately. It was an explosion of colors among the other buildings.

After buying pink peonies—her mom's favorite—she made her way to the graveyard.

"Hi mom," she whispered as she put the bouquet on the gravestone. Leah looked at the engraved inscription, feeling her heart squeeze painfully.

No matter how many times she visited, every time felt like a blow.

She bit her lip and took a deep breath as she sat beside the headstone.

Although she missed her friends and old school, she was still glad they moved to Bellevue. She could visit her mom as much as she wanted.

"I miss you, Mom," she said, wiping a tear that fell on her cheek. She wondered when she'd be able to come here with a smile on her face, feeling peaceful, and not as if her heart was being torn into pieces each time.

She heard birds chirping in the branches, but couldn't

see them through the thick, green foliage. She wondered if it were blue jays. Her mom loved blue jays. And she loved autumn. Especially when the leaves turned different colors. Trying to rival a rainbow, she used to say with a grin, her eyes shining.

She missed her mom so much, the pain felt acute.

Blinking away tears, she looked at her phone and saw it was time to go home. She already felt depressed by all the work that was awaiting her.

"I'll visit soon," she said, and as usual, only the silence answered her, the marble of the gravestone glinting in the sunlight.

CHAPTER THIRTEEN

Hayden

"Hayden, we need to talk," his dad said as he came into the kitchen.

Hayden looked in the fridge, trying to decide what to eat. "What about?"

He was annoyed that his dad chose this morning of all mornings to try to talk to him.

Not that another day would have been better, but still. Hayden had gotten used to their routine of avoiding the topic. He hadn't talked to his dad for days and had only recently come around to answer his questions with monosyllabic responses.

After everything he had learned, he felt his dad should be satisfied and not push his luck further, but apparently, he had other ideas.

"Hayden, if I could change what I've done, I would have, trust me," said his dad. He sounded as tired as he looked.

Hayden noticed his shirt was a bit rumpled and he felt a pinch in his stomach. His father was nothing short of meticulous, his appearance always ideal. The fact that he hadn't even bothered to iron out the creases of his shirt spoke volumes.

"Can we talk another time? I'm going to be late for school," said Hayden as he grabbed a couple of granola bars and put them in his bag.

"I made scrambled eggs," said his dad, watching the snacks with a frown.

He knew he wouldn't be able to eat breakfast. Not after feeling like a vice was squeezing his stomach.

"I can't, I have to go," said Hayden, not meeting his eyes.

He'd just get something more filling at the cafeteria at break time.

"Don't wait for me for dinner, I'll be at Kane's place," said Hayden, getting out.

"Boys, dinner is ready," Kane's mom said from downstairs.

Hayden and Kane were working on their homework, and while Kane was doing most of the work, Hayden kept thinking whether he should bring up the topic of his mom.

He didn't know how Kane would react and he dreaded speaking the truth. All day he tried to pretend everything was fine, but it was getting tiresome.

Yesterday morning, he had woken up late and remembering he had swimming class, he had decided to skip the class altogether.

He knew he'd be called into the principal's office again, but he didn't care. Anything was better than facing the humiliating experience of not being able to dive into the swimming pool.

"Hayden, you coming?" Kane asked. Hayden noticed he had already gotten up and was at the threshold while he was still sitting on the bed, his notebook in his lap.

He was looking at Hayden with an inquisitive air, his eyebrow raised.

"Yeah," said Hayden, pretending to not notice his look.

"You okay?" Kane asked, watching him. "You've been spacing out a lot these days."

Trust Kane to notice.

"Yeah, just tired," Hayden said. "Let's go eat, I'm starving."

Without waiting for Kane's reply, he went downstairs.

Aunt Kim had already set the table and Kai was putting out the cutlery.

She smiled when she saw them come in.

"Where's Dad?" asked Kane.

"He'll be in later," his mom said as she put the meat and potatoes dish in the middle of the table. The smell was mouth-watering.

Hayden took his seat beside Kane and wondered what it would have been like if his mom had never left.

"Hayden?"

Hayden looked up and saw that Kane and his mom were looking at him.

"Do you want some sauteed zucchini?" asked Aunt Kim, extending him the plate.

"No, thank you," Hayden said.

He felt Kane nudge him with his elbow. "Mate, you sure you okay?" he asked.

Hayden nodded, trying to act nonchalant.

"Kai, sweetheart, please put away your phone," Kane's mom said. The boy sighed and put it in his pocket.

Hayden suddenly, inexplicably, felt an urge to cry. He looked at his plate and tried to swallow through the lump in his throat.

After soccer practice was over, Hayden made his way to the café where his grandma had asked him to meet her.

He went in and she smiled when she saw him.

"Sorry, am I late?" asked Hayden, giving her a kiss on the cheek.

"No, right on time," smiled his grandma. "I took the liberty to order the apple pie you like so much for us, hope you don't mind?"

"I'm starving, I'll eat anything," chuckled Hayden as he took a seat in front of her. "And all their pies are good, anyway."

His grandma smiled again, but she seemed distracted and kept looking at the door.

"Are you waiting for someone else?" asked Hayden.

He had been surprised when she had asked him to join her at the cafe after school. They used to come often to eat their pies on the weekends. But never on a school day.

She looked at him, her expression suddenly so serious he was disconcerted.

However, before she could answer, a movement on his peripheral vision caught his attention and he turned to see his mom walk toward them, her expression unsure.

He turned toward his grandma, his shock rendering him speechless. He couldn't believe she would set him up like that. Especially when he had told her he didn't want to see her.

"Aviannah, please take a seat," said his grandma, scooting over on her bench to make space.

She smiled at his mom, and he clenched his fist. Why was she pretending everything was normal?

His mom sat across from him and tried to smile.

"Hayden, I'm so happy you agreed to come," she said, her voice soft.

"I didn't," said Hayden, not bothering to hide his anger.

His mom looked at his grandma who shot him a glance.

"I was going to tell him," she said.

"Hayden," she said, turning toward him, her voice firm, but something akin to pleading in the tone. She was asking him to not make a scene.

"It's important that we sit together as a family and talk things through," she said, extending her hand to take his.

He put his hands on his lap to hide their shaking and stared at the table.

"Hayden," sighed his grandma. He looked up and met her stare.

"Since we're talking about being a family, aren't families supposed to stick together?" he asked his grandma, refusing to look at his mother, though he could feel her eyes on him.

He heard her soft intake of breath, and suddenly, he lost his appetite. He knew he wouldn't be able to sit there and pretend. He wasn't going to play their game.

"I have to go," he said, not looking at them.

"Hayden!" He heard his grandma call after him, but he didn't stop. He needed to get away.

When he got home, he went to his bedroom and took out the old box case he kept under his bed. He moved the Pokémon cards, the dirty tennis ball, the old, blue glove—the only one remaining after he had given up on boxing after a few weeks back in the days—and finally found what he was looking for.

He grabbed the thin notebook and opened it. On the

pages, he saw his childish scribbling, where he had written countless times when he was small.

My mom loves me

My mom watches over me in heaven

My mom forgives me

My mom still loves me

He tore the pages, reducing them to small pieces until nothing was left but a small, white pile of little pieces on the floor.

He watched them, feeling his breathing slow down and, slowly, his hands stopped shaking.

He gathered them all in his hands and threw them in the recycling bin by his desk.

That's it. He was done feeling guilty.

His mother had made her choice all those years ago, and he just made his.

Sitting at his desk, he tried to focus on his homework, but he had been rereading the last paragraph for the third time, and still didn't get it.

He sighed, pushing the textbook away. Just then, he heard a soft knock.

"Come in," he said.

His grandmother came through the door, looking so apologetic, he had no heart to tell her to leave.

"Hayden, I'm sorry, love. I should have asked you first if you wanted to meet your mom. But I thought hearing her out would help."

"How? What would it change?" asked Hayden, his eyebrow raised.

"Everyone deserves a second chance in life, don't you think?" asked his grandma, her voice gentle.

"Not really. Sometimes, it's just too late."

"I understand your anger and your pain, Hayden, sweetheart. I can only imagine how you felt when you saw your mom."

Hayden looked at his grandma, wondering how she expected him to just accept the whole situation if she understood his emotional state.

"Then, why did you never tell me? Why did none of you ever tell me the truth?"

"Your dad thought it was for the best. He was scared that the truth would destroy you."

Hayden scoffed, shaking his head. He felt his temples throb again and clenched his jaw. He couldn't go on like that.

"I don't want to talk about it anymore," he said, getting up.

I know you're angry at your dad for not telling you about your mom, but he's really sorry, you know?" said his grandmother, looking at him with worry.

Did his dad ask her to talk to him? He wanted to scoff. Typical Dad. Who was it going to be next? His Grandpa?

But even as he thought about that, he knew his grandfather wouldn't even try to convince him to see his mother. He seemed adamant that she stay out of their lives.

And what irritated him was that he didn't know how it made him feel. Shouldn't he be relieved his grandfather was on his side and that he was supporting his anger?

"Hayden, please talk to your dad, he's miserable with your silence. You know you mean the world to him, my love," said his grandma.

Hayden looked at her and shrugged. He looked at the window, feeling his irritation return. And the feeling of betrayal.

"I hope you'll be there for the company's anniversary party? It's this Friday."

Hayden had completely forgotten about that.

"I don't know. I have a lot of things to do," said Hayden, avoiding her gaze.

"On a Friday night?"

"I promised Kane I'd help him with a project," said Hayden, glancing at his grandma quickly to see if she could tell he was lying.

Her raised eyebrows and skeptical expression let him know she wasn't buying it.

"You can at least come up for a couple of hours, don't you think?"

"Yeah, I guess, I'll see," said Hayden noncommittally.

His grandma looked so sad he almost wanted to say yes to make her happy, but he kept quiet.

She rose and approached him. She put a hand on his cheek, forcing him to look at her.

"Hayden, that anger that you're feeling will only end up hurting you more. Please, let it go. Forgive your parents.

For your own sake. So you can be happy."

He looked at her pale, gray eyes and saw the same love there since he had learned to recognize that feeling when he was small.

He used to believe his grandma would protect him from all harm and that her arms would soothe all his hurt.

He put his arms around her and hugged her hard, afraid to let go. He felt like he was five again, seeking refuge in his grandma's arms, expecting her to soothe his hurt.

CHAPTER FOURTEEN

Leah

Leah looked around the reception hall and sighed. She was already regretting her agreement to accompany her uncle Eric to the corporate anniversary.

The firm, which was specializing in the installation of the irrigation system, was celebrating its thirtieth anniversary, and as Leah had learned from the speech given by the president of the company earlier in the evening, the Rainbird Company had become the leading irrigation contractor in the region, servicing both residential and commercial accounts for thirty years now.

Her uncle, who was one of the managers in the residential sector, was busy talking with his colleagues, and Leah was sitting alone at the table. Just then, the doors of the reception hall opened loudly, attracting the attention of some people.

Leah thought she was going to fall from her chair when she saw who exactly it was who walked in.

Hayden Hemingway in all his glory was making his way to the front of the room. His dress shirt was unbuttoned at the top, and he hadn't even bothered wearing a tie or a blazer. Needless to say, his entry caused quite a stir. Leah could see people whisper as they followed him with their stares. Knowing him, she would bet anything he had done it on purpose. She was sure he was the kind of person who enjoyed being the star of the show.

She tried to hide in her seat and wondered how she would be able to escape without being seen. She didn't know why, but she dreaded having to talk to him. Seeing as they were both among the youngest people there, she knew he would notice her soon enough if she didn't disappear right now.

And what was he doing here anyway? Maybe he was accompanying his father or mother, but she had a hard time picturing him doing so. He just didn't seem like the kind of child who would voluntarily accompany his parents to their corporate party. He probably spent all his weekends partying with his friends and getting wasted, she thought disdainfully. And yet, there he was. On a Friday evening.

It had been a week since he dropped her home and since then, they never spoke in school, except for the awkward nod if ever their paths would cross, which happened very rarely. Leah made sure of that.

She hadn't told Riley how he gave her a lift home, feeling too weird to even attempt to bring it up. She was still perplexed by his kindness and wary of it.

She saw her uncle then, and as luck would have it, he was a few feet away from where Hayden was standing, his back to her, talking to some man she couldn't see the face of, and an elderly couple.

She sighed once more and poured herself more orange juice.

"Leah Driscoll. What a pleasant surprise. Again."

She had been so deep in her thoughts she hadn't heard him approach. She startled, and slowly turned around, hoping against hope she was mistaken, and that it was someone else. No such luck. Hayden was looking at her, his head tilted slightly to the left, his eyebrow raised in a silent question.

"Oh. Hey. Hi." *How articulate, Leah.* She wanted to kick herself. He sat beside her.

"Hi, yourself. So, what brings you here?"

She was about to answer when her uncle approached the two of them.

"Hey, Leah. Sorry about that. When Andy gets into one of his lecture modes, there's no stopping him."

He then noticed Hayden sitting beside her. He shot Leah a questioning look and turned toward Hayden. But before he could say anything, someone called up his name, and excusing himself, he went away.

"Was that your dad?"

"My uncle. I came with him because my little cousin is sick, and Aunt Kristina had to stay home," she said, wondering why she was explaining herself. "Anyway, what are *you* doing here?"

He raised an eyebrow and couldn't have looked more arrogant had he announced he was made king. "In case it escaped your notice, Driscoll, the company is my dad's. Liam *Hemingway* is my father." The way he put emphasis on the last name made her feel stupid, and she chided herself for not making the connection sooner.

"Oh, I'm sorry. I didn't realize your family was the only one in the entire universe with the last name Hemingway."

He smiled that half-smile of his, and she wished she could come up with something smart to wipe off that smirk of his face. His stare was starting to make her feel uncomfortable, and she had to refrain herself from fidgeting in her seat. To hide her discomfort, she occupied herself with her glass of orange juice.

"Do you want to dance?" he asked suddenly.

"What? No. I don't dance."

"Everyone knows how to dance."

Before she could understand what was happening, he took her by the arm, and literally dragged her to the dance floor.

"Hey, let go!"

"Don't be such a coward."

"I'm not a coward! I just don't like to dance!"

She tried to free her arm, but it was like his hand was made of iron.

"Stop making a scene. Everyone's watching," he whispered into her ear, as he put his arms around her waist.

His proximity was disconcerting. She looked around and saw that he was right. People were watching them. She stopped her struggle.

"Then, let me go," she said quietly.

"One dance, and you can go."

She scowled, and he flashed her a patronizing smile. The nerve of him! She wondered if Uncle Eric would forgive her for maiming his boss's son. Probably not. Life was so unfair. Oh well, there were other, less obvious, ways. And with an innocent expression, she stepped on his foot. Hard.

"Sorry!"

"It's okay."

From the way he was looking at her, she knew he knew she did it on purpose. She tried to hide her smile under a contrite look.

"I never thought you'd be such an ungraceful dancer," he added with a smirk.

Her smile froze on her face. Jerk.

"Nice dress, by the way. The color suits you."

She had put on a dark blue dress that reached her knees, with three-quarter sleeves, and her hair was up in a simple, low bun. Simple, yet elegant. At least, she hoped she looked that way.

"Thank you. It's my favorite color."

He smiled, a twinkle in his eyes, and she realized belatedly that his eyes were the same color and became mortified.

"Mine, too. Who would have thought we would have so much in common?"

She could hear laughter in his voice and thought of his dark blue Audi. Had fate become really mischievous with her these days?

"One color doesn't constitute as 'so much,'" she felt the need to point out.

"Who knows? Maybe we share similar tastes in many other areas."

"I highly doubt that," she muttered under her breath.

"Well, actually, I can already name at least one other thing we have in common: we are both hot-headed. You got very lucky that my best friend Kane convinced me it was not worth getting in trouble to get retaliation for that article. Although, I can say that you're far more vindictive than I am, and you have another big flaw: you don't know how to forgive others."

She glared at him. "My actions were justified. If you had shown up like we had agreed and hadn't insulted me for something that wasn't even my fault to begin with, I would never have published such an article about you."

"I already apologized for that."

Even in her irritation, she instantly noticed the change in him. His demeanor became cold and lost its easiness. Yet she didn't heed the warning. "Yeah, well, you didn't even explain why you didn't come for the interview. It's not like you had to go somewhere. You were in your house and napping at that."

She didn't even try to hide her contempt. If he thought he could get away with anything just because he was good-looking, and some people treated him as some celebrity in their school, it was time to wake him up. Plus, she still resented him for making her miss the opportunity to write for the student newspaper.

She wanted him to feel guilty so she could feel less petty about that article.

As the ugly realization hit, she realized that she was making things worse, but she couldn't stop the words. They were a deluge.

"And because of your immature behavior, I lost the opportunity to write for the student newspaper. It was important to me. I could have gotten good recommendations later on for that. Because, unlike you, some of us have to work hard to get through life. But what would you know? Your mom probably still pampers you like a baby, and you think you can throw a tantrum, and be forgiven after, no matter what. Well, let me tell—"

All this time, he had been listening to her silently, an indecipherable look in his eyes. But, at her last comment, he sent her such a murderous glare that the words died on her lips.

"Are you done yet? Because if you are, I would like to

tell you one thing and listen well, 'cuz I'm not going to repeat myself. Never assume to know me, okay? You think you can bullshit crap about me, and you feel justified in your assumptions because I bruised that little ego of yours? It's high time you open your eyes and grow up. Not everything is as you assume it to be."

Without waiting for her reply, he turned and walked out of the room.

"Leah, what was that all about?"

She turned and saw her uncle standing beside her, watching her, worried. In her indignation, she didn't realize that she was still standing on the dance floor, looking like an idiot. She looked around and saw that some people were staring at her. She also saw Liam Hemingway look at her curiously.

It seemed Hayden Hemingway had a talent for making her look like a fool.

"You never mentioned you knew Mr. Hemingway's son," said Uncle Eric as they drove back home.

"Yeah, we have one class together."

"He looked kinda angry when he stormed out of the reception."

Leah knew it was his way of asking what had happened

between them. "He's weird. I think he's bipolar, to be honest."

There's no way she would tell her uncle about the article fiasco as he would tell Aunt Kristina and her dad.

He laughed, shaking his head.

Before he could ask her more details, she asked him about the Hemingway family to divert his attention. She was trying to figure out what she had said to make the boy go from all teasing and relaxed to an angry bull in less than two minutes. Another thing was bothering her, a detail she hadn't picked up on immediately. The fact that Mrs. Hemingway was conspicuously absent from the party.

"Uncle Eric, why wasn't Mr. Hemingway's wife at the party? Are they divorced?"

"It's a complicated story. Some in the company say she left many years ago when their son was only a baby, while others say she passed away."

"What do you mean?"

"I don't know the details. No one really talks about it, but the rumors started because, apparently, there was no funeral. So, it got people's tongues wagging. You know how it is," said her uncle, sighing.

Leah stayed silent, too shocked to say anything. Her uncle spoke up again.

"I think Mr. Hemingway never got over his wife, either. He might be all smiles, but whenever he thinks no one is looking, he gets a haunted look in his eyes. It's sad, really.

He's such a good man. I wonder what really happened. But I guess we'll never know."

Leah wished she had just kept her mouth shut at the party. Or the time she went to his house. Why did she bring up the topic of his mom every time she was venting? God, she was such an idiot.

CHAPTER FIFTEEN

Hayden

On Saturday morning, Hayden went jogging. The laps made him feel good. He could feel he was outrunning his thoughts, leaving them far behind, if only for a few hours.

The achy muscles were a familiar comfort. In their second soccer match, his performance had been less than stellar, and his coach was perplexed and disappointed.

You need to focus more, Hayden, he said during practice.

He wished he could make up his mind about the whole situation. Since his mother's visit, it's like he could feel her invisible presence surrounding him. It was so oppressive, he felt claustrophobic in his own head, like he was stuck in some kind of tunnel, constantly trying to outrun all the conflicting feelings.

He sprinted up the hill, running as fast as he could,

the blood pounding in his head, blotting out every thought.

He stopped, feeling a stitch in his side. He put his hands to his knees. No matter how fast he ran, she was always around him. He wanted to scream in frustration.

Exhausted, he turned back and forced himself to run even faster. Soon, he had to stop because his legs were burning, and his lungs were screaming in agony. He sat on the sidewalk bench, feeling the warmth of the sun.

He had been so angry last night when he came home that he went straight to bed to avoid any questions his dad might have.

Leah Driscoll had a tendency to always say the thing that would push his buttons. He sighed as he remembered the day she had come to his house. He had felt guilty for yelling at her and had tried to make up for his rude behaviour since then.

He wanted to tell her he was trying to make up for acting like a jerk. He knew it wasn't her fault what happened on Saturday. But the words didn't come. And then she had managed to anger him again last night.

He put his fingers through his hair, feeling them damp with sweat.

He wasn't proud of how he acted yesterday, but it was either him leaving or rendering her to ashes with his ire. Well, at least he had tried to be nice. It wasn't his fault the girl didn't know how to keep her tongue in check. He better stay away from her for his own peace of mind.

As Hayden went into the kitchen, he saw that his dad already ate.

"Good morning, Hayden. You're up early today. Anything special?"

"No, just went for a jog."

"I made some scrambled eggs and hash browns."

Hayden poured himself orange juice and sat at the table with his breakfast.

"So, what was that, yesterday?" asked his dad, looking at him over his cup of coffee.

Hayden scowled. Why did his dad have to bring that up when he was trying to forget it?

"Hayden?" His dad looked inquisitive.

"What do you mean?"

"Who was that girl?"

"Urgh, don't remind me of her existence, please."

"You seemed to enjoy her presence yesterday. That is until you decided to storm off," said Liam, a hint of a smile on his lips.

Hayden rolled his eyes. "Her name is Leah and she's just this really annoying girl who thinks she can dish it out but can't take it. Anyways, I don't want to talk about her."

There was silence as Hayden ate his breakfast. Finally, he looked up at his dad and saw that he was watching him.

"Hayden, I know you don't want to talk about your

mom, and you're angry at me for hiding the truth, but it pains me to see you hurting"

Hayden tried to remain impassive. He had promised himself he wouldn't be thinking about her anymore. He needed to move on. He looked at his food, wondering if his dad could tell that he had been thinking about his mom almost every waking hour of his life since she came back.

"I don't think talking would change anything or make things better."

He wondered if his dad knew his grandma had tried to make him meet her.

His father sighed and rubbed his forehead. "Your mother didn't have an easy life, you know? We were best friends, so I was there, and I saw how she was hurting."

"Then why didn't you try to help her?" Hayden looked at his dad, trying to not look accusatory.

"I did, I did the best I could, but her behavior was getting too erratic and impulsive."

Hayden kept silent, unsure of what to say.

"But people change, Hayden. They do things they regret, but they can also become better," said his dad.

Hayden glanced at his expression, and it hurt him to see the pain in his eyes.

"Thank you for breakfast, Dad," he said at last. Without giving his dad a chance to reply, he headed out.

"Hayden, you're not focusing on the game," complained Kane as he completely pulverized his opponent in the Deadly Duty video game.

They were sitting in Kane's living room, playing Hayden's favorite video game but he couldn't focus.

"What's going on, Hayden?"

"What do you mean? I'm fine, just tired,"

"Mate, you try to act as if everything is fine, but I know something is up. Olivia thinks it has to do with that article written by that new girl. You've been weird since then," said Kane, watching Hayden closely.

Hayden couldn't help it, he laughed. "Gosh, trust Liv to come up with such an explanation."

"She even went to see that girl to tell her what she did was wrong," said Kane with a little smile.

"I wonder how Leah took it," said Hayden with a little smile, shaking his head, as he tried to picture the scene. "But it was just a stupid article, I'm past that."

"So, then what is it?" asked Kane, looking determined to get the truth.

Hayden wondered if he could say it. He took a deep breath and decided that he could confide in his best friend. "Something happened that Saturday. Something that made me forget to show up for the interview. And which caused the whole mess with Leah." He stopped.

"What happened?"

Hayden rubbed his face with his hands. "You won't believe it, but my—"

"Kane, we're home," Kane's mom's voice carried from the doorway.

Kane groaned. He gave Hayden an apologetic glance.

His younger brother came into the living room and his hazel eyes lit up when he saw the video game. "I'm playing, too!" said Kai, throwing himself on the couch, disturbing the sleeping cat who, hissing and looking indignant, fled the room. The teenager took the game console from his brother's hand, and got completely absorbed in the game, his lanky figure sprawled all over.

His mom followed. "How are you, Hayden?" she asked with a smile.

"Hi, Aunt Kim. I'm good."

"I'm making chicken for dinner; I hope you're staying."

"Sorry, I have to leave, my dad needs my help," lied Hayden. He didn't think he could watch their happy family again and pretend everything was fine.

Kane looked at him in surprise, but Hayden didn't meet his questioning gaze. "Hayden, didn't you want to tell me something?"

"I'll talk to you later, Kane, I completely forgot I have to go help my dad," said Hayden.

Bidding his goodbyes, he left quickly before they could

stop him. As he sat in the driver's seat, Kane came out on the front porch, but he drove away before he could reach his car.

He could see the figure of his friend in his side mirror as he sped away and felt guilty.

He thought he could talk about his mom, but something got stuck in his throat and it was hard to swallow. As if something heavy had settled in his chest. He feared neither Kane nor Olivia would understand. They had perfect, whole families where both their fathers and mothers had always been there for them.

He sped up faster, trying to chase the gloomy thoughts away. Feeling lonelier than ever.

CHAPTER SIXTEEN

Leah

Saturday morning, Leah opened her eyes, an overwhelming sadness filling her chest as she realized it was her mother's birthday.

They all promised themselves that they'd celebrate this occasion to remember her mother and not wallow in misery as she wouldn't approve of it. But it was hard. All she wanted to do was hide under the blanket and cry the day away.

She felt the tears sting her eyes and roll down her temples as she watched the ceiling. *You can do this, Leah. You're strong, remember? For your dad. For yourself.*

They were going to bring flowers to her grave today, and then spend time at her grandfather's farmhouse. Uncle Eric and his family would be there too.

Her phone beeped with a text from Anaya that said, *Thinking of you and your mom.* She had added a heart and praying hands emoji and Leah smiled despite the pain.

The primary reason why they had decided to move to Bellevue was that her mom wanted to be buried near her mom, and it was her birthplace. And with her grandfather and the rest of the family living here, it only made sense.

They had moved to Montreal when she was six years old as her mom was a professor of English literature at McGill University and when she passed away, there was nothing holding them there anymore.

Gathering all her courage, Leah got up from bed and went to take a shower.

After breakfast, Leah and her dad went to buy pink peonies for her mom again. As they drove to the graveyard, her dad was quiet, and she didn't have the heart to say anything either. They drew strength from each other's presence like they always did.

She still remembered the night her mom passed away, the thunder, the pouring rain. You never forget that kind of pain. As if your heart had been ripped from you, and then crushed some more.

They were staying at Uncle Eric's place, and she had been in complete denial for weeks until she finally broke down. That night, when pain had been too intense, and the constant April rain made it feel as if she would never know happiness again, she had run out of the house to the cemetery, and lying on her mom's grave, she had fallen apart and started crying.

She didn't know how long she had been there, but she felt her dad's strong, warm hands take her by the shoulders.

Even though he was as drenched as she was, she could see the tears on his face, and the pain and fear in his eyes pierced her. She realized then that she had completely forgotten about her dad and his suffering. She had been so absorbed in her own grief that she had felt entitled to it, as if only she was allowed to suffer, not thinking about what her dad was going through, he who had lost his life companion.

She didn't know it was possible to cry any harder, but when she embraced her dad, she felt she could never stop, as if a deluge had opened within her, and was flooding everything. Or maybe it was cleansing all the pain, all the suppressed feelings of anger and resentment at the whole world that had dared to go on, and be happy when her mom was no longer there?

She kept apologizing to her dad as he held her tight, saying how sorry she was for being so selfish, how she hadn't known she was hurting him with her withdrawal. And he had simply rocked her in his arms, kissing her head, and offering refuge and forgiveness.

She looked at her dad now and saw he was lost in his thoughts, dealing with his own grief in his own quiet way. She saw with a painful squeeze of her heart that his temples had started graying.

"Dad, I'm really happy we have each other," she said, smiling through the tears that started falling.

"Me, too, pumpkin. Me, too," he replied, taking one of her hands in his and holding them tightly.

As Leah watched the blue sky, she tried to smile for her

mom's sake. She would keep her promise and be strong.

Uncle Eric and Aunt Kristina were already at their grandfather's place with their five-year-old daughter, Jamie, and had set up the table.

After greeting and hugging everyone, they sat at the table and her grandfather said a prayer as they held hands together.

Leah felt her heart swell with love and gratitude.

I know you're watching, Mum. I love you so much.

Jamie stayed solemn as she sat at the table. She used to love her aunt so much and probably wondered where she went. She was a bright, little girl but even for her, the concept of death was too hard to grasp.

Leah squeezed her little hand and smiled at her when Jamie looked at her.

Later, when they went to the backyard, Jamie sat beside Leah on the swings and whispered, "I saw Grandpa cry today."

Leah felt her heart squeeze. "He told me he had been chopping onions, but I knew he was lying because there were no onions," said Jamie, her small face serious.

"Grandpa is sad today," said Leah.

"Are you sad too?" asked Jamie.

"Yes, very sad," said Leah, trying to smile.

Jamie got closer and put her arms around her neck and Leah hugged her, her tears sliding down her cheeks.

CHAPTER SEVENTEEN

Hayden

Monday morning came way too early, and as Hayden made his way to his classroom, he saw a familiar brunette come from the opposite direction. Should he take it as a bad sign for his test?

Their eyes met, and he saw her eyes widen in surprise. He decided he didn't want to spoil his mood so early in the morning and simply ignored her.

He thought she was going to simply pass him by, but to his disbelief and utter irritation, she made her way toward him. *Great. Just what he needed. A lecture and it wasn't even ten in the morning yet.* He hadn't even had coffee yet, for God's sake.

"Hayden!"

Praying he would keep his calm, he turned toward

her. "Leah, can we talk later? I need to get to my class now."

He was giving her a chance to turn tail and flee with her head attached to her shoulders. But either the girl was very brave or very stupid because she still proceeded to talk.

"It won't take long. I just needed to say something."

He noticed then that she seemed uncomfortable and almost bashful and couldn't seem to look him in the eye. That was interesting.

"Look, about what I said on Friday night. I wanted to say that I'm sorry."

"You said a lot of things on Friday night. Care to be more specific?"

"All of it. I shouldn't have brought up the interview or the article when you already apologized for it. And the things I said about you. You're right. I don't know you, so I shouldn't assume things I know nothing about. So, yeah, I'm sorry."

He blinked. That was unexpected. He had been prepared to have her rant and accuse him of spoiling her Friday night on top of all the other wrongs he had already done to her. But an apology? Never in a million years. Maybe he had heard her wrong?

"Did you really just apologize, Leah Driscoll?"

"I can admit my mistakes and own up to them. No big deal."

But he could see that it was a big deal for her. She probably wasn't used to being in the wrong. He smiled. "It's okay. No hard feelings."

She looked up at him, a relieved smile appearing on her lips and illuminating her whole face. He wanted to say she should smile more, it really suited her. But he kept quiet.

"Okay, then. Bye."

He nodded, and she left, waving. He followed her with his eyes till she turned around the corner and shook his head. Unbelievable. The girl was something. Just when he thought he had her figured out, she went and proved him wrong. He went to his class, a small smile on his lips.

Until he remembered that he had a test waiting for him.

The week flew by in a flash, and Hayden found himself once again running on Saturday morning. He was starting to enjoy those morning runs.

All week, he kept reassuring Kane that he was fine. When his best friend asked him what he had wanted to tell him at his place, he lied, saying he had had a fight with his dad about schoolwork.

Kane had looked him in the eyes, trying to see if he was lying, but then Olivia showed up and he didn't mention it again. Olivia, who was always worried about him, was relieved when he told her the same lie that he told Kane.

Watching her relief, he had felt like the biggest jerk on Earth, but he dreaded telling them the truth. Something inside of him curled up in shame just thinking of saying the truth out loud.

He continued to run faster until he reached the beach shore. It was empty at such an early hour, and he enjoyed the peace while walking on the sand, even with the chilly breeze of early October.

The sun was dazzling, and he looked on the horizon to take in the full splendor of the view.

His eyes stopped on a hooded figure in a windbreaker who was bending to pick up something on the ground, and when she turned around, he was surprised to see it was Leah.

She looked as surprised as he felt, and he didn't know what to do at first, but he didn't have to decide as she started walking toward him, removing her wind-blown hair away from her face.

"Hayden Hemingway, I would never in a million years have guessed you like to take strolls on the beach on a Saturday morning," she said, grinning.

"Told you there are many things you don't know about me," he replied. He looked at her hands and saw she was holding seashells.

She followed his gaze and extended one to him. "Aren't they beautiful? I always liked collecting them when I was little. My mom and I would see who could find the most interesting shell whenever we would go to the beach," she said, a happy smile on her face at the memory.

He took the small, gray seashell, and liked how smooth it was in his palm.

"That's cool. She didn't come today?" he asked, looking around.

"She passed away," she replied softly, her serene expression marred by sadness.

"I'm so sorry. I didn't know." He wished he had kept his mouth shut.

"It's okay. It gets a bit easier with time, but I still miss her terribly, and I know I always will," she said, biting her lower lip.

He wanted to offer words of comfort but was at a loss of what to say. She seemed to feel his discomfort, for she tried to smile, even though her eyes seemed too bright.

"It's quite windy this morning," she said, pulling her jacket higher around her neck. She glanced at his light sweatshirt hoodie and running pants. "You're not cold?"

"No, I went for a jog this morning, and before I knew it, I was on the beach."

"And here I thought you were coming every weekend," she teased him.

"No, it's the first time I've come here so early. It's beautiful," he admitted.

An awkward silence settled in, and he wondered how to break it. Before he could ask her how she liked her new school, she looked down at her watch.

"I have to go. It was nice seeing you, Hayden. Enjoy the rest of your walk."

"Thanks. Have a nice day."

She waved as she walked away. More people had started

gathering on the beach, mostly elderly couples or families with small kids who were running around, laughing loudly. Feeling out of place, he headed home, too.

CHAPTER EIGHTEEN

Leah

"Anaya, can you go get the popcorn while I buy the tickets? It will save us time." That was the problem with Saturday evenings. All the lines were super long.

Anaya had come to visit for the weekend, and they decided to go to the movies. Leah had missed her friend so much and had been looking forward to having her at her house for the first time since they moved.

Her mother was going to pick her up tomorrow, but until then, they were going to enjoy each minute until they saw each other again.

Finally, Leah's turn came, and she got two tickets for *The Wanderer*. The critics had all praised the movie, and she couldn't wait to watch it. As she went to look for her friend, she dropped one of the tickets, and as she picked it up, she bumped into someone.

"Sorry!"

"It's okay. I already know you can be clumsy," said Hayden with a smile.

"Hayden!" She was too surprised to even reply with something witty.

"Hello, Leah."

"Hayden?"

The two of them turned as his friends approached them with a questioning look on their faces.

"Guys, this is Leah. Leah, this is Kane and Olivia," Hayden said, pointing to the dark-haired Asian boy who nodded to her, an amused expression in his eyes.

"We know each other," said Olivia, giving Leah a friendly smile.

"Seriously, Leah, that article was brilliant. It was time someone took Hayden down a peg, or two," said Kane, laughing slightly.

"Ha. Ha. Very funny. You should become a humorist, Kane," deadpanned Hayden.

Kane didn't have time to respond because Anaya appeared just then. "There you are! I was looking for you everywhere!"

"Sorry," said Leah before she proceeded to introduce her friend to her classmates.

"Nice to meet you, guys. Wait." She turned toward Hayden, as if suddenly realizing something important. "You're Hayden *Hemingway*?"

"Yeah," he said, looking slightly surprised.

Leah had not filled Anaya in on everything that had happened since the article fiasco; she was waiting to tell her everything in person, as she felt it wasn't something she could discuss over the phone.

"But I thought you guys hated each other! Weren't you the one who got Leah fired from the journal team?" She looked at Leah, as if saying, *You've got a lot to explain, Missy.*

"That was before. We're okay now. We cleared up the misunderstanding, right, Leah?" Hayden was looking at her with an amused expression.

She acquiesced and looked at Anaya with an apologetic look that said, *I'll explain everything later.*

"Which movie are you going to?" asked Kane.

"*The Wanderer*, and you?" replied Leah.

"*Kings and Men*, if there are enough tickets," he said.

"We should get them now," said Olivia and each group went in their own directions after saying goodbye.

While the two girls waited for the commercials to end, and the movie to start, Leah filled in her best friend about the recent developments that had happened between Hayden and her, ending with how just last Saturday morning, she had run into him on the beach and since then, they were somewhat friendly at school.

"Maybe it's a good thing," Anaya said.

"What do you mean?" asked Leah, confusion coloring her tone.

"Well, you have to admit that he is very cute," Anaya teased.

"What does that have to do with anything?" exclaimed Leah, stupefied.

"Oh, come on. Don't tell me you didn't wish you had started on better terms when you saw how good-looking he was?"

"No!" exclaimed Leah. The thought had never crossed her mind.

"What no?" asked a voice behind her, and Leah was so startled she almost dropped her popcorn.

Hayden was sitting down behind her, joined by Kane and Olivia.

"Nothing!" replied Leah rapidly, before Anaya could embarrass her further. She was glad for the darkness that hid her flushed face.

"What are you guys doing here? Didn't you say you were going to watch the other movie?" asked Anaya.

"There were only two tickets left, and *The Wanderer* was our second choice, anyway," answered Kane.

Leah noticed how Hayden was holding Olivia's bag and passing her stuff when she was seated. *Are they together?* she wondered. *So what if they're together? Why should that be my concern?*

She turned in her seat and focused on the screen. She was not going to let Anaya's words mess up with her mind.

"And then he punched me for taking what he had decided was his toy. Of course, I wasn't about to let him beat me, so I punched him back. The kindergarten teacher put us in the corner for fighting. And we bonded during our detention. As the saying goes, nothing strengthens friendship as much as sharing the same plight, and thus, our friendship began," concluded Kane.

"You mean, nothing strengthens a friendship as a good fight does," said Hayden as everyone was laughing at the story.

They were sitting at a table at a coffee shop, drinking coffee–tea for Leah–and eating doughnuts. After the movie ended, they all agreed dessert was in order.

Leah noticed that the three of them were very close, and Olivia seemed to be very doting on Hayden especially. She almost groaned.

Brain, what is wrong with you? Why are you even thinking about this?

"Leah?"

She looked at Anaya who was looking at her. "Sorry, yes?"

She realized she had zoned out while they were all talking.

Anaya tried to hide her smile, and Leah feared she had seen her watch Hayden and Olivia. "Kane asked you how you like school?" repeated Anaya.

"Oh, it's really nice!" said Leah, trying to sound cheerful.

Just then a group of teenagers came in, among them Riley.

Their eyes met and she saw him break into a big grin before his smile faded as he saw who exactly she was sitting with.

Everyone at the table turned to follow her gaze and she felt guilt assuage her as Riley looked back, a perplexed expression on his face.

Leah realized how the whole scene must look to him, her enjoying time with Hayden Hemingway, of all people.

Like with Anaya, she hadn't told him anything about Hayden, and now felt like the biggest fool. She could feel her face flushing.

Riley said something to his friends before making his way toward them.

"Hey, Leah, what are you doing here?" he asked as he approached their table.

Before she could reply, Hayden spoke up, "I think it's obvious, Connors, but if you need to be stated the obvious: she is spending time with her friends."

He had never looked so arrogant as he did now. The way he emphasized the last word was meant as a provocation, and Leah winced, wishing he wasn't so provocative.

Riley's gaze shifted to Hayden at his words, his expression turning cold. As she saw the two young men look at each other with barely hidden hatred, she understood that the term "not the best of friends" had been the understatement of the century.

Riley looked back at her, as if expecting her to deny everything.

"Yeah," she cleared her throat, finding it too dry suddenly. "We met at the movies and decided to get some coffee afterwards."

The atmosphere was so tense she tried to think of something to say to alleviate it. She saw that Kane was also watching Riley with careful caution, whereas Olivia completely avoided looking in Riley's direction. Their eyes met, and Leah saw discomfort in the redhead's green eyes. *Why did she seem so uncomfortable around Riley?*

"I see." Riley nodded. Looking back at Leah, he said, "Well, then, I'll see you around, I guess."

As she watched him leave, she felt like the most horrible person ever, and wondered how she'd be able to explain herself. His upset expression made her realize how terrible of a friend she was, and before it was too late, she got up and ran after him.

"Riley!"

He turned around as she approached him.

"I'm so sorry about that. I should have told you that Hayden and I made peace and today we met unexpectedly." Her face was contrite.

He smiled kindly. "It's okay, Leah. You can be friends with whoever you want, and just because Hemingway and I don't get along, doesn't mean you can't be his friend. I just don't want to lose you as a friend, that's all."

She looked at him, confused. "Why would you lose me as a friend?"

Riley cleared his throat. "Just keep in mind that not

everything Hemingway might say is true," he said cryptically.

"What do you mean?"

"He can be very biased."

Leah smiled. "Don't worry, I won't let him talk bad of you."

Riley looked at her with a strange gaze, as if wanting to say something and thinking better of it. "Anyways, my friends are waiting, so I better go," he said at last, looking over his shoulder.

She watched him leave with his friends, feeling strangely sad. She hoped she wasn't going to lose him as a friend.

When she came back to their table, there was an awkward silence.

"You and Connors are friends?" asked Hayden. But his expression wasn't fooling her. He knew they were friends; he had seen them at school more than enough.

"Yes. We are very good friends. He was actually the one who dropped me at your house the day of the interview," she added, to gauge his reaction.

Why was she baiting him? Why was she bringing up the bad memories again?

"I see." He tried to be nonchalant, but Leah could tell that something was bothering him.

"May I ask why you two don't like each other so much?"

"We've never been fond of each other."

"Yes, Riley told me the same thing. But why? You can't just hate a person without a reason."

"Oh, believe me, I have plenty of reasons to hate him."

"I really hope for your sake that it wasn't a stupid fight about some girl."

She felt Kane shift uncomfortably, and Olivia went completely rigid.

Kane cleared his throat. "Hey guys, someone want to try their caramel latte? I've heard it is really good."

Leah realized that he was trying to divert their attention from the current conversation, and she felt bad for being so intrusive. Clearly, something bad had happened between the two of them, and a girl was concerned, Leah was certain. She would be lying if she said that curiosity wasn't killing her, but she knew that she had no right to ask.

"Me!" exclaimed Anaya, who had understood, and was also trying to dispel the tension.

Kane and Anaya got up to get their drinks and nobody mentioned Riley again.

"I had a lot of fun. It was really nice meeting you all," said Anaya.

"It was a pleasure to meet you, too," replied Kane, smiling broadly at Anaya, and Leah got the impression he was talking for himself. She met Hayden's eyes, and they both tried to hide their smiles.

"We should meet more often, now that Hayden and Leah are such great buddies," added Kane, a twinkle in his eye.

Olivia smiled, but it seemed contrived. She had been quiet since Riley came and hadn't seemed happy since then.

"Absolutely," agreed Anaya enthusiastically, and Leah shot her a sideways glance, trying to convey to her that she was overdoing it.

"Bye, Anaya, hope we get the chance to meet again," said Hayden.

"Don't worry, I'll come visit often," said Anaya and looked at Leah sideways with an amused smile.

"See you in school, Leah."

"See you," said Leah. It would be a very interesting week, she realized, as she thought of Riley and their intense rivalry. She wondered if she'd ever find out what happened.

CHAPTER NINETEEN

HAYDEN

When Hayden got home, he saw that his dad was asleep on the sofa, his glasses askew and a book on his lap. He put the book and his glasses away, being careful to not wake him up, as he covered him with the blanket they always kept on the couch.

As he looked at his sleeping form, he wondered how he was dealing with the situation with his mom. He hadn't tried to bring up the subject of his mom again since last Saturday, but Hayden could see his preoccupied look. He missed their old days, before his mom came into the picture, shattering their peaceful existence.

Hayden sighed, annoyed at himself for always thinking of his mom whenever he looked at his dad.

"Is everything alright, Hayden?"

He startled.

"Yes, Dad, just came in. You fell asleep."

His dad looked at the blanket and smiled. "There's some leftovers from dinner if you're hungry."

"I'm good, I already ate. I'm exhausted, I'm going to bed. Good night."

"Good night, Hayden."

Hayden woke up, disoriented, eyes blinking to adjust to the darkness, the digital clock glinting 3:33 a.m.

This time, the dream was different. He was watching as his mother went into the water while he watched helplessly until the water swallowed her.

He touched his cheeks, feeling the wetness of his tears.

The more he tried to avoid thinking about his mom, the more intense and scarier his dreams were becoming. As if punishing him for daring to avoid her.

He sighed and raked his fingers through his hair, damp with sweat.

He fell back on his bed and watched the ceiling, feeling as if he was out of his body, floating somewhere above.

His bedroom door opened, and his dad came in.

"Dad? What happened?" asked Hayden, confused and worried. Why was his dad up at such an hour?

His dad kept watching him in silence, and Hayden got up from bed, hurrying to see what was wrong.

"Dad, what's going on?" he asked, grabbing him by the shoulder. His hand met empty air.

Startled, he looked up and saw that he was all alone on some island as everything–water and sky–turned black around him.

He woke up with a scream. "Dad!"

He tried to get out of bed and, getting entangled in his sheets, fell off the bed.

His door opened and his dad ran in. "Hayden, son, you okay?"

Hayden wanted to weep from the relief. His dad was beside him, alive and safe. He wanted to speak but was too choked up. He could only nod. He didn't want his dad to worry, and as his dad switched on his nightstand lamp, he felt safe, foolish, and embarrassed by his reaction.

"Sorry, I just had a bad dream," he said, not looking his dad in the eye.

"Do you want a glass of water?"

Hayden thought he must look pitiful sitting on the floor, sweaty, his facial expression a strange combination of scared and relieved.

"No, I'm good, sorry that I woke you up, Dad, you can go back to sleep." Hayden sat back on his bed. He didn't trust his legs to support him just then.

"You sure? You look shaken up. Do you need something?"

"I'll survive."

His dad's gaze lingered on him, and he opened his mouth to say something, but he seemed to change his mind at the last minute. "Okay, son, get some sleep, I'll see you tomorrow."

That had been the first time he ever dreamt of losing his dad. His dad had always been his constant. Always present for him. He couldn't even imagine his life without his dad.

His thoughts went to his mom, and he wondered how she was. She hadn't come to see him since that Saturday morning, and it had been a month already.

He remembered his dad's conversation on the phone and turning pale with fear when he saw Hayden. He wondered if they had seen each other since then. He wondered if his mom had given up...

Judging by the fact that she hadn't tried to come see him again, she probably realized he didn't want anything to do with her. He didn't know how that made him feel. He couldn't bring himself to feel the relief he had assumed he would feel.

He put his blanket over his head and tried to fall asleep.

When he went to the kitchen in the morning, still groggy from the lack of sleep, his dad was already up.

"Morning," he said as he went to serve himself a glass of juice.

"Morning, Hayden, slept well?" he asked.

Hayden saw that his dad looked just as tired as him and felt guilty as he realized he probably hadn't been able to go back to sleep either.

"Kinda. Sorry for that, you probably weren't able to get any sleep after that, right?" asked Hayden with a sheepish expression.

"Hayden, as long as you're alright, that's all that matters," his dad said. His voice was affectionate, and Hayden felt his guilt increase, remembering how much of a hard time he had given him.

As Hayden sat down at the table with his scrambled eggs, his dad cleared his throat. "Hayden, the principal called me on Friday. He said you've been missing your swimming classes since the beginning of school."

Hayden had been expecting this conversation. "Sorry, Dad, I meant to tell you, I want to drop the swimming class."

"Why, Hayden?" His dad was calm as usual.

"I hate that class, and I already know how to swim anyway, so it's useless. I can spend that period on some other subject instead," said Hayden.

"Hayden, do you know why I always forced you to go to swimming lessons since you were young and were always crying that you didn't want to go?"

Hayden felt he already knew the answer. It seemed a lot of his answers had to do with his mom.

"I think I do," said Hayden, lowering his gaze to his plate where the scrambled eggs lay, forgotten.

"I wanted to make sure you were never again in a situation where you'd be helpless in the water," said his dad quietly, confirming his guesses.

"I know, Dad, but since I already know how to swim, I just don't see the point of going to the swimming class," said Hayden, deciding he will still get what he wanted.

There was no way he was going to expose himself to

ridicule like that first day of school.

Kane had asked him a couple of times why he was not going to the class, and Hayden was running out of excuses. He didn't want to admit he was scared because he had a childish fear of drowning whenever he felt his feet no longer touched the floor.

"But the swimming classes will only help you get better and stronger," said his dad, frowning, not understanding his reticence.

"Dad, I don't want to go to swimming classes, they're not helping me. Not anymore," said Hayden, his voice firm. "If anything, they make me feel worse," he added.

His dad looked at him with a pensive look, as if realizing something he should have realized a long time ago. "Hayden, I'm sorry, I didn't know that's how swimming made you feel. I should have known. I just didn't think you remembered that incident, you were so small. A two-year-old toddler." His dad raked his hair with his fingers.

Hayden wanted to smile. He recognized that gesture, a gesture he himself made often. "I don't remember, not consciously, at least. But I don't know how to say it, it's like my body freezes when I'm in the water. Even though I know perfectly well I can swim, and whenever I'm above the water, I'm fine, I can do the laps. But the teacher always asks me to dive into the water, and I hate that. It messes me up."

Hayden let it all out, feeling relieved he could tell

his dad the truth, no longer caring if he sounded like a coward. He hated the feeling of powerlessness that being underwater gave him. He'd rather not have to experience it if he could.

"Why didn't you tell me before?"

"I didn't want to be a coward. Especially since the fear of drowning seemed so unreasonable. But when you told me what happened, I understood," said Hayden, feeling light as the truth left his chest.

"I'll talk to the principal, my son. I'll explain everything and see what class you can take instead to complete the requirements," said his dad, looking at him the way he always did whenever he wanted to show him he was there for him.

"Thank you, Dad," said Hayden. He wondered why he had waited so long to tell his dad the truth when it had been so easy.

He had assumed his dad would be angry and would force him to go back, but he had forgotten how fair his dad always was.

"Hayden, can you pass by the pastry shop and get some pastries for tomorrow?" asked his dad as he got up from the table.

He had forgotten about the Thanksgiving supper. His grandma always made a feast for the occasion.

"Sure, I'll pass by later today," said Hayden.

CHAPTER TWENTY

Leah

"Thank you so much, Leah," said Aunt Kristina as she and Uncle Eric prepared to leave, leaving Jamie overnight.

"I was looking forward to spending some time with Jamie. Since school started, I almost haven't seen her at all," said Leah with a smile at her cute little cousin.

Anaya had left this morning, and her uncle and aunt were going to a wedding outside the city, coming back tomorrow for Thankisgiving as they were planning to have dinner at her grandfather's place.

"Bye, Mommy, bye, Daddy," said the little girl, waving at her parents, her plush unicorn under her arm.

"It's such a beautiful day, what do you say we go to the park and then get some cake?" proposed Leah enthusiastically to Jamie who nodded, jumping in excitement.

Like Leah, she had a very sweet tooth, and whenever they came to Montreal to visit Leah and her parents, they always went to the café Rockaberry to enjoy their famous pies.

Leah missed the café and was delighted to find a café nearby that had almost the same desserts she loved. She had found it by chance as she was navigating through the city the first week, trying to get used to the new environment.

"Dad, we're going out," said Leah, calling to her dad who, being an actuary, was in his office as he had to submit some risk assessment report for his company.

"Okay, pumpkin, enjoy your outing and be careful. Bye my princess," shouted her dad through the open door of his study.

"Bye Uncle Aaron," yelled Jamie, ready to go outside.

When they arrived at the park, Leah saw that many had decided to enjoy the sunny day. Despite the bright sun, it was quite windy and Leah was glad they were dressed warmly enough.

Jamie ran to the swings, the leaves flying under her little feet, her blond curls bouncing on her shoulders. The cold was turning the leaves orange and red, and Leah smiled, enjoying the beautiful view.

"Tadi, can you push me?" asked Jamie, trying to propel herself.

"Hold tight, I'll be pushing very high," said Leah with a smile.

"Higher, higher!" yelled Jamie, swinging her legs excitedly.

"What if you fly away?"

"That's silly, Tadi. I don't have wings. How can I fly away?"

Leah laughed. Her little cousin was too smart for her own good.

"Jamie, be careful to not eat the cake too fast or you'll have a tummy ache," said Leah as she watched the little girl taking a big bite of her dessert.

"This is delicious."

"Yes, it is. I see that you learned another big word. Did you learn it in kindergarten?"

"No, Mommy did. Look, that's the word cup," said the child by pointing at the wall in front of her where words like *coffee love, perfect cup, like home, mama's pie* were painted in capital blue and red letters.

"Yes, you're right," smiled Leah.

Café Gourmand had a very colorful interior. All the round tables and chairs were a vibrant red, while the long sofa along the wall was white, and the cozy decor made it a quaint place.

"Oopsie… I dropped a piece," Jamie said, and was about

to get off her chair to get it, but Leah stopped her.

"It's okay, sweetie, I'll get it."

She grabbed a napkin and collected the fallen piece under the table. As she sat back, her attention went to the front door as it opened and none other than Hayden Hemingway came in.

Their eyes met, and she smiled.

"Is it becoming a tradition of ours, Leah?" he inquired as he approached their table.

Before she could reply, Jamie spoke up, "What is tradition?"

"It's like a habit," explained Leah.

"Like brushing teeth? Daddy says that brushing teeth is an important habit."

"Yes, sweetie."

"Who do we have here?" asked Hayden, smiling at Jamie.

"Jamie," said the child. "And this is my Tadi." She pointed at Leah.

"That's a nice name, Jamie. I'm Hayden."

"Hi, Hayden. Your name sounds like my best friend's name! Her name is Jaiden," said the little girl, excited.

"Jamie and Jaiden, you really sound like the best of friends."

She nodded seriously. "Best friends forever. She even gave me a bracelet. Look."

She pointed to her tiny wrist where she wore a delicate bracelet with two small charms, a flower and an infinity symbol.

"Mommy said that means forever," Jamie said solemnly, pointing at the horizontal eight charm.

"Your mommy's right."

"Do you wanna take a seat?" asked Leah, gesturing at the table.

"With pleasure," said Hayden.

"I'm eating Oreo cheesecake," said Jamie. "Do you like it?"

"That's my favorite. That and the choco-brownie one," answered Hayden, grinning. "Would you like one?"

"Yes!" Jamie's whole face lit up at the prospect of more dessert.

"No, thank you, I don't even think she'll be able to finish this slice," interjected Leah. "The portions are huge."

Jamie looked crestfallen.

"You'll try it another time, sweetheart, ok?" Leah appeased her.

"I'll order one, and you can try it," said Hayden.

The little girl looked at Leah, afraid she would say no.

"One small bite won't hurt, now, will it?" Hayden continued, his expression asking Leah to agree.

"Okay," conceded Leah. "I guess a tiny bite won't hurt, but only one."

"Yay!" giggled Jamie.

After ordering, Hayden turned toward Jamie. "My grandma always told me that you can tell a person is nice and kind if they like sweets," he said, winking.

"Really?" exclaimed Jamie, her eyes round. "So, I am a very nice person," she said. "And Tadi, too," she said. "And you, too!" she added with a happy smile.

"Yes, we're all a happy-go-lucky, kind bunch, indeed," said Hayden while Leah rolled her eyes, smiling despite herself.

When they were done, Hayden excused himself and while they waited and put on their jackets, Jamie tried to find more words on the wall.

"Look, it's the word love!" she said as she pointed at the red letters on the wall.

"Ready to go?" asked Hayden, appearing at their table with a white pastry box he showed Jamie.

"The choco-brownie just for you," he said with a smile.

"Cake!" exclaimed Jamie, clapping her hands.

"Oh, you didn't have to get her anything," said Leah.

Hayden winked at Jamie. "Of course I did. That's her prize for getting all the words on the wall."

Leah made her way to pay, but Hayden stopped her. "I already paid," he said.

"That's really nice of you, thank you," said Leah, feeling completely surprised and touched by such consideration.

He smiled and opened the door for them as they went out.

"Thank you, Hayden." Jamie grinned.

When he heard they had walked to the place, he told them he'd drop them home. "Don't argue, it's getting late, and Jamie is getting tired."

Leah saw that Jamie was yawning. It was time for her nap.

They sat in the back seat, and soon Jamie was fast asleep on Leah's lap. At the red light, Hayden looked over his shoulder and smiled when he saw the sleeping figure.

"Why does Jamie call you Tadi?"

"It means Aunt in Estonian. Her mom is Estonian, and she read her a story about a little girl and her aunt, and since then, she's been calling me that, thinking I'm her aunt."

"She loves you a lot."

"I don't know what I would do without her and my aunt, uncle, and grandfather. After Mom passed away, Aunt Kristina was so supportive and despite us still living in Montreal, she and Uncle Eric would come visit often to make sure Dad and I were okay."

Hayden looked at her through the rear-view mirror, and Leah turned her gaze away when she realized she had tears in her eyes.

"Jamie was so little then. I can't believe how fast time flew by. I remember her being this tiny, little baby, and now she's going to kindergarten," she babbled, hoping to hide her emotional reaction.

He stopped the car, and she saw they were in front of her house.

"Wait, I'll carry her home," said Hayden, getting out of the vehicle. He made his way to her side and opened the door. As he bent to her level to take the sleepy child, he turned his head and Leah stopped breathing. Their faces were mere inches away and she blushed hard when she saw his gaze go to her lips.

"Sorry," he mumbled and, turning his face quickly away,

carefully picked up Jamie in his arms.

She opened the door for him to get into the house.

"Leah–" Her dad didn't get the chance to continue as his daughter put her finger in front of her mouth.

"Shh…" she whispered, pointing at Jamie who was sleeping in Hayden's arms.

"You can put her in my room," Leah whispered, indicating the stairs while giving the box of cake to her dad.

In Leah's bedroom, he carefully put Jamie on her bed, and Leah proceeded to remove her light coat and shoes. She then proceeded to put pillows on the side of the bed so the child wouldn't fall off.

She turned around and found herself face to face with Hayden who was standing behind her all this time. She was so close she could see his eyelashes.

"Sorry," he apologized and stepped aside.

She hoped he couldn't see her blush as it was getting embarrassing at this point.

They made their way downstairs and entered the kitchen.

"Dad, this is Hayden Hemingway. Hayden, this is my dad, Aaron."

"Nice to meet you, sir," Hayden said, extending his hand for a handshake.

"The pleasure's all mine, Hayden. Dinner will be ready soon; I hope you're not in a hurry."

"Oh, thank you, but I don't want to impose."

"Don't be ridiculous. That's the least we can do after you

treated us to dessert today, and bought this cake on top of that," said Leah. "Do you need help, Dad?"

"Everything is almost done, except for the salad."

"I'll do it," she said.

"I can help set up the table," offered Hayden, feeling useless, standing in the middle of the kitchen.

"I love soccer," said her dad when Hayden told him that he was playing as a striker for the school's team. "Didn't you have to write an article on soccer for school, Leah?"

Leah regretted now asking him all those questions and telling him it was for an article.

Hayden almost choked on his glass of water and started coughing.

"You okay?" asked Leah.

"Yes, sorry for that, it went down the wrong way," said Hayden, slightly red from the exertion.

"I hate when that happens," said Aaron with a smile.

"So, what happened with that article?" asked her dad again, turning toward her.

"Oh, it didn't work out, they found someone more qualified," said Leah, lowering her eyes.

"Don't worry, pumpkin, I'm sure there will be other opportunities, and you hate sports, anyway," said her dad, comforting her, and she felt ashamed for lying.

Hayden had remorse in his eyes. She smiled, letting him know it was all good.

Jamie appeared at the entrance of the kitchen.

"Look who's awake," said Leah and got up from the table to serve her a plate. "Did you wash your hands?"

"Yes, I did. What's for dinner?" she asked as she climbed on the chair with the double cushion.

"Meatballs and rice."

"No meatballs!" grimaced Jamie. "I want lasagna."

"Your mommy said you already had lasagna yesterday, Jamie, you can't eat it every day."

"Yes, I can," affirmed Jamie.

"Unfortunately, there's none today, so you have to eat what's for dinner tonight," said Leah with a tone that invited no argument.

"Then, just rice. I don't want meatballs," pouted Jamie.

"I'll add a bit of sauce as plain rice will be too dry."

"What if you break the meatballs into tiny pieces and mix them with rice? Then, you won't feel them at all," suggested Hayden.

Leah could see Jamie was torn between her dislike of meatballs and her desire to have Hayden's approval, as she was accustomed to people praising her. Finally, the need for praise won over, and she agreed to try one meatball. Leah smiled.

As she accompanied Hayden to the door later that night, she almost had the urge to pinch herself to make sure she wasn't dreaming. She still couldn't believe Hayden Hemingway, someone she thought she'd despise for the rest of her life, had spent the evening at her house.

He must have been thinking along the same lines, for

she heard him chuckle and shake his head in disbelief. "Who would have thought, eh?" he said, looking at her with an amused expression, and that half-smile of his that she had come to associate with him, and realized she didn't mind it at all now.

"Indeed," she said with a voice full of mirth.

"Thank you for having me for dinner."

"Thank you for the cake. Jamie is already excited for tomorrow because of it."

"Next time, I'll get her the triple-chocolate mousse cake, she'll love it."

"That's kind of you, but her parents are going to kill me for giving their daughter cavities," she said, amused.

"It's only baby teeth, they'll fall out anyway."

"I can already see what kind of dad you'll be," she said, and they laughed.

There was a small silence as neither knew how to say goodbye.

"Well, then, I guess I'll be seeing you in school. Good night," Hayden said finally.

"Good night."

She watched as he walked down the pavement and saw him look at her and wave before getting in the car and driving away.

She went back inside and joined her dad and Jamie in the living room, taking a seat on the loveseat. They were watching *The Lion King*, and Leah watched the heart-warming scene of Simba and Mufasa playing under the starry night. Jamie, who had her head in her uncle's lap and her favorite plush unicorn under her arm, was riveted to the screen. Her dad looked up at her, and they shared a smile.

CHAPTER TWENTY-ONE

Hayden

As Hayden drove home, still trying to process everything that had happened, he felt a small smile on his lips.

He had been pleasantly surprised at how at ease he felt with Leah, which was weird considering their bad beginning. He wondered how things would be at school and frowned when he thought of Riley. Should he tell her not to be friends with him? He knew what a douchebag he was, but she obviously didn't. Should he tell Connors to stay away from her?

He snorted. *Hayden, who do you think you are? Her boyfriend? I'm not sure Leah will appreciate being told with whom to be friends.*

He shook his head, trying to get rid of the weird thoughts and remembered he forgot to get the pastries for tomorrow's dinner. He hoped they were open tomorrow or he'll have to explain why he didn't get the pastries like he was supposed to.

As Hayden went to put his soccer bag in the back seat of his car before school, something small glinted in the floor and he took it. It was a small, golden hoop. Leah's earring. He smiled, putting it in his pocket.

Arriving at school, he went to his locker to deposit his bags and retrieve his textbooks. He had a free period because he no longer needed to go to swimming class, so he took advantage of that period to go to the library and study.

Entering the quiet place, he saw a few students already working silently on their laptops while some were in the comfortable blue armchairs, reading.

He sat at a table and proceeded to work on his assignment. He wanted to finish his paper, even if the deadline was only in one week.

As he thought about his next paragraph, Olivia sat beside him. "Hi," she whispered with a smile.

"Hey, Liv, what are you doing here?" he asked.

"Same as you, I came to study," she said.

"What about your class?"

"It was canceled, the teacher got sick, and they couldn't

find a substitute," she said, taking out her laptop. "So, how have you been?" She gave him a quick side glance as she typed her password in.

"Good, how was your weekend?"

"I helped Mom in the store, and then went to my tennis lesson. My shoulder is still hurting," she said, rubbing her upper body.

"Poor you, you should use some heating cream or a heating pad," he said, looking at her with empathy. He knew all about sore muscles and pain.

"It's okay, I took some Advil this morning; hopefully, it will help," she said. "Anyways, how was your weekend?"

"It was good," he said, debating whether to tell her he was at Leah's house.

"I texted you, but you didn't reply. I was worried something happened," she said.

"Sorry, I was at Leah's and forgot to answer after that," he apologized.

He saw her freeze and her smile disappearing as she blinked twice. "You were at *Leah's* house?"

"I know, right, I was surprised myself," he chuckled. "We met at Café Gourmand on Sunday, and after dropping her at her house, she and her dad invited me over for dinner."

"That's… uhm nice," said Olivia, suddenly looking at her laptop, a frown on her face.

"You should definitely apply some heating cream, only then will the pain get better," said Hayden, looking at her as she pinched her lips.

"Yeah, I should," she murmured, fixing her laptop screen.

Hayden went back to his essay.

"We should get to class," he said when the first period ended. Olivia nodded, packing her stuff.

She was quiet the whole time and he realized she was upset. He had agreed to go to the movies after they had begged him as he had already bailed twice before when they went out, and here he was, spending the evening with a girl he had met only last month. Whereas he knew Olivia even before he had met Kane. They started at the same preschool when they were only two years old.

"We should go to that La Poutinerie place this weekend," he said.

He wanted to make up for the times he refused to go out with them those past few weeks.

"Yeah, okay," said Olivia. She sounded disinterested.

"Liv, I'm sorry, I know I've been acting weird these days, but school and soccer have been hard these past weeks, and I didn't want to fall behind," he apologized as they stopped in front of his locker.

Olivia sighed. "Hayden, you don't have to be sorry, I was just worried, but I guess you're okay, right, since you obviously have time for other friends," she said, looking down at her nails, avoiding his gaze.

He didn't like the bitterness in her voice. Guilt gnawed at his guts. "You and Kane always come first, you know that," he said, hurt by her reproach. What was he supposed to do now? Stop making new friends? Liv was being a bit unreasonable.

"And that's why I want us to spend time together this weekend, like old times," he said with a small smile.

"Hey guys," said Kane.

Olivia turned her gaze away from Hayden and greeted Kane.

"What's with the gloomy face?" asked Kane, always coming directly to the point.

"Nothing," replied Olivia as she looked at the students passing by, completely refusing to look in Hayden's direction.

Kane looked at Hayden with a raised eyebrow. He knew that expression. *What's wrong with her? Did you guys fight?* Kane was asking non-verbally.

Hayden shook his head lightly and made a gesture that he would tell him later.

"You were at *Leah's* house?" asked Kane, standing at Hayden's locker, waiting for the latter to get his soccer stuff.

Hayden didn't know whether to laugh or be annoyed.

"Yes, and Olivia didn't take it well," said Hayden, sighing as he passed his fingers in his hair.

Kane grimaced at the words, and Hayden dreaded he'd be upset with him, too.

"I told her we should go to La Poutinerie this weekend," said Hayden, hoping his friend would agree.

Kane nodded, keeping quiet.

"So, you won't say anything?" asked Hayden when his best friend continued to stand silent.

"What do you want me to say?" said Kane, but not spitefully.

"I don't know, are you upset I spent time with Leah yesterday evening?" asked Hayden.

"No, the more you'll spend time with her, the more chances I'll get to see Anaya again," said Kane with a sly smile.

"Sucker," said Hayden, punching his friend in the shoulder.

"Hey, didn't you notice how cute she was?" said Kane, laughing.

"Ugh, don't get all lovey-dovey on me." Hayden rolled his eyes good-naturedly.

"Look who's talking," snorted Kane.

Hayden gave him a puzzled look. "What do you mean?"

"I mean, Mr. Blind, that you have a crush on Leah," said Kane with a triumphant smirk.

"Yeah, *right*," said Hayden sarcastically.

Kane looked at him with a knowing look, as if to say, *you really want me to believe that?*

"Kane, I just had dinner at her house, I didn't ask her to be my girlfriend," said Hayden, annoyed.

As soon as the words were out, he realized he should have just kept quiet. Now Kane will bug him that he wants Leah to be his girlfriend. *Ridiculous. We just met last month.*

"Anyways, I don't have time for your foolish suppositions for I need to go to practice, or else Coach Franck will have my head," said Hayden.

"Be sure to focus on the game and try not to think of a certain someone we shall not name," yelled Kane as Hayden ran down the corridor.

Hayden didn't pay him any attention, making sure to not bump into the other students who were leaving the building.

When they were done, he almost flew home, he was that tired. He went to take a shower and as he got dressed, his sore muscles reminded him of Olivia's shoulder, and he smiled. He knew how to get her to forgive him. He would buy her a tube of heating ointment and pass by the chocolate store to get her favorite box of chocolate, and, hopefully, he'd get back in her good graces again.

If he hurried, he'd be home before his dad and would try to make some dinner.

When he stopped in front of Olivia's house, the white and beige bricks as familiar as his own house, he rang the door, and soon enough, Olivia opened the door.

"Hayden, what are you doing here?" she asked, and although he could see she was still miffed, she was also happy to see him.

"Can't I come by to say hi to my best friend?" he asked sweetly, and she rolled her eyes.

"Please, don't overdo the cheesiness, it doesn't suit you," she said.

"Come in." She moved to make room for him to enter the house.

"This is for you," he said, giving her the bag with the chocolate and the ointment.

"What is it?" she asked, looking inside the bag. "You got me chocolate!" She looked up, a big smile illuminating her face. That's how he was used to seeing her. Radiant and happy.

He nodded, smiling back.

"What are you doing?" he asked as they went into the living room.

"I was working on my history assignment," said Olivia and he saw her textbooks and laptop on the coffee table in the middle of the room, the series *Heartland* playing on TV.

"I can't believe they're still running that series," said Hayden, remembering how it used to always air on CBC when he was younger.

"It's really good," said Olivia.

Hayden shrugged, he much preferred watching fantasy and adventure movies.

"You won't sit down?" asked Olivia as she sat on the couch, folding her legs under her, the way she always used to sit whenever they were watching a movie.

"I can't stay long, I need to go home before Dad is back from work," said Hayden.

"Oh, okay, I thought you were going to stay for dinner," said Olivia, slightly disappointed.

Hayden heard the reproach again in her voice.

"Next time, I promise," he said, his hands in his jeans' pockets.

Olivia turned to the TV, frowning.

"Well, I better go," said Hayden, suddenly feeling uncomfortable.

He didn't understand why she was so touchy these days.

"Hayden," said Olivia, sitting straight, putting her legs down.

"Yeah?" he asked when she didn't continue.

"Are we okay?" she asked, looking up at him, removing her hair from her eyes.

With half of her hair out of the ponytail, hair messier than usual, she looked younger than her age, and Hayden got the impression they were back in time, when they were twelve and planning their next prank.

Back then, things were simple. He missed those times.

"Of course," he answered, looking at the TV screen and the table, but not her eyes.

He felt a weird sensation in the pit of his stomach that felt strangely like guilt, even though he had no idea why he should feel guilty. He hadn't done anything wrong.

"It's just that you've been so distant these days," said Olivia slowly. "Withdrawn."

"School and soccer, you know," he said, but even to his ears, the excuse sounded lame.

"I mean you've distanced yourself from me," said Olivia, looking him directly in the eyes.

"I don't get it, what do you mean?" he asked, confused.

"I think you do," she said softly, looking at her hands on her lap, her bangs covering part of her face.

"Liv, look, I'm sorry if you thought I was being distant, I didn't mean to, it's just that I have a lot of things on my plate right now," said Hayden, hating to see his friend so downcast.

"I understand," she said at last, but she didn't look like she did. She looked even more hurt. "You should go, or you'll be late," she said, smiling at him. The sadness in her smile made his stomach twist painfully.

He felt like he was slowly losing her friendship, and he didn't know how to fix things. No matter how much he tried, he found himself unable to tell the truth.

Something inside of him was ashamed to admit the truth.

He took a step toward Olivia, wanting to tell her that he wanted things to be like they used to be before, when there were no secrets between them nor this weird tension that had slowly crept between them since this summer.

Since that night at the party.

He knew from her gaze that she was thinking about that night, too. "Bye, Hayden," she said, her eyes sad.

He opened his mouth to apologize, to say something, but the words got stuck in his throat. "Bye," he said, turning and leaving like the coward he was.

CHAPTER TWENTY-TWO

Leah

As Leah made her way to school, she passed through the parking lot to shorten the distance.

A dark blue Audi parked not far away, and Hayden emerged from his vehicle, his blond hair glinting under the bright sun of the chilly October morning, his dark leather jacket open.

Their eyes met, and he smiled, and before she could stop herself, she found herself grinning back. He met her halfway.

"Hey, you," he said with a small smile.

"Good morning," she replied and watched him take something out of his pocket and extend his hand to her.

The sun caught the glint of the gold circle in his palm. She frowned and squinting her eyes against the rays of sunshine, looked up at him. Why was he giving her a ring?

"Is that some sort of proposal or bribery, Hayden Hemingway?" she asked.

He blinked, a look of confusion etched on his features. "What?" Then, comprehension dawned on his face, and he smiled that smile of his. "That, Leah Driscoll, is your earring. Had it been a proposal, I would have done it with more style, and had it been bribery, it would have been more enticing."

His voice held amusement as he looked down at her, mirth twinkling in his eyes.

She felt like the biggest idiot ever and tried to stave off the blush she could feel was creeping on her cheeks. Why did she perpetually have to be red around him? But she had walked into that one herself.

She took the golden hoop and examined it. "How come it's with you? I thought I had lost it outside."

"You dropped it in my car on Sunday evening. I was going to give it to you yesterday, but I didn't see you the whole day."

"Thank you. I didn't think I'd find it again." She put the earring in her pocket.

Inside, she stopped in front of her locker and saw with surprise he leaned on the locker nearby. Was he going to wait for her?

"You're not going to take your stuff?" she asked.

"It's all in my bag, and since we have English together now, I figured I might as well wait for you," he replied.

"Okay," she said, trying to squash the happy feeling inside of her and not to grin like a fool. *Thank God Anaya is not here to see me right now.* She took her textbooks and as she was going to close her locker, someone called Hayden. It was Kane. He approached them, a smile on his lips and an amused glint in his dark eyes. "Hey guys, how are you?" he asked.

"Hi Kane," she said, noticing how Kane smiled mischievously toward Hayden who gave him a warning look.

Just then, she saw Riley at his locker.

"I'll be back," she told Hayden and went to see Riley.

"Hey, how's it going?" he said.

"Hi, good, and you?" she replied.

"Good," said Riley, but he looked distracted. She saw that he was looking over her shoulder, and it didn't take a genius to guess at whom he was looking.

She turned and saw Kane say something to Hayden as the latter frowned, looking annoyed yet amused.

"You guys friends now?" he asked.

"Well, yes," she said. She wondered if she should tell him about the fact that Hayden had dinner at her place but decided that she didn't want to add fuel to the fire.

"We have English now, so he's waiting for me to go to class together," she said.

"Okay, I'll see you after, then," said Riley and went away before she could say anything else.

She tried to not get annoyed, but she felt it was a bit rude of Riley to just leave like that. *Well, Leah, what did you expect? That he'll be super happy that you're friends with his enemy?*

She tried not to feel guilty, but deep down, she could understand why Riley was upset. After all, he had befriended her first. He was there for her when she needed someone by her side.

She sighed and went to join Hayden who was looking at her. She ignored his look, not wanting him to see she was upset.

"You okay?" he asked quietly as they sat at their desks.

She shrugged. "Yeah, fine," she said.

"Good morning, students," said their teacher when the class began. "As we are almost done with our books, I want to let you know that we will soon be working on a project where you'll be paired in teams."

Everyone started turning around, looking for potential partners, when the teacher's words doused their enthusiasm.

"Teams," he paused for emphasis, "of my choosing."

Some students groaned and Leah wondered who she'd be paired with. She didn't know anyone besides Hayden, having barely spoken a few words to some of the students. She wasn't able to meet anyone with whom she felt like she could develop a deep friendship.

He started calling out the names of the teams, and soon it was Leah's turn.

"Leah, you will be paired with Hayden," he said.

Leah blinked. Did she hear right?

"I guess we'll be working together," said Hayden as he

leaned forward on his desk.

She turned to meet his gaze and smiled. She was glad.

As the teacher proceeded to explain what the project entailed, Leah dutifully took notes. She wanted to make sure they got it right.

"So, when do you want to start working on this project, partner?" asked Hayden as they made their way out of the class.

"We can start tomorrow," suggested Leah.

"Sounds good to me," said Hayden. "After school?"

"Works with me," she said.

"I'll see you after," he said as he went to his other class, and she went to hers.

As she sat down to eat her lunch, Leah opened her book, wanting to get to the end of her book, *I Know Why the Caged Bird Sings.*

"What are you reading?" asked Riley as he sat in front of her with his own lunch.

"You weren't supposed to be working on your science project?" asked Leah as she showed him the orange cover.

"It was cancelled, half of the team couldn't make it," he said. "I heard of that book; apparently, it's very good," he said.

"It's amazing, you should read it," she replied, putting it aside.

As she looked over Riley's shoulder, she saw Hayden give her a small wave, accompanied by Kane and Olivia.

She smiled back.

Riley turned to look at them, too, and Leah noticed that his gaze lingered on Olivia's especially. It was obvious something had happened between them, and Leah wondered if that was the reason for the enmity between Hayden and Riley.

She didn't know how that knowledge made her feel.

He turned back, looking at the cafeteria's lunch—chicken patty bun and a meager salad on the side—as if debating whether to speak.

"Were you and Olivia friends before?" asked Leah before she could stop herself.

"You can say that, yeah, we were kinda friends," he said, not looking as carefree as he did a couple of minutes ago.

"What happened, if you don't mind me asking?" she asked.

Riley shrugged and looked at her, his stare a strange mix of annoyance and challenge.

"Hemingway happened."

Leah didn't know what to say. She had almost expected this answer, but she hadn't expected Riley's reaction. He looked almost angry, and it was an unsettling sight, for even though she had known him for only a month, she knew he wasn't hot-headed or prone to get angry easily.

"I'm sorry," she said at last.

"Why are you apologizing for him?" he asked. He sounded defensive.

"I'm not, I'm sorry for whatever happened that hurt you so much," she clarified. She saw his frown go away and the tension leave his shoulders. It must have been pretty serious, whatever the thing was that happened between the three of them.

"It's all in the past now, anyway," he said. "I've moved on."

Leah didn't say anything because if there was one thing she knew, it was that he didn't look like he had moved on.

"We need to come up with our main themes so we can see which book would be the best choice," said Leah as Hayden and she made their way out of school.

Their English project wasn't due until mid-November, but Leah preferred to have it done before so she wouldn't get overwhelmed with the other projects.

She looked at Hayden and saw that he was staring ahead, a frown on his face. She followed his gaze and saw Riley and Olivia talk outside, near the entrance.

As they approached them, Leah saw that Olivia's eyes widened while Riley seemed annoyed. His usual expression whenever Hayden was around, Leah had noticed.

"What's going on?" said Hayden, his voice cold.

He was looking at Riley, a defiant look on his face. Leah looked at Olivia whose anxious expression made her worry that things might get out of hand.

She knew Riley was usually self-possessed, but she had witnessed Hayden's temper and knew it wasn't pretty.

"Nothing that's your concern, Hemingway," replied Riley, raising his eyebrow as a challenge.

"Hi, Riley. Hi, Olivia," said Leah, trying to sound cheerful.

She might as well have spoken to deaf ears.

"Look, I don't know what your problem is, but if I were you, I'd leave Liv alone," said Hayden, taking a step forward.

"Hayden, please," said Olivia, putting her hand on his forearm.

Leah saw Riley look at Olivia's hand, his expression turning sourer. Before she could come up with an idea of how to diffuse the tension, Kane came up beside Hayden.

"Hayden, come on, let's go, it's not worth it."

Hayden looked at Kane and back at Riley before stepping back.

"Whatever," he said. "Let's go, Liv," he said. Olivia seemed to hesitate, biting her lower lip as she glanced at Riley before following Hayden and Kane.

Leah hadn't missed the apologetic look in her eyes as she had looked at Riley.

"You coming, Leah?" asked Hayden, looking at her.

Leah looked at Riley and back at Hayden.

"No, I'm staying," she said.

Hayden frowned and she saw his jaw tighten before he shook his head and left with his friends.

"Are you alright?" Leah asked, turning toward Riley.

"Yeah, I'm fine," he said, his voice flat.

He met her gaze and sighed, rubbing his neck. "Sorry, Leah."

"Don't apologize. What Hayden said was uncalled for."

Not for the first time, she wondered why Hayden got so angry whenever Riley was concerned and why the latter got so defensive.

"Well, nothing new here. Hemingway's a jerk that likes to meddle in other people's affairs."

"I'm sorry."

"Let's just change topics, okay? Thinking of Hemingway spoils my mood and makes my blood boil."

"Let's get something at Timmie's," she said, grabbing his sleeve. "I'm pretty sure they have the Pumpkin Spiced TimBits already."

"Leah, you don't have to do this," said Riley.

"But I want TimBits."

"No, I mean, I appreciate your support, but you don't have to baby me like I'm a wounded child. I'm fine."

"Riley, you're my friend and I want to spend time with you. What's wrong with that?"

Riley seemed reluctant to move.

"Hey, now, I'm getting offended. You don't want to spend time with me?" Leah asked, trying to look upset.

"Alright, let's go before you start bawling," said Riley, rolling his eyes. He pushed her gently on the shoulder as she grinned.

CHAPTER TWENTY-THREE

HAYDEN

After the end of classes, Hayden went home, glad that he didn't have soccer practice so he could catch up on his assignments.

As he went to open the door, he saw a box wrapped in beige paper on the front steps. It was addressed to him, with his name delicately written in cursive letters.

The writing didn't seem familiar.

What was that?

The box wasn't heavy, but it seemed something solid was inside. When he tore the wrapping, he saw a dark green box under it and as he opened the lid, his eyes fell on letters. His heart started beating faster. With shaky fingers, he took one envelope and took out the folded paper.

He felt like he already knew what he was going to find.

Dear Hayden,

Again, I didn't get the courage to post the letter to you. I don't even know if I can. But I'm not giving up hope. I'm working on myself. To be better for you. So I can one day come and see you. I don't want to think about any other possibilities right now. I'm just focusing on one day at a time. One small step at a time. It helps whenever I get overwhelmed. My therapist is always encouraging me to not hide from my emotions. To confront them. The pills are helping, too.

My beautiful son, I need you to know how much I love you. You are my stars in the darkest of nights. The reason I keep fighting. Why I keep carrying on when everything is dark around me, and inside me.

I keep imagining myself holding you in my arms, looking at your eyes that were always filled with wonder, your delightful smile, and I find I can breathe again. I find the strength to get out of bed and face another day.

For you, my son. Only you.

With love,
Mom.

A tear dropped on the letter and Hayden wiped his eyes. His throat was burning, and it was hard to breathe. A thousand little shards seemed to have lodged themselves in his chest.

He took a deep breath and looked at the other letters.

He was afraid to open them. The pain was too great.

He sat on his bed, his elbows on his knees, and put his face in his hands.

He wanted to erase the letters. He had worked so hard to suppress the conflicting emotions of the past weeks, his anger at his mom, his desire to see her, the feeling of betrayal he got every time he thought of her.

It was too much.

A couple of hours later, having taken a shower, he sat down to do his homework. He felt calmer.

He could almost pretend nothing had happened again. At this point, he was becoming an expert.

His eyes went to the closet where the box was hidden, buried under his clothes.

He turned back to his homework. *Focus.*

It seemed his mind was becoming volatile these days as he kept hearing his coach telling him to concentrate during practice and all his teachers complain about his careless mistakes and lack of attention. He wished he could erase his memory.

All these years, he had imagined what it would be like to have his mom in his life and now he couldn't think about her without feeling as if his heart might explode. Why was the truth so painful?

He sighed.

"Hayden?" he heard his grandma call him from downstairs. Hayden looked at his clock, surprised it was already past 7 p.m. and he had done nothing on his school work.

He took a quick look in the mirror. He looked decent so he went downstairs.

"Hi, Grandma, how are you?" asked Hayden, giving her a kiss on her cheek.

He was still upset that she had tried to force him to talk to his mother, but since she had been so sorry, he pretended that everything was fine. No matter how much he wanted to be angry with his grandmother, he didn't think he'd be able to bear it if they stopped talking.

"I'm good, my love, how was your day? Your dad said he'll be in late tonight; he has a last-minute meeting. Did you eat?"

"Not yet," he replied.

"I'll fix us dinner," she said.

"Grandpa didn't come with you?"

"No, he's still at work," she said, looking up to smile at him. She frowned as she looked closer.

"Are you okay? You look pale," she commented.

"I'm good, just tired," he replied evasively.

"That's because you're not eating properly," said his grandmother. "Do you want pasta for tonight?"

"Yeah, sure," shrugged Hayden.

"Grandma, I don't want to see her. I don't see what's the point," sighed Hayden. He was annoyed at his grandma for bringing his mom yet again.

He felt a headache coming. Like every time he thought about his mother.

His Grandma put her hand on his across the kitchen table.

"Hayden, I completely understand your pain and your anger, but I think you need to hear Aviannah out. She's your mom, after all," his grandma said.

He knew she was disappointed when he had stormed out of the café after seeing his mom sit at their table.

Before Hayden could reply, he heard his grandfather's voice behind him. He turned and saw him standing on the threshold.

"Anne-Marie, Hayden already said no, I don't see why you keep pressuring him," he said, his voice cold.

He was looking at his grandma with a warning in his eyes. Hayden had often seen this look, but it was mostly directed toward his father or him. Never toward his grandma.

He squirmed, feeling the tension, and hating feeling responsible for it.

"Vincent, I didn't know you were here," said his grandma, having recovered from her surprise.

"Where's Liam?" she asked. She either didn't hear his comment or was simply ignoring it. With his grandma, it was hard to tell.

"He's still in the office. I came back early," his grandpa said.

He looked at Hayden and gave him a small smile, although Hayden could see that he was still irritated.

"I have to finish my homework," said Hayden as he got up, hating himself for running away like a coward.

"Do you want some tea?" asked his grandma, looking at her husband.

As Hayden made his way toward his bedroom, he heard his grandpa speak up again, and stopped. He knew it was wrong to eavesdrop, but he couldn't help himself.

"Why are you trying to reconcile them?"

"Because she's his mother, something you seem to forget," his grandma replied, her voice sounding tired.

"And you seem to forget that this woman left him when he was only two years old. She made her choice and should be dealing with the consequences."

He could tell his grandpa was getting angry.

"You know as well as I do what she was dealing with," his grandma answered.

"I don't care. All I know is that she shirked her duties as a mother. So why should she expect forgiveness now?"

Hayden felt something twist inside of him. He knew his grandpa meant well and only wanted to protect him. And didn't he tell the same thing to his grandma? So why was he feeling angry now? Why did it hurt to hear those words?

He was getting worried for his sanity. Was he becoming bipolar?

And his grandpa spoke the truth. His mother had left him. Without looking back. Sure, she felt guilty now, but she was too late.

He knew then that their broken bond could never be

repaired. Something inside him twisted painfully.

He leaned against the wall, and putting his head back, closed his eyes. He felt queasy.

You lived without your mom all your life. What's different now?

Get a grip and stop being such a fool. She'll probably change her mind again, anyway. Next thing you'll know, she'll already be gone.

Opening his eyes and making sure to be as silent as possible, he went up to his room.

CHAPTER TWENTY-FOUR

Leah

The next morning, as Leah made her way to her locker, she saw that Hayden was already there. Waiting for her.

"Hey," he said as she approached him.

"Hi." She didn't respond to his smile. She was still annoyed by his childish and mean behavior from yesterday.

"Look, I'm sorry, but when I saw Liv with Connors, I got angry," Hayden said.

"That, I saw. But I also saw that Riley was doing nothing wrong, so I don't get why you got angry," said Leah, watching his face for any clue.

"Look, there are many things you don't know," sighed Hayden.

"All I know is that Riley is a good guy and he's my friend."

Hayden snorted, his expression derisive. "Connors, a

good guy. Right."

"Hayden, I don't know what your problem is, but you need to stop acting like that."

She was getting fed up with his condescending and judgmental attitude toward Riley.

"Exactly, you don't know what my problem is with him, so you can't judge me," Hayden retorted, frowning.

"Then, tell me. Explain it to me," snapped Leah, closing her locker.

"I can't, it's not my place to tell," he said.

Leah looked at him and bit her lip. She didn't want to make him the bad guy, but his behavior was irrational, and she found it annoying.

"I better go to class," she said at last and walked away.

She didn't turn back for she had a feeling he was watching her leave.

Before she could enter her class, she felt him grab her arm.

"Leah, look, I'm sorry, I wish I could tell you everything, but I can't. But I don't want you to think I'm some psycho, I'm just trying to be a good friend."

"Hayden, I understand you mean well, but, sometimes, misunderstandings can happen."

The bell rang.

"You should go, or you'll be late for class," she said.

She could see by his expression that he didn't agree with her, but he didn't argue further.

"See you later," he said, walking away.

On Friday afternoon, Leah and Hayden went to the Tim Horton's near their school so they could work on their English project.

"Let's take that spot in the corner on the benches so we can have some quiet," she said, pointing to the red and beige seat in the back.

After getting coffee and Timbits, they opened their laptops and started brainstorming.

"Did you think about which book you want to present?" she asked him. She had made a small list, but she wanted to hear his suggestions first.

"Not really," admitted Hayden sheepishly.

"I made a list," she said, taking out her notebook and, opening it to the page where she put a purple sticky flag note, showed him the titles.

"I haven't read any of them," he admitted.

"Then you'll get the chance to read a new book," she teased him, smiling as she bit into a chocolate glazed TimBit.

She might still be annoyed at his attitude with Riley, but she told herself she had to be fair with Hayden, too, and not judge him too harshly. He was right; she didn't know their story.

"Which is your favorite?" he asked, taking a birthday

cake TimBit and indicating the list of suggestions.

"I don't really have a favorite, I like each book for different reasons," she replied.

"I prefer fantasy books and movies," said Hayden.

"I love fantasy, too," she said with a grin.

"*Lord of the Rings* is my favorite!" they said at the same time and laughed.

"I think I've watched it ten times," admitted Hayden with a grin.

"I watched it even more," said Leah with a satisfied smile. "What about *The Hobbit*?" she asked, wondering if he shared her opinion.

"It was okay, not great. I mean, it's still a good movie, but something was lacking."

Leah nodded. "I know, right? It didn't have the magic of *Lord of the Rings*, it felt dull."

"Dull, exactly!" said Hayden, wiping his fingers to remove the glazed sugar.

After talking nonstop about a thousand unrelated things, they finally started working on their project, mostly arguing as they couldn't even agree on a book, let alone which themes to focus on or how to go about the presentation.

While Hayden wanted to make it original, Leah was more worried about the quality of the content they were going to present.

"Oh man, I have to go to work, it's almost six," said Hayden, looking at the time.

"Already?" exclaimed Leah, surprised that time had

flown so fast.

"That's what happens when you're in such good company." Hayden flashed her a smug smirk.

She rolled her eyes. "Or when you're not being productive," she retorted as they picked up their bags.

"I'm going to send you the outline I did tonight," said Leah as they made their way toward the parking lot.

They walked to his car as he was supposed to drop her home.

"Okay, thank–" Hayden stopped short.

Following his gaze, Leah saw he was looking at a beautiful woman with long, straight blond hair. She was slim and tall, and in her black paletot, she looked very elegant.

She was looking at Hayden with such an expression that Leah felt something twist inside her. She stopped in her tracks, realizing exactly who the woman was and her gaze went to Hayden who kept his eyes riveted on his mother.

There was no mistaking their resemblance.

A moment passed, and neither of them spoke. Leah could feel Hayden's tension and it made her nervous.

As if breaking from a trance, his mother spoke, "Hayden." Her voice was soft and light.

Hayden's stunned expression turned to an angry frown.

"Leah, may I present to you my mother. The woman who left her son years ago and has decided to grace us with her presence now."

His eyes never left his mother's as he spoke, and his

voice held such cold anger, Leah flinched.

His mother's eyes filled with tears, and Leah had to refrain from reaching out to her. She could feel the woman's pain, and the atmosphere got so tense, it was hard to breathe. The blond woman turned toward Leah, a silent plea in her eyes. She wished the earth would open underneath her feet and swallow her whole. She had never felt so awkward and out of place in her life.

His mom opened her mouth to say something, but she never got the chance, because suddenly Hayden took Leah's hand and dragged her away. Too stupefied to protest, Leah threw one last glance at the other woman, who was watching them leave, her hand raised in a gesture that seemed to indicate she wanted to stop them.

Hayden didn't speak at all as they got in the car, but even Leah, who hadn't known him for very long, could see how hard he tried to suppress his fury. His hands shook as he held the steering wheel, and she realized that it was not his anger he was trying to hide, but his pain. Like a wounded animal. She thought about the pain she had witnessed on his mother's face, so raw and sincere, and felt her own eyes sting.

The whole ride was silent as Leah didn't know what to say. She didn't want to hurt Hayden even more and wondered how he'd be able to go to work.

"Are you still going to go to work?" she asked quietly, glancing at him.

He nodded.

She observed his profile and his pinched lips and turned away.

Soon, they were at her house, and she had a sense of déjà-vu, but, then again, the circumstances and the atmosphere were so different that she felt like a lifetime had passed since the last time he had dropped her home.

She opened the car door. "Hayden. If you need to talk–or if you need anything really–you know you can talk to me. Anytime."

He tried to smile, but it was a pitiful attempt. "Thank you, Leah."

It was a long time before Leah managed to fall asleep. Flashes of what happened in the parking lot kept appearing in her mind.

Something told her it wasn't the first time he had seen his mom since she left. He had been upset by her arrival, but not surprised to see her. She wondered if his mom had tried to talk to him before, and he had refused.

His mom's hurt expression kept playing in her memory. She felt bad for the woman. Yes, she probably deserved it, but then, her repentance had been so genuine, Leah thought that it was wrong of Hayden to refuse to hear her out. He might not get another chance of making up with his mom again, and he was throwing it away without even giving it a second thought.

She took the frame on her nightstand and looked at the picture of her mother. Even after all this time, it still hurt to look at her face. Even now, she could feel her heart squeeze painfully. She put it to her chest and looked out of the window at the stars. "I miss you, Mom."

CHAPTER TWENTY-FIVE

HAYDEN

The next morning, as Hayden pulled up in front of Leah's house, he saw Leah come out. She closed the door and put on her beanie.

When she saw him, she stopped in her tracks, surprise evident on her face. "Hayden, what are you doing here?"

"Good morning to you, too. I'm very good, thank you for asking," he answered with a cheeky grin.

She rolled her eyes. "Hi Hayden! How are you? I am so happy to see you!"

"A simple 'hi' would have sufficed," he replied. "And to answer your question, you were the one who invited me to see your sunrise."

She had told him she sometimes watched the sunrise at the beach and was planning to go tomorrow, and he had said he'd come.

"I didn't think you were serious when you said that," she said.

"I'm always serious," he said, feeling like he deserved an award for waking up so early, even if he had barely managed to get any sleep.

She grinned.

"Get in or we're gonna miss that sunrise of yours," he said, a smile of his own appearing on his lips. Her smile was contagious.

As they drove to the beach, she didn't mention yesterday evening or try to talk about his mother and he was glad. He wanted to pretend everything was normal.

As they walked along the beach, Leah picked up a seashell and toyed with it. It was getting colder, and he was glad he had put on his jacket. The beach was deserted, save for the two of them.

He looked at the water and took a deep breath of the cool air. The sky was still dark, except for a purple-pinkish streak of light on the horizon.

"I never realized how peaceful the beach is. Whenever I used to come, there were always so many people that I never noticed how nice it is."

Leah smiled at him. "I know what you mean. Whenever my mom and I used to visit my grandpa, we would come here. We would observe a five-minute silence. It was our little ritual. And during those moments, I felt as if the water was giving me its tranquility. I felt one with it. I could feel it run through my veins. I didn't know where it ended, and I began. We were one. I felt so safe here."

She stopped abruptly, and a frown creased her forehead.

"I believed, naïve that I was, that it would always be like that. I couldn't picture it otherwise. Then, my mom got sick. And after a while, she got too sick to travel, so we stopped. When she died, I couldn't bear the thought of visiting this beach alone. But Mom asked to be buried in this town, beside her mom. My dad decided we needed to move here to be able to always visit her and be closer to Grandpa and Uncle Eric and his family."

She told him how many times she no longer saw the reason to carry on. She didn't find any meaning to life anymore. Then, she saw how much her father was grieving, but was trying to hide it for her sake, living for her. She realized she had to make it through, not for her own sake, but for her father's sake, who would be completely shattered if he lost his daughter, too.

"I knew then that Mom wouldn't want me to give up on life, and, slowly, I found the will to live again."

She had a far-off look on her face, and the rising sun was bathing her face in a golden glow. She looked like a child, peaceful and soft. He admired her serenity. Her strength.

"Look," she said quietly, placing her hand upon his and pointing at the view in front of them. He turned and saw the sun filling the sky, slow and majestic. And it felt as if it was filling his whole chest, illuminating a fire within him.

He watched as Leah watched the sunrise, his heart beating steadily and painfully slow. He felt like the rising sun; he, too, was waking up finally, after a long slumber he hadn't known he was in.

"You know," she said, her voice oddly quiet as if afraid someone might overhear her–the water, or the sun, or the wind maybe? "I feel so alive when I watch the sunrise. Like it's making me realize that maybe I have the whole world at my feet, open for me to dive in and that no matter how dark it might become in my life, the dawn will always be waiting around the corner. No darkness is eternal, the sun will always come rising, and even one ray of sunshine is enough to show you the path."

The light had turned her eyes amber, and they seemed to be filled with the warmth of the sun itself.

"Thank you," he said.

"What for?"

"For sharing this moment with me."

She smiled and took his hand, squeezing it gently. He squeezed it back, touched by the simple gesture.

As they watched the sunrise reach its full splendor, Hayden didn't know what it was, maybe Leah's confession, her hand in his, or even the hypnotic power of the sun, but he confided in her.

He told her how he always thought his mother had died during childbirth only to learn that she had left when he was two and how she had showed up at his door the day they were supposed to have the interview.

He told her how betrayed he felt, seeing his mom alive. As if he had lost her all over again when all he had ever dreamt about was to know how it would have felt if she was alive and he was growing up with a mom.

He told her how she had given him the letters she had been writing all these years and how much pain she went through and how she tried to get better so she could see him again. How, whenever he read them, he wanted so much to talk to her. But his fear that she would leave and hurt him again if he forgave her was too great. He didn't think he'd be able to bear it if she did it again.

"Maybe. But you need to give your mom a chance to prove herself," said Leah gently.

"What if she changes her mind and leaves me again?"

"That you don't know. Maybe she will, maybe she won't and will always be there for you from now on. Just give her a chance. Because the days you will be able to spend happy with her are worth it. It might not be perfect. You might still fight and maybe your hurt won't go away at once or even completely, but give her a chance. Give both of you a chance. You deserve it, Hayden," she said.

"I still can't forget that she left me when I was small," said Hayden, looking at the horizon.

She smiled gently. "You can be angry at her for leaving for so many years. You can feel hurt. It's normal. But you can't say your mom doesn't love you. She never gave up on you. So don't give up on her now. Don't turn your back on her when she is trying so hard to be part of your life again."

"I thought I'd be so happy if only she was in my life, but it turns out that the only things I feel are anger and bitterness," he confessed.

"I get it, you feel rancour toward your mom because the story you believed to be true happened to be false. But it doesn't change the fact that your mom still loves you. Yes, she might not have been the ideal mom by the regular standards, nor was she present most of your life, but she fought for you. She got better for you. That's love, Hayden. That's caring. Caring enough to want to be in her son's life, even after everything she went through."

Hayden stayed silent. The silence felt comfortable.

"I need to go home," said Leah after a while, taking a look at her watch.

"Do you have any plans this afternoon?" Hayden asked.

"I'm going to visit my grandfather," she said. She paused before continuing. "Do you want to come?"

"Yes," said Hayden, not even stopping to think about it, surprising them both.

When Hayden parked in front of her house, she looked at him and said, "Thank you."

"For what?" he said, mirroring her words earlier.

"For coming with me. You didn't have to, but you still came. You know, I never thought I'd say this, but I was really wrong about you. You're not at all how I perceived you to be. And I'm sorry for that. Now that I know the truth, I wish more than ever that I had never written that awful article."

"You don't have to apologize for that, you had no way of knowing. And I acted horribly. Consider us quit."

She smiled, getting out of the car.

"What time should I come?" asked Hayden.

"I was thinking at 1:30 p.m., is that okay?"

"Okay, see you soon, then," said Hayden.

She waved and closed the car door and he drove away. He was happy she had invited him to visit her grandfather.

Her company made him forget everything he tried to not think about, and if he was being honest, he really liked spending time with her.

He could already see Kane's smug face and wanted to groan. That boy was way too perceptive for his own good.

CHAPTER TWENTY-SIX

Leah

"Morning, pumpkin," said Leah's father. He was sitting at the kitchen table, reading the newspaper, sipping his coffee.

"Good morning, Dad."

"You're up early," he said.

"Yes, I went to see the sunrise with Hayden," she said.

"He's coming with me to see Grandpa this afternoon," she added as she put bread in the toaster and took out peanut butter.

"Sounds like a wonderful idea."

"Hayden is a good friend, Dad," said Leah, rolling her eyes at his mischievous smile.

"I never said anything else," he replied with an innocent look.

"You implied it with your tone," she said, raising her eyebrow as she took a plate for her sandwich.

"I didn't. I just wanted to say what a wonderful friend Hayden seems to be," said her dad.

She could hear he was trying not to laugh, and his amused expression warmed her heart. It had been a long time since she had seen him so carefree.

Before Leah could reply, her dad took his cup of coffee and headed out. "Say 'hi' to Grandpa for me. Oh, and to Hayden, too. Tell him he can come for dinner anytime again," he said with a grin.

"I will, Dad. I will," said Leah, hiding her smile as she took a bite of her delicious sandwich.

After finishing her breakfast, she made cookies for her grandfather and did homework. As she sat at her desk, she remembered Hayden's happy expression at being invited and smiled. She caught a glimpse of her reflection in the mirror and groaned. She was being a fool. They were friends. Only friends. *No point getting carried away, Leah. Focus on your homework.*

She could already picture Anaya's smug face as she told her everything. Sometimes, her best friend knew her better than she knew herself.

She tried to quell the feeling of excitement but didn't succeed. She couldn't wait until this afternoon.

She sighed as she looked at the time. Since when were mornings this long?

She wondered what she was going to wear and slapped

her forehead as she caught her train of thought.

She was going to visit her grandfather, not go to some fashion show.

She read the sentence again. And again. Her brain seemed to have forgotten how to make sense of phrases.

She went to sit on her bed and took the picture of her mom.

"You would have liked Hayden a lot, Mom," she whispered to the smiling portrait.

The glass caught the light of the sun coming through the window. The picture seemed to wink in agreement.

She wondered how her grandpa would find Hayden and if they would like each other.

Oh Leah, stop it. You're being ridiculous.

She tried to get back to her homework, but it made her think of school, and school made her think again of Hayden.

It also made her think of Riley and her guilt increased. She felt like she had let him down. She wondered if she'd ever find out what happened between him and Hayden this past summer. Did she even want to find out?

From what she had observed, she felt like Riley liked Olivia, but did that mean that Hayden liked Olivia too and they fought over her?

The thought made her depressed. She didn't want to think that Hayden and Olivia were more than friends. From what she had seen, they seemed like they were very close friends. Or maybe that's what she was hoping for?

She groaned. *Just stop thinking, Leah. Focus on your homework.*

It was already almost noon. She needed to hurry up if she wanted to be done before one o'clock.

CHAPTER TWENTY-SEVEN

Hayden

After driving for almost half an hour, they finally reached the farm. They got out of the car, and entered the house, which was surprisingly cozy and clean, despite being maintained only by an old man.

"Grand-père, c'est moi!" said Leah, putting the container of cookies on the kitchen table before proceeding to the living room with Hayden.

It was interesting to hear Leah speak in French. She had told him about her mother's side being mostly French, and as he looked at her now, he had the impression this was a new, more carefree Leah.

"Léa! Quelle bonne surprise! Comment va ton papa?" said her grandfather, getting out of the salon.

She hugged him and laughed. "Dad's good," said Leah.

Seeing Leah's grandfather, Hayden was a little surprised. Yes, he had the required gray beard and almost all his head was white, but it was his vitality that surprised him. The way he talked, the way he walked spoke of unbound energy. He was average in height and build, but his features told the story of a man who had seen and been through a lot.

In the car, Leah told him he had lost both of his parents when he was sixteen, lost his wife when he wasn't even fifty yet, and then lost his only child as well. Yet, despite all this, his eyes held a twinkle of humor and told the world that this was a man who loved life and didn't give up on it. A man who hadn't stopped seeing the beauty of life despite all its cruelties and sorrows.

He noticed Hayden standing behind, looking at them.

"Hello, sir." Hayden shook the older man's hand.

"Hello, jeune homme." His voice held a questioning tone.

"Grand-père, this is Hayden Hemingway," Leah said, reverting to English for Hayden's sake. "Hayden, this is Roland Rousseau, my grandfather."

"A pleasure to meet you, sir."

"The pleasure's all mine. Are you Leah's boyfriend?"

"Grandpa! He's my friend." Leah went red to the roots of her hair.

Hayden smiled.

"Okay, I'm going to get some refreshments. I'll be back in a sec," said Leah, sending him an apologetic look.

She left the room, leaving the two of them alone.

"You have a nice farm." He had seen it on their way inside, and it was vast and well-maintained. Roland looked at Hayden inquisitively, and he tried not to feel intimidated.

"Have you ever ridden a horse, Hayden?" he asked.

"I did some horse riding when I was small."

"Want to try one of my horses?"

"With pleasure." He knew that refusing wouldn't gain him favors. And he didn't know why, but he wanted to be liked by Leah's granddad.

Just then, Leah came back with their drinks and a tray of cookies. "Where are you headed?"

"I'm going to get a horse for Hayden. He wants to take a ride."

"You know how to ride horses?" She sounded as surprised as she looked.

"A bit," Hayden said, trying to not appear too confident in case he ridiculed himself. Even if he did some horse riding when he was thirteen, it had still been a while, and he wondered if he would feel comfortable.

"Do you want to try my cookies before?" asked Leah, extending him the tray.

"You made them?" asked Hayden, taking a bite of the soft chocolate cookie and being surprised by the delicious taste.

She nodded.

"Wow, I love it," said Hayden with raised eyebrows as he felt the chocolate melt in his mouth.

She smiled and blushed. He smiled and put the rest of the cookie in his mouth. It was really good, chewy with just the right amount of chocolate chips.

He took a sip of his lemonade glass. "I better get going, your grandfather must be wondering where I am," said Hayden.

"Have fun!" said Leah with a smile.

When the horse was saddled, Hayden mounted the animal, and realized that the technique was coming back to him. His teacher had always told him he had potential.

As he rode the beautiful, black horse, the old memories came back. He remembered feeling like Zorro, as powerful and fast, with no one able to catch him. The feel of the wind, the steady and powerful feeling of the animal's movements, its mighty back, all of it was familiar and comforting. He was startled at how much he had missed it. When he got down, he helped the grandfather's assistant unsaddle the horse and stroke the smooth fur like he had been taught.

The grandfather's assistant led the animal away, and he approached Roland Rousseau. "You know how to ride a horse, alright. You're very good at it, Hayden."

"Thank you," he said, and although he didn't let it show, he was relieved and not a bit proud inside. Hayden felt he had passed some unspoken test.

They spoke for some time—about horses and what formidable animals they were. About Leah and how he had wished his granddaughter would share his enthusiasm, but although she loved them, she absolutely refused to ride them. Hayden smiled, trying to picture her on a horse.

Thierry, the grandfather's assistant, called him, and excusing himself, the old man left.

"Why, Hayden, you never cease to surprise me." He turned, and saw Leah approach him.

"What can I say? I'm gifted at everything I do."

She rolled her eyes. "I'm surprised you didn't fall from the horse. What with that big head of yours." She was grinning, her eyes full of mirth.

"You're just jealous. By the way, your grandpa said you don't ride?"

"I'm afraid of heights, and the horses can feel my fear, which makes them nervous and agitated."

"Would you ride with me?" he asked suddenly.

"No, sorry. It's not that I don't trust your abilities, but I don't even ride with Grandpa."

"Just give it a try. You'll like it, you'll see."

"No, thank you, I already know what my strong points are, and horse riding isn't one of them."

The rest of the day went by quickly, and after dinner, they got ready to leave.

"It was a pleasure to meet you, Hayden."

"The pleasure's all mine, sir."

"Call me Roland. And do visit again."

"I will." As the words left his mouth, he felt surprised that he really meant them. He had truly enjoyed himself.

It had been a long time since he had felt so peaceful. The atmosphere made him forget all the unpleasant things he was trying to not think about.

Leah hugged her grandfather at the door. "Dad said that it's your turn to visit us this time," she said with a smile.

Her grandfather laughed. "My horses won't be able to bear my absence for a whole day. Thierry might be a good help, but he still has a lot to learn. No, better you come visit me."

They bid their goodbyes and went to the car.

CHAPTER TWENTY-EIGHT

Leah

As they drove back, Leah leaned against the window and watched the vast fields being left behind as they neared their town.

She thought about her grandfather and his refusal to come live with Dad and her. Like that, they would always be together, and he wouldn't be lonely anymore. But her grandad was a proud man. And he liked his house and ranch too much to even consider the idea of moving.

Leah had asked him once why, and he said that the house held all the memories that were dear to him. His wife and he had spent the best years of their lives there. His daughter was born there. His house was filled with the best moments of his life.

"Penny for your thoughts?"

Leah was startled out of her musing. “Oh sorry, I was thinking about my grandpa.”

“He’s a good man. Can I ask you a question?”

“Sure.”

“You said your grandma passed away when she was young. Your grandpa didn’t remarry after?”

Leah smiled. “I asked him the same question, and I’ll always remember what he told me. ‘You don’t cease to love a person just because they went away.’ That he didn’t marry my grandmother on the condition that she would live longer than him. And when I asked him if he ever felt lonely, he said no, because she was with him every moment. In his heart.”

“He’s an amazing man,” said Hayden, with respect and wonder in his voice.

“I know. I wish people today were more like him.”

“Sorry to break it to you, but people nowadays are selfish and driven by self-interests. I don’t think they even know how to feel a love as pure as your grandfather does.”

“And there goes my dream of ever finding Mr. Right.”

“Well, if you’re going to compare them to your grandfather, you need to admit your standards are pretty demanding.”

“True. My grandad is the strongest person I know. The older I get, the more I admire him for his strength, his unwavering faith, and his undying love.”

“He is. Some people are just born strong, I guess,” said Hayden with a thoughtful look.

"I think strength is a choice we make," said Leah.

"Maybe. But sometimes it feels as if some have more of it to begin with than others."

Leah was silent.

"Don't worry, your Prince Charming is going to be just like your grandfather," said Hayden with a smile.

"What?" asked Leah, confused.

"You said earlier you were afraid you'll never find your Mr. Right. I'm telling you, you will," he clarified.

Leah laughed. "Oh yeah? Weren't you the one who said that people nowadays are selfish and weak?"

Hayden nodded. "The majority yes, but you'll get your *rare perle*. How do you say it in French again, that one-in-a million jewel?"

"*Perle rare*," Leah corrected him. "The adjective comes after the subject in French. Didn't Madame Boisvin teach you that?"

"She might, she might have not. I tend to zone out during her classes. She has an amazing gift of making the most interesting subjects sound deadly boring," said Hayden.

Leah laughed. "Or maybe if you actually tried to learn, you'd see that it can actually be very interesting."

Hayden shrugged. "As long as I pass the class, that's all I care about."

"I can help you with your French homework, if ever you need it," said Leah.

"I knew there was a reason I became friends with you,"

he said with a big grin.

Leah punched him on the shoulder. "I take back my offer, you lazy bum."

"Hey, that's mean. I'll help you find your Mr. Right in return."

"How sweet of you, but no thanks. You'll just end up spoiling everything and scaring him away, if anything. Can't take such a risk, now, can I?" said Leah, laughing and shaking her head.

"You seriously underestimate my matching skills. Many of my friends will attest that it was thanks to me they got their girlfriends."

"Good for you. I've heard that matchmaking is a really prosperous business. You should open your own. 'Hayden Hemingway: Savior of Lost Souls.'"

"Now I know what to do if my father's business goes bankrupt."

"Yup, and if my Prince Charming doesn't show up by then, I'll be your first client. And I expect a 100 percent discount."

"Why? If I start making discounts from the beginning, how do you expect my business to prosper?"

"The idea was mine, so that's the least you can do."

"Leah Driscoll," he said with a disappointed expression. "It's a question of your life, of your soul mate, and you're being so stingy?"

"Shut up. And I won't need your help anyway because I'll know when I will have found him."

"You still might need my help to make him fall for you," said Hayden with a confident look.

Leah rolled her eyes. "Right, because you'll know what he will like?"

Hayden smiled. "You never know. What if he's like me?"

"Oh God, please no, I won't be able to endure such a big ego as yours."

"Hey, my ego is justified. I can't help it if I'm so awesome," said Hayden, looking offended.

"Wow, I am seriously impressed at how you're still able to walk around with such a big head," she said, shaking her head.

"Another talent of mine," laughed Hayden.

He stopped in front of her house, and she smiled. "Bye, Hayden."

"Thank you for inviting me today, Leah, I really enjoyed it," he said, his expression sincere.

She smiled. "Thank you for coming with me. I'm glad you liked it."

As she was about to get out of the car, Hayden spoke up, "Leah, I was wondering… That is, if you're free, of course, I thought maybe we can go for dinner tomorrow?"

Leah felt her heartbeat speed up and felt her cheeks heat up. She tried not to grin like an idiot as she nodded. "Yeah, sure, why not?" she said, trying to sound calmer than she felt. She didn't want him to see how excited she was.

"Yes?" repeated Hayden happily. "I can pick you up at 7 p.m. tomorrow. I know a nice place where they make the best desserts."

"Okay," said Leah, gripping the handle of the car.

"I'll see you tomorrow, then," said Hayden with a big smile as she got out.

"See you tomorrow," she said. She could feel her cheeks getting red. She waved through the window, no longer caring to hide her own smile.

He drove away and she watched the car turn at the corner of the street before going inside. She felt as if a stampede of butterflies huge as buffalos were wreaking havoc in her stomach.

CHAPTER TWENTY-NINE

HAYDEN

When Hayden got home, he saw that Kane had texted him many times. He dialed Kane's number.

"You alive, mate?" asked Kane as he answered the phone.

"Of course, why?" asked Hayden.

"You've been pretty much AWOL since yesterday," said Kane.

Hayden could picture the frown on his face. "I was working on a school project," said Hayden. "With Leah," he added.

"Ahhh, that explains everything then," said Kane, and Hayden could hear his suppressed laughter.

"No, you don't understand, we were working on the English assignment." He didn't think Kane needed to know that only one of the days was spent working on the school project.

"For two days straight. How dedicated of you. I never knew you had such a passion for school, Hayden," snorted Kane. He was no longer hiding his laughter.

"Stupid," said Hayden, but he could feel his own big grin and was glad Kane couldn't see him. There would have been no end to his teasing then.

"What are you doing tomorrow?" asked Kane.

Hayden winced. "I… uhm… invited Leah for dinner," he said finally.

Kane howled with laughter. "You're whipped, man," he said when his laughter subsided.

"I just wanted to be nice. She invited me to see her grandfather's ranch today. That's the least I could do," protested Hayden, wincing at his lame excuse.

"Ohh, you went to see her grandfather's ranch? Wow, things are going pretty fast."

"We're friends, Kane. Just friends."

"Sure," said Kane. "What about your old friends, then? I don't see you spending every hour of your weekend with us anymore."

Hayden stayed silent, guilt assuaging him.

"I'm kidding, Hayden, chill," said Kane. "Leah is a nice girl. And I do hope next time you go on a date, it will be a double date, with you guys and me and Anaya," he added.

Hayden could hear the cheeky grin in his voice.

"Sucker. And you're saying I'm whipped," said Hayden, feeling lighter.

"Hayden, maybe it's better not to mention it to Olivia for now," said Kane, his tone more serious.

Hayden felt his smile slip as the guilt came back. He sighed. "Yeah, better not," he said quietly. He rubbed his neck.

"Don't worry, Hayden. She just needs time to adjust," said Kane.

"Yeah, maybe," mumbled Hayden. He hoped Liv wouldn't stop being his friend if ever he and Leah—

"Okay, I was just checking in. Enjoy your date tomorrow. Make sure to not drool too much in front of Leah," said Kane, his voice back to cheerful.

"Don't worry, I'm not like you," retorted Hayden.

Kane laughed as he hung up. Hayden smiled. His best friend always knew how to bring up his mood.

Sunday morning, Hayden woke up, a nervous pit in his stomach. He hoped everything would go well this evening. He went downstairs to see if his dad was home. Finding the kitchen empty, he went into his father's study. Through the open door, he saw that his dad was sitting in his big, leather chair, looking out of the window. He looked lost.

"Dad?" said Hayden, leaning on the doorframe.

Startled, his dad turned to look at him.

"Hayden, you're up early?" asked his dad, looking at the clock on the wall.

"You okay, Dad? You seemed lost," asked Hayden, observing his dad's face. He looked tired.

"Yes, yes. I was just thinking about work," he replied, looking at the papers on his desk.

Hayden felt sad. Sad that his dad was trying to deal with his pain on his own. That he was trying to be strong for him, not letting him see how much he was suffering. He wanted to tell him that he was sorry for how he had acted and that he shouldn't have ignored him for so long, but words failed him.

"I just wanted to say to not wait for me for dinner tonight. I'm going to eat dinner with a friend," said Hayden.

"Kane, Olivia?" asked his dad, distracted, going through some documents. His desk, usually tidied up, looked messy with papers all over.

"No, Leah," said Hayden, after debating whether to tell the truth.

"The Leah you left standing on the dance floor in such a gentlemanly manner?" asked his dad with a small smile.

Hayden winced at the memory. "Yes, Leah. We're okay now, we're friends now," he said.

"It must be so if you're going for dinner," replied his dad with a teasing smile.

"Yes, friends can have dinner," said Hayden, rolling his eyes. "Have a nice day, Dad."

"Have fun, son," he said as Hayden went out.

Just then, the front door opened and in walked his grandfather. Hayden was still trying to forget his grandfather's attitude toward his mother, and it annoyed him that it was bothering him so much. He knew he was being a hypocrite. His grandfather was always strict and cold, and Hayden had never been really close to him, but these days, he felt easily irritated by his controlling attitude.

"Hayden," his grandfather greeted him.

"Hi Grandpa," said Hayden.

"How's school?" asked his grandfather, stopping beside him.

"It's going well," said Hayden.

"I hope you are thinking about universities," said his grandpa, observing his expression.

"A bit," lied Hayden, looking at the wall.

"Hey Dad," said his father as he got out of the study. "I'm going to make some coffee. You want some?"

"We don't have time. We better hurry," said his grandfather.

"Hurry?" asked his dad. He seemed confused.

"The meeting, Liam. Did you forget?"

"Oh yes, of course, I'll just grab the papers and we can head out," said his father.

Hayden watched his dad walk back into his study to grab the documents and wondered why he always let his father talk to him like he was incompetent. Quelling his anger, he went back into his room.

The day flew by quickly and when Hayden saw that it was already 6 p.m., Hayden went to take a shower and tried to decide what to wear. He didn't want to be a show-off, but he wanted Leah to be pleased with his appearance.

He groaned. *She's just a friend. Right.*

After going through several outfits, he finally settled on a nice black polo sweater and dark pants. While the weather was surprisingly mild for October, evenings could become chilly very quickly.

As he made his way downstairs, he saw that his dad and grandpa were back and were talking in his study. Before he could stop himself, he approached the door quietly, wondering if they'd be talking about his mom.

"Life doesn't like weak people, Liam, remember that," said his grandpa with his authoritative voice.

"Dad, life is not some battle you need to constantly win," his dad said. He sounded annoyed.

"All I'm saying is that if you show even one weakness, the competitors will eat you alive. There's a reason why our company became the leading company in the region in the last few years. Because I never compromised. I never showed any weakness the others could exploit."

Hayden shook his head and went quietly away. He was so foolish. Why did he even assume that they would be talking about his mom? His grandfather was being his usual, domineering self, trying to impose his opinions and views on everyone around him. He resolved not to think about his mom at all and enjoy tonight's date.

CHAPTER THIRTY

Leah

Leah was having a dilemma: she didn't know what to wear. She had spent the last two hours rummaging through her wardrobe. She wanted to look nice, yet not too overdressed as to give him ideas that she was head over heels for him. She sighed at how ridiculous she was being. She had always looked down at those girls who would go in a frenzy over what to put on for a date, and here she was, no better.

Urgh. Ce n'est pas sorcier, Leah, just wear something presentable. That's all.

She was tempted to put on black skinny pants and a dark, indigp blue blouse, but she feared he would read too much into it. But it wasn't her fault that most of her nice clothes were actually the same color as his eyes! She wanted to bang her head against the wall, but refrained, as going on a date with a lump the size of a plump on the forehead wasn't the best way to impress. Plus, he would comment about her clumsiness again.

She glared at the blue blouse as if it was responsible for her current impediment. *Oh, forget it.* She was going to put it on and let him think what he wanted. She wasn't going to let the nice top sit at the back of her wardrobe because of Hayden Hemingway and his blue eyes.

She wondered if she should wear eyeliner. But what if she forgot and rubbed her eyes, and ended up looking like a raccoon? No, it was best to forego eyeliner. She let her hair down and applied some lipstick. She put on her silver necklace. It was simple and went well with her outfit.

Sighing in relief, she looked up at the clock and saw that she still had half an hour to go before seven o'clock. She went downstairs and poured herself some water.

"What's the occasion? I thought you were going out just as friends. 'Hang out,' I think was the word you used."

Leah whirled around, almost dropping her glass of water, and saw her dad in the doorway, watching her with a small, knowing smile.

"Dad, you scared me! Aren't you supposed to be at Uncle Eric's?"

"Yes, but he was feeling ill, and it's not like I could miss something as important as my daughter's date, now, could I?"

"It's not a date. We're going to eat. As friends."

Her dad opened his mouth to respond, but the phone rang, and he went to answer it instead. Leah looked up at the time. Fifteen minutes left. She hoped her dad wouldn't embarrass her. Maybe she could leave now and ask Hayden to meet her somewhere down the street?

She went to put on her jacket and ankle boots, and as she was opening the door, remembered her scarf and went to grab it.

"Leah, you're forgetting your bag." *Darn.*

"Thanks, Dad. I was about to take it."

"Ah, okay. I thought you forgot about it, what in your hurry to leave." He smiled sweetly.

Leah didn't have to reply because just then the doorbell rang. *Great*, she thought, resigned.

"Hey," she tried to smile, but seeing his slightly puzzled look, it probably came out as a grimace.

"Hi. You ready?"

"Yes," she said, zipping her boots.

Hayden looked over her shoulder and saw her dad coming out of the living room. "Good evening, Mr. Driscoll. Hope you're having a nice evening."

"Hi Hayden, good to see you again. Enjoy your dinner."

"Thank you."

"Okay, bye, Dad," said Leah before he could say something to embarrass her as she didn't like the mischievous glint in his eyes.

"Don't forget the curfew, pumpkin." She just knew it. Her Dad would never pass the opportunity to make fun of her.

"Don't you worry, Mr. Driscoll, I'll bring her home before the clock strikes twelve," said Hayden, an amused expression on his face.

"Ha, ha. You seem to forget Cindrella here can hear you," said Leah, rolling her eyes.

"The curfew is at eleven. Better not take chances to have the car turn into a pumpkin," her dad said, laughter evident in his voice.

"Eleven it is, then," replied Hayden, grinning.

Leah looked at her dad, signaling he was laying it on too thick, but her dad grinned and winked. As he closed the door, she could hear him chuckling, and her annoyance was short lived. She loved her dad's laugh, even if it was at her own expense.

"Your dad is very funny," said Hayden as if reading her mind.

"I know. He always makes fun of me."

"I guess it's in the family, your grandpa, your dad," chuckled Hayden.

"Speaking of Grandpa, Dad told me that he really liked you."

"Really?" He looked pleasantly surprised, and this, in turn, baffled Leah. Even someone like Hayden Hemingway worried about making a good impression.

"I'm glad," said Hayden, and Leah felt a pleasant and warm feeling in her stomach.

They arrived at the restaurant, and when she saw the place, Leah worried she was too underdressed. She should have put on some nice dress, she chided herself. No, she had to let her pride get in the way.

"You okay?" He seemed to have noticed her discomfort, and was looking at her, worried.

"Yeah. It's just that–I mean, it's nothing."

"Tell me."

"It's silly, really. Just forget it."

"If you don't like the place, we can always leave."

"No, it's not that. I just feel like I'm not dressed well enough for such a nice place."

"You look really nice, Leah." His gaze was so bright and blue, it was dazzling. Like the sky at night.

She lowered her eyes, feeling herself blush. Thankfully, he had enough tact to not tease her.

After finishing their meal, they went for a walk and stopped at the end of the dock. The place was really beautiful and right by the lake.

Leah felt the wind on her face, and her hair flew behind her. She felt like she could fly away. She closed her eyes, and smiled, sighing happily.

When she opened her eyes, Hayden was staring at her. His eyes were like the sea under the moonlight. Intense and beautiful. Could her brain get any cheesier yet? She wanted to cringe at her own sentimentality, but she couldn't help herself. It's like her brain was stuck on some loop.

"It's a beautiful night," he said, looking at the stars. She almost sighed in relief when her brain didn't supply any corny comparison with his eyes yet again.

"My mom used to love starry nights like this one. In Montreal, we would go to Mont-Royal to see the stars better. In the city, we can't really see them because there's too much light."

"Do you miss Montreal a lot?" asked Hayden, looking at her.

"Yes," said Leah. "Very much. I miss Anaya and her family. My old house. My old school. My old life," she said, watching the dark water beneath the dock.

"I'm sorry," said Hayden quietly.

"I know it's foolish, but if I was granted a wish, I would have wished to go back in time. Not to change things but only to be more grateful while I had them. I wish I was more appreciative of everything I had that I took for granted," said Leah, gripping the metallic, black railings that were on each side of the dock.

Hayden stayed silent beside her, his eyes watching the calm waters reflect the shine of the moon. Leah hesitated before continuing. The soothing water and the darkness seemed to coax the truth out of her.

"But above all, I wish I had spent the last days with my mom laughing and making her as happy as I could. Instead of wasting the precious time I had with her crying and lamenting at the unfairness of it all," she whispered.

Hayden lifted his hand and wiped the tears she hadn't even been aware had started falling.

"Your mom knew you were hurting, Leah. Don't feel guilty for hurting when your mom was sick. You're only human," he said softly, looking in her eyes.

She closed her eyes, feeling more tears escape and let out a shuddering breath.

She felt his arms envelope her in an embrace and she clung to him tighter, letting her tears fall.

When she calmed down, she let out an embarrassed laugh.

"I'm sorry for being so depressing. It's probably not what you were expecting. I promise, I'll be more joyful from now on," she said, wiping her tears away.

He gave her a handkerchief.

She looked at the piece of cloth with a puzzled expression. "You're carrying a handkerchief with you all the time?" she asked incredulously.

Hayden smiled. "I was raised by my grandma, and she believes in etiquette. She always told me that a gentleman ought to carry a handkerchief on him when he's with a lady," he said, his eyes twinkling with good-natured humor.

"Wow, my hat goes off to your grandmother for raising such a perfect gentleman," said Leah with hardly feigned amazement.

Hayden laughed. "I'll let her know, thank you," he said.

Leah's heart filled her chest. She loved hearing him laugh. Oh God, she was a goner. She looked at the dainty handkerchief, feeling bad for ruining it with her tears and snot, and tried to be as delicate as possible when blowing her nose, but was there really a way to do it elegantly?

Something wet landed on her forehead.

"It's gonna start raining," said Hayden. "Let's go before it stars pouring," he added. October rains could be unpredictable.

He took her hand and didn't let go until they reached his car in the parking lot. As they got inside the car, it started raining harder.

"I've always wanted to dance under the rain," she said, smiling, putting on her security belt.

"Really? Why?"

"I don't know. It seems so wonderful in movies. But I never got the courage to do it, lest people think I'm a nutter."

"Life is too short to think about what others will think, don't you think?" said Hayden with a big grin.

Leah nodded, smiling.

He suddenly opened his door and stepped out.

"Where are you going?" asked Leah, confused.

She watched in befuddlement as he opened her door, and extending his hand in a gallant gesture, asked her, "Shall we dance, Miss Driscoll?"

"What? It's raining! We'll get sick!"

"Oh, come on, don't be a spoilsport!" He took her by the hand, and Leah had a moment of déjà-vu as he dragged her out of the car.

"You're crazy, you know that?"

"I know. But, seriously, what's the point of denying ourselves our wishes? We live only once. Might as well enjoy it to its fullest!"

He whirled her, and she forgot all about common sense, and cars driving by, and people looking at them as if they had escaped from the asylum. She let it all go and enjoyed herself. She felt like she was a kid again. She looked toward the sky and laughed. She heard Hayden laugh, too, and saw that he was watching her with a twinkle in his eyes.

Her heart lurched. Hayden had never looked as good as he did now, with hair darkened by the rain, and eyes darker still, looking at her with a small smile, droplets of rain clinging to his eyelashes.

She put her arms around him and hugged him tight. She felt safe in his arms. He held her like he would never let her go, and she wished he never would.

CHAPTER THIRTY-ONE

Hayden

Hayden woke up, feeling the sunlight on his face and, looking at the clock, saw it was past nine o'clock. As he got dressed, he thought about the events of yesterday evening and smiled.

He had wanted to kiss Leah so bad, but he didn't know how she'd react. Holding her felt almost as good.

"Liam, I can't believe you still haven't finished the proposal. The deadline is in less than three days, and you have nothing to show for."

As Hayden made his way downstairs, he could hear his grandfather's voice from his father's office. He sounded irate. As usual.

"Dad, I'm sorry, it completely slipped my mind. I'll get on it right away. I still have time," his dad said, his voice sounding more tired than usual.

His father had a tendency to shrink in front of his father, and Hayden wondered when he'd finally remember he was an adult as well.

His grandfather's imposing personality was intimidating, but sometimes, Hayden just wanted to tell him to back off. He was being too much.

As he made his way to the kitchen, his father and grandfather came out of the office.

It was always the same routine with them. Hayden wondered what they would do if their company disappeared.

"Good morning," said his dad, smiling. Hayden could see his eyebags.

"Morning," said Hayden.

As his grandfather made his way to the door, his dad stopped and looked at him. He pulled at his tie.

"Hayden, do you want to order some pizza tonight?"

Hayden wanted to say no, that he had already plans, but seeing his dad's hopeful expression, he simply nodded.

"Yeah, sure," he said, shrugging with one shoulder. He'll take advantage of the day off — their school had a PA day— to work on his assignments.

"Okay, great, so I'll see you later, then," his father said, giving him a small smile.

Later, as he sat at his desk doing his homework, his dad came into his room.

"Pizza should be here soon," he said. "Hope you're

hungry. I ordered some chicken wings as well."

Hayden nodded. "That's great."

As the doorbell rang, his dad smiled and went to answer the door.

Hayden sighed. As much as he was angry at his dad, he also hated seeing him so low and demoralized.

As he took a bite of his pizza, Hayden remembered how he used to feel so excited whenever they had a pizza night with his dad when he was little.

They would watch movies and his dad allowed him to stay late. He was never a strict parent.

Unlike his grandfather.

"It's been a long time since we had a pizza night," said his dad, as if reading his mind.

"Yeah."

Hayden focused on his slice, wondering why his dad always let his father dictate his life.

"So, did you finish your project on time?" he asked.

"Yeah, almost done," said his dad, swallowing his own morsel.

"I'm sure Grandpa must be glad. He seemed ready to blow up a fuse this morning."

His dad gave him a small smile.

"I know Dad can be strict sometimes, but it's his personality. He means well."

Hayden shrugged. "Yeah, maybe. But he doesn't have to be such an— so annoying about that," he said, taking a chicken wing.

It was crispy, yet tender, just like he liked them.

"He has always been like that, you know that."

"And that makes it okay?" asked Hayden, raising an eyebrow.

His dad looked at him across the table, putting his slice on his plate.

"What's gotten into you, Hayden? You seem easily irritated with your grandpa these days," said his dad, his expression serious.

"All I'm saying is that you don't always have to agree with everything he says. He can't always be right, can he?"

It came out snappier than he had intended.

"Hayden," said his father, "I know it's hard for you to see it that way now, but a lot of times, parents do know best."

"Aren't you a parent yourself? Shouldn't that give you some say?"

"But I'm also still my father's son," said his father, giving him a small smile.

Hayden kept quiet. There really was no point arguing. His grandfather was never going to change, nor was his father, for that matter.

CHAPTER THIRTY-TWO

Leah

"I can't believe it's Halloween soon. Time flew by," said Leah as they walked in the park.

She had asked him if he wanted to take a stroll in the park after school and he had agreed.

She was glad she had on her warm coat and scarf as the wind was chilly that day.

The trees were already turning golden, brownish red and yellow leaves littering the ground.

"Yeah," nodded Hayden.

She saw that he was looking at a woman who was swinging her child on the swings as children played with a ball on the grass.

He had a thoughtful look in his eyes.

"What are you thinking about?" she asked, wondering

why he was so quiet since they arrived at the park.

"Nothing, just—-" he stopped, raking his hand through his hair.

He zipped his coat and put his hands in his pockets.

"I just remembered something," he said finally.

She wondered if she was allowed to ask.

"Do you want to leave?" she asked. She could see he seemed upset.

He shook his head. "No, I'm fine, really. It's just related to my mom," he said.

As he told her about the strange, elderly woman he had met with Kane and Olivia on the first day of school, Leah could only imagine how he had felt when he had realized the woman wasn't mistaken after all, and that he had been lied to all along.

He was looking at the children running after the soccer ball, frowning. He wasn't seeing them at all, lost in his thoughts.

"Hayden, I think you should give her a chance," she said, looking him in the eyes.

He looked at her, his eyes widening, before he scowled. "Not you, too. Why is everyone trying to make me do it?"

He sounded exasperated, but Leah wasn't ready to back down. It was too important.

"Because it's the right thing to do," she answered.

"She left, she abandoned me," said Hayden.

"Hayden, you told me yourself she was sick," said Leah. She felt a tightness in her chest, not liking his reaction.

"Leah, please, let's not talk about this anymore," he said, his voice flat.

"Please," he repeated, his voice a warning as she was about to protest.

She knew that continuing would only antagonize him further, so she kept quiet.

"Look, I'm sorry, I didn't want to snap at you," he said, sighing. "It's just that I can't…" he trailed off, seeming unsure of what to say.

"I'm sorry, I wish I hadn't asked you to come here," she said, resuming to walk.

"Hey, don't worry about it. I can't avoid this park forever just because my mom used to bring me here when I was a baby. I'm fine," he said, tugging at her arm and making her stop.

She turned and looked at him and he smiled. She wanted to tell him that he wasn't fine and probably wouldn't be unless he forgave his mother, but she knew he didn't want to hear that, so she said nothing.

It was a sunny, bright day, despite the cold, and the air felt crisp. His hair shone in the sunlight and his eyes seemed brighter than usual.

They were standing so close she could see a small, faint beauty spot on his left cheek, just under his lower eyelashes.

He stopped smiling as his eyes lowered to her lips and he took one step closer, bringing their faces inches away from each other.

She felt her breath catch as she watched him lower his

face toward her. Her eyes fluttered, closing, and she lifted her face slightly, waiting—

"Ow," she exclaimed, feeling the impact of something hitting her against her back as he caught her in his arms.

"Leah, are you okay?" asked Hayden, looking at her with worry.

"Yes," she said, disoriented and looking behind her to see what had hit her.

She saw a ball at her feet and a boy running toward her, his eyes wide.

"Sorry, I didn't mean to hit you," he said, sounding contrite.

He was no more than ten. She smiled.

"It's okay, no harm done," she said, taking the ball and throwing it at him.

She turned back toward Hayden and smiled.

"Are you sure alright?" he asked again.

"Yeah, I was just surprised," she said.

She looked around them, trying not to blush as he put his hands in pockets again and gave her a small smile.

"We should probably head home, it's getting cold," she said, playing with her scarf.

"Yeah, let's go," said Hayden.

As they made their way out of the park, she felt his hand take hers and she smiled. His hand felt warm around hers and it didn't feel so cold suddenly.

CHAPTER THIRTY-THREE

Hayden

"I want you to give your best," the coach said on Friday evening.

They were playing a game against the Bulls—a redoubtable team—and Hayden was prepared to give his all. He might have had a few bad practices, but he wasn't going to let them down tonight.

As they went on the field, he looked in the stands and saw Leah with Kane and Olivia. His Dad couldn't come tonight, he had too much work.

Leah smiled and waved when she caught his eyes on her.

It had been almost a week since their date. Hayden smiled at the memory. Since then, Leah had started spending more time with him and his friends and he could never hide his joy when she was with them. He bore Kane's smug smirk and teasing with as much dignity as he could muster. He smiled at his friends and turned his attention back to the game. He had someone to impress tonight.

The Bulls were a strong team, and from the beginning, it was tight. By the time they got to halftime, the Bulls were leading 3-2.

"It's okay, we can still turn it around," encouraged their coach.

Hayden felt a stitch in his side and tried to take deep, even breaths. He needed to keep his strength so he could score a goal. He wanted them to win. He needed it to be an amazing game.

"Ok, let's go back on the field and show them who the Lions are," said their coach when the fifteen-minute interval ended.

As Hayden ran back on the field, a familiar silhouette caught his attention. He stopped and saw his grandmother accompanied by another woman taking a seat in the stands.

His mother.

Surely, he was imagining it? How could his grandma bring his mother to his game?

His heart beat painfully against his chest as he tried to not get overwhelmed.

"Hayden!" said his coach.

Hayden turned, still in a daze.

"Focus, son. I need you to be focused on the game," said his coach. "Now is not the time to be distracted."

Hayden nodded, avoiding his eyes, and went to take his position.

He felt like he was underwater. He had a hard time hearing his teammates and his hands were shaking. As he ran on the field, he felt anger replace his numbness.

Why did she come to his game? To show everyone that she was not dead after all? So people would realize that his mother had simply left him when he was small? He could already guess what people were going to say. He could hear the whispers in the corridors.

His heart was burning with so much anger, he felt the fire would consume him whole.

"Hayden!" screamed his teammate. He turned to the side and saw that Kurt was making a pass.

His feet felt heavy like lead, but he managed to catch the ball and run to the opposite side. He sprinted as fast as he could, dodging the players from the other team. He looked at the sides. Time was running out and he was trapped. He knew he had to make a pass, but his brain seemed to have forgotten how to play. He could barely make out his friends from the players of the other team. He couldn't make a pass now. He feinted to the side and took a shot. The soccer ball flew in the air and went over the goalpost. The referee blew the whistle.

Game over.

They had lost. Hayden lowered his head in shame, crushed under the weight of disappointment.

His coach shook his head in disapproval and his

teammates dragged their feet off the field. He had failed them. The pain was so acute, every breath hurt.

As he went to join his team, his coach gave him a brief squeeze on the shoulder.

"I know you'll do better next time, son," said his coach. His tone was filled with pity and disappointment.

Hayden hated feeling like a loser.

"Hayden," his friends called him.

He turned and saw them standing behind him. Kane, Leah, Olivia, his grandma and her.

She was looking at him with pity. He scowled. He was done being pitied. How dare she show up and spoil his concentration? It was all her fault. If she hadn't been here, he would have played well. He would have scored that goal.

"Hayden," said his grandma, approaching him with a gentle, hesitant smile.

"Grandma," said Hayden. He tried to keep his cool, but he was hurt she would do this to him again.

She frowned when she saw the look in his eyes.

"It's okay, Hayden, it's only a game. You can't always win," she said.

Hayden stayed silent.

"Your mom came to see you play," she added, a cautious tone in her voice. She seemed to sense his anger.

"I saw," replied Hayden curtly before turning to leave. He was done being understanding with his grandma. She had betrayed him yet again.

"Where are you going, Hayden?" asked his grandma,

putting a hand on his arm.

She was looking at him uncomprehendingly, and he almost wanted to laugh at how oblivious she was being. He saw Kane's and Olivia's expressions; they had a hard time processing what they had just heard. Leah looked apprehensive and worried.

He could also see the curious glances some of his teammates were giving him.

"Away from her," replied Hayden before he could stop himself.

He tried to keep his cool, not wanting anyone to see how upset he was, but he was so angry he was shaking.

"Hayden," said his grandma, lowering her tone. It held a warning.

But he didn't heed it. If anything, it made him angrier. "Why did you bring her?" His grandmother opened her mouth to reply, but he snatched his arm away. His grandma's hurt expression made him almost want to laugh.

"Why did you come?" he asked, turning towards his mother.

She lowered her gaze, looking like she regretted coming.

"I asked her to come," answered his grandma. "For you."

"Well, you shouldn't have," snapped Hayden. He was tired of his grandma trying to fix everything. Didn't she see she couldn't fix it? Fix them? It was too late.

He could see his grandma getting upset and he almost felt guilty. He couldn't remember a time when he had been angry with her.

"Hayden, love, your mom is trying to make an effort for you. She wanted to support you today because I told her how important soccer is for you," his grandma said, sounding upset.

Hayden scoffed.

"I don't want her support. She only made things worse. I wouldn't have missed the shot if she hadn't come," said Hayden and hated how lame he sounded as soon as the words left his mouth. He was so angry he felt as if thousands of needles were prickling his skin.

"Hayden, that's ridiculous," said his grandma, frowning.

"The whole situation is ridiculous!" exploded Hayden, feeling something inside of him snap. "I never wanted her to come to the game! I didn't ask for her to come! I didn't ask for her to come back into my life unannounced! Expecting for me to simply accept her. As if it's an everyday thing, to leave your child and come back years later, expecting to be forgiven. While all this time, this child was suffering. Feeling guilty. Believing he was the reason for his mother's death."

He was shouting at this point, and everyone was looking at him, but he was beyond caring.

"How do you think I felt all those years? Growing up without a mother? Did you even care?" asked Hayden, looking her straight in the eyes.

Tears fell down her cheeks. She looked crestfallen and he wanted to scream. He could feel his own eyes sting, but he'd be damned if he cried in front of her.

"Why did you come back and ruin my life? You shouldn't have come back," he said, watching his mom as tears rolled down her cheeks.

Hating her for being weak and crying. Hating himself that he cared. That her tears were stabbing him inside.

He turned and met his friends' stares. They were looking at him as if they didn't recognize him. As if he was a total stranger.

He felt like a stranger to himself, too. He needed to get out of there. He didn't stop when his grandma called him. He didn't even look back.

Did she really think he was going to be overjoyed that his mother, the one who was never there for him when he grew up, had come to see him play soccer?

Hayden didn't know how long he ran, but his lungs were two hot coals inside of him by the time he stopped.

He saw that he had come to the park. How ironic. The sun was setting, and the air was cooler. But not cool enough to cool his anger.

He sat on the bench, his elbows on his thighs, his face hidden in his hands. His temples were throbbing painfully. He wanted the hurt to stop. He didn't know how long he stayed like that until he heard his name.

"Hayden."

Hayden looked up and saw Kane. His expression was cautious, unreadable.

"Kane, I don't want to talk," said Hayden.

"It's okay, we don't have to talk," answered Kane, taking a seat beside him.

Hayden clenched his hands. Of course, Kane wouldn't understand. He had a perfect family. A mom that never left him. That never made him believe she was dead.

Kane must be thinking Hayden's family was psycho. He felt the sharp needle of shame in the pit of his stomach. The fire was waking up again.

"You can say it," said Hayden.

"Say what?" asked Kane.

"That you pity me for having such a mom," snapped Hayden. He was done being babied.

"Why would I think that?" asked Kane.

"Why wouldn't you?" counteracted Hayden.

"Because maybe I'm your best friend. Something you seem to have forgotten."

Hayden heard the accusation loud and clear. "Don't you dare make me the bad guy here," said Hayden, his voice contorted with anger.

"Make you the bad guy? Hayden, do you hear yourself?" exclaimed Kane, incredulous.

"Don't you see how messed up the whole situation is?" asked Hayden.

"Messed up? Hayden, all I know is that your mom, who you thought was dead, came back into your life. And you're being an asshole. That's all I'm seeing," replied Kane, looking him straight in the eyes.

"*I'm* an asshole?" Hayden felt like he had been punched.

"Yes, an ungrateful asshole. I don't know what happened because obviously you didn't trust me enough to tell me the truth, but from what I saw earlier, you were being a jerk," said Kane calmly.

"How dare you?" asked Hayden, his voice shaking.

"How dare I what?" asked Kane. He had a cold look in his eyes.

"Blame me. And you dare accuse me of not telling you when obviously you would never have understood what I'm going through. Your mom never left you," said Hayden accusingly.

"So, now I have to apologize for that, too?" asked Kane. He was looking at Hayden as if he didn't recognize him or didn't like what he saw.

"So, you're saying you would have understood had I told you?" scoffed Hayden.

"No, I'm saying I would have acted like a best friend and tried to support you," Kane said.

Hayden turned away and looked at the trees. The sun had completely disappeared, and it was dark now.

"Yeah, I can see your big support. You telling me I'm being jerk, is that what you call being a best friend?" asked Hayden. He sounded snide and he knew it.

"You know what, Hayden? Screw you. I'm done trying. I'm not gonna sit here and try to explain myself to you. When you don't even care about our friendship. I don't even know why I bothered," said Kane as he got up and left.

Without looking back.

Hayden clenched his teeth to keep from screaming. Suddenly, the cold was unbearable, and he could feel it seep through his clothes. Settling in his bones.

Hayden watched Kane leave and he had never felt so alone in his life. He couldn't remember a time where Kane had walked out on him. Sure, they fought, like all best friends do, but Kane had never left. They would always make up right after.

No, I can't let this happen, thought Hayden, but his feet seemed glued to the ground. He could only watch helplessly as Kane got farther and farther.

Stop him, his brain kept yelling at him, but his legs wouldn't move.

It was too late. Kane was gone.

CHAPTER THIRTY-FOUR

Leah

As she made her way toward the beach on Saturday morning, Leah wondered if Hayden would be there.

She didn't know whether she wanted him to be there. She had texted him, telling him she'd be at the beach tomorrow, but he hadn't replied to her. She hadn't stopped thinking about what happened, and the more she thought about it, the angrier she felt toward Hayden for acting like such a jackass.

She had left after Kane went to find him. He had asked them not to come with him, and Leah and Olivia knew it was best.

Hayden's mother had been so hurt when Hayden was so cruel in front of everyone.

She said goodbye to Olivia and went home, feeling

completely shocked and disappointed. She had tossed around all night, trying to fall asleep, and only managed to get a few hours of sleep before she woke up, feeling restless again.

She hoped walking outside would help make her feel better and headed to the beach. She doubted Hayden would show up, but she still wanted to take her chances.

She pulled her jacket tight. It was a windy, gloomy morning. The beach was empty—save for a lonely silhouette. Before she even registered it, her feet were carrying her toward Hayden.

"Hayden," she said.

He turned to look at her, his expression unreadable. He looked like death warmed over.

She almost took pity on him. "Why are you acting like this, Hayden? Can't you see how lucky you are?" She had tried to speak calmly, but the words came out too earnest. Almost accusing.

Hayden looked at her incredulously. "I–*I* am lucky?"

"Yes, you *are* lucky. At least you still have your mom." He scoffed, but she continued, determined to speak up her mind. "Yes, she might not have been the greatest mom, but she worked on herself. She fought against her depression and mental illness. For *you.*"

Hayden hunched his shoulders, whether defensively or because he was cold, Leah couldn't tell.

"I thought you of all people would understand me," he said, his voice low.

"Well, I would do anything to have my mom back in my life," said Leah adamantly.

"You don't understand, it's completely different. Your mom never left you of her own will. She cared about you."

"Your mom cares. You just don't see it because you're so blinded by your anger you don't want to admit the truth."

"My anger is justified."

"Hayden, I'm trying to open your eyes and make you realize that you're being selfish and resentful, and losing the opportunity to have a happy relationship with your mother out of your own pettiness. By holding onto your anger, you're not gaining anything. What are you trying to prove? That you can hold a grudge your whole life? You can't live with anger all your life. It's gonna eat you up."

"So, now you're telling me I'm being a drama-queen, a whiner when everything is so fucking perfect in my life? Is that what you're telling me?" said Hayden, his anger as sudden as thunder. It seemed to erupt out of him like fire.

Leah looked at him, incredulous, frowning. "No, Mr. Dramatic, I never said that you have no reason to be hurt. I'm saying that your mom is trying to make it up to you. Yes, I know she abandoned you!" she exclaimed when she saw he was about to interrupt her again.

He shut his mouth tight, anger wrinkling his eyes, a stubborn expression on his face.

"You're here, acting all high and mighty, feeling like the world owes you something just because your mom left you when you were a child. That's not how life works, Hayden.

Grow up already. Be grateful enough to acknowledge how lucky you are that your mom is trying to make amends and be a part of your life again."

Hayden scoffed. "Easy for you to say."

"Easy for me? For me who lost my mom when she never deserved to get sick or die so young," exclaimed Leah. She felt like her heart was trying to come out of her chest.

Hayden was pale, lips pinched, arms by his side. Looking desolate and upset.

But Leah was tired of his attitude. She just wanted to shake him until he came to his senses. "Don't you ever dare, Hayden, to say that again. Not when you have not experienced the loss I did. Yes, your mom left you, yes, she caused you pain, but she is ALIVE! Alive and trying to be in your life again! And you, what are you doing? You're pushing her away, playing the victim, not ever thinking or caring how you're hurting her with your behavior. She is only a human, for God's sake! Everyone makes mistakes, but your mom is trying to make up for it."

She looked at Hayden and realized a wall stood between them. He was all by himself in his little island of misery and she had no interest whatsoever to join him there.

"I was the one to suffer for the mistakes she made," he said with cold anger.

Leah was stunned. "You know, Hayden, I'm really disappointed in you. I didn't think you were so resentful."

As she spoke, Hayden's face turned white and two red

splotches appeared on his cheekbones. He seemed livid, but she didn't care.

"How dare you make me the bad one when she's the one who left me?" he whispered. His voice sounded strangled under the anger. She could hear the tremble in it.

"Haven't you listened to a word I said?" she sighed, feeling her exasperation rise. "Your mom was sick, for God's sake! She was unwell! She got better for YOU! She fought her battles for you! So she can be a good mom for *you*!"

His nostrils flared. "Whenever a mother leaves her child, she can no longer be called a good mother. I don't care what her excuse was," he said, his voice flat.

"Then, you don't deserve to have a mother at all, if you can't even be compassionate enough to share her suffering," Leah snapped.

As soon as she had said the words, she knew she had gone too far. He took a step back as if she had punched him. He was hurting, too. His pain was making him irrational.

"Hayden…" she said, stepping toward him to apologize.

"Don't," he said, putting his hand up. She saw it was shaking.

Without another word, he turned and left. She watched as he huddled against the wind, walking fast to get away from her.

Why had she been so cruel? She hung her head low and bit her lip to prevent herself from crying. Her legs felt weak. She sat on the sand and put her arms around her legs. She watched the seagulls flying in the gray skies. Soon, she felt as numb from the cold as from her conflicting emotions.

Slowly, she got up and made her way back home, feeling the cold of the wind seep through her coat inside her bones.

CHAPTER THIRTY-FIVE

Hayden

On Monday afternoon, Hayden dragged his feet to the locker room. He had been in a bad mood the whole day. He felt irritated by everything, and he dreaded seeing his teammates after Friday's fiasco.

Kane and Leah had completely ignored him, and Olivia was awkwardly silent around him. He had spent all day avoiding the stares of his classmates. After classes ended, he headed to soccer practice. He knew his coach expected him to show up no matter what.

As he got inside the room, he heard some voices on the other side of the lockers, in the right corner.

He stopped when he heard his name.

"I always knew Hemingway was a screw-up anyway,"

said Tyler, in that arrogant voice of his.

Hayden tightened his fists. He had always hated Tyler and his condescending attitude, and now he felt his hate get sharper.

"It's not surprising, now that we know that his mom is a screw-up too. It's in the blood," continued Tyler.

There was some nervous laugh.

"Shut your mouth, Tyler, you're the one who is messed up," said Kurt.

Tyler didn't get the chance to reply as Hayden appeared in their view.

He saw Kurt and the other boy–Carter, someone he had thought of as a friend.

Tyler's eyes widened before they narrowed in contempt.

"What did you say about my mom?" asked Hayden, quietly. Too quietly.

"Nothing that's not true," replied Tyler with a smirk. "A screw-up," he continued, his voice pregnant with malice as he watched Hayden's reaction.

The boy didn't even have time to blink before Hayden's fist connected with his face. Hard.

"Hayden, stop!" screamed Kurt, trying to keep him away from the other boy. Tyler was stunned at first, but it was quickly replaced by rage as he tried to punch Hayden as well.

Hayden wanted the pain to go away. The hate, too. At that moment, he wasn't sure who he hated more: Tyler or himself.

Hayden tackled Tyler to the floor as the other tried to push him away.

"Repeat that again, you motherfucker," whispered Hayden, heated as he grabbed his teammate by the collar, his voice distorted with hatred.

Tyler looked at him with anger, blood seeping from his mouth.

"Last time I saw, you weren't mama's boy," replied Tyler with his arrogant smirk.

"Hayden, stop!" cried Kurt again.

Hayden was grabbed by the two boys, and the moment of distraction was enough for Tyler to punch Hayden in the eye as Hayden was lifted away.

The pain was blinding.

"What the hell is going on here?" bellowed their coach, approaching them quickly and grabbing Hayden by the shoulder.

Ah crap, thought Hayden.

"Why are you fighting?" demanded their coach.

Hayden remained silent as did the others.

"Detention for the rest of the week!" announced their coach.

"But we have a game this Thursday!" protested Tyler, hissing with pain.

"Then, you should have thought about that before you started fighting," said their coach with barely contained anger.

"I didn't start the fight. He was the one who punched

me," exclaimed Tyler, pointing an accusatory finger at Hayden.

"Hayden, is that true?" asked his coach.

"Yes," said Hayden flatly, maintaining eye contact.

"You're going to the principal with me, boy," said the coach, clearly irritated by Hayden's attitude.

Hayden kept quiet. He saw Tyler smirk surreptitiously while the others avoided his eyes.

As he sat in the principal's office, Principal Macey sighed deeply. "You have no idea how disappointed I was to hear that you started a fight, Hayden," said the principal, looking sad.

You're not the only one, trust me, sir, Hayden thought. It seemed he was on some fast-track record to get as many people disappointed in him as possible.

He looked at his entwined hands on his lap.

"I'm sorry to tell you that you'll be suspended from playing for the rest of the season," the principal said.

Hayden nodded.

"Is there something you want to say?" asked Principal Macey, not unkindly.

"No, sir," said Hayden.

"I think it will do you good to speak with our counselor, Mrs. Desjardins," said Principal Macey.

"I don't need to, I'm fine," said Hayden.

"I wasn't asking, Hayden," said Principal Macey, his tone leaving no room for argument. "I'll ask her to schedule you for an appointment this week." Hayden stood up and opened the door when the principal spoke up again. "Don't waste your opportunity, Hayden," he said, looking at him with a piercing look.

Hayden gave a curt nod before going out. He made his way to his locker to take his stuff. He looked down the corridor and saw his coach walk toward him rapidly.

"Hayden, son, Anderson told me the truth. Why didn't you say anything?"

Now we are back to son, thought Hayden, still remembering how he had addressed him as a boy less than an hour ago.

Hayden shrugged. "Would it have changed something?"

"Of course! Obviously, I don't condone violence, but since you were provoked, you wouldn't have been punished unjustly. Don't worry, I'll explain everything to the principal, and I suspended Tyler from playing for the next game. I'm expecting to see you at the training Wednesday after school," said his coach with a paternal smile and a tap on the shoulder.

Hayden stayed impassive.

"See you then," said his coach after a short silence, uncomfortable.

"I'm not coming," said Hayden and without waiting for his coach's reply, he turned and left. He felt hollow.

As he made his way to the parking lot, his right eye throbbing, he saw Riley walking to his own car, and he saw red. He had seen him with Leah all day and it had pained him to no end to not be able to talk to her. Even if he was still upset at her words. His mind was a minefield where he felt anything might trigger an explosion.

A desolate, lonely minefield.

"Connors, if I were you, I would stop playing with Leah," said Hayden, approaching Riley.

Riley turned around, looking confused. "What?" he said.

"You heard me. You think I don't know you?"

Riley narrowed his eyes in contempt. "Exactly, you don't know me at all, so you don't know what my intentions are with Leah."

Hayden scoffed with disdain. "What can a scumbag's intentions be but bad? You think I forgot what you tried to do to Olivia in the summer? Thank God I came on time. I don't want you to hurt Leah or you'll regret it. So I'm warning you"

Riley almost growled in frustration. "You are such a blind, self-absorbed fool. I wonder how you can walk with that empty brain of yours. Look, I'm tired of repeating myself, so I'm going to ask you to leave now before you make things worse. My patience is wearing thin."

"I'm serious, Connors, leave Leah alone. Or I will tell her the truth," said Hayden, grabbing Riley by the collar.

Something seemed to snap in Riley's eyes. He pushed Hayden's hands away, so hard Hayden stumbled back.

Riley advanced, anger punctuating each of his words.

"Oh yeah? And what exactly do you think is the truth? Did it never occur to that thick brain of yours that maybe not I, but you are the one who hurt Olivia that night?

Who keeps constantly hurting her with that irritating, egotistical attitude of yours?"

Hayden was taken aback and didn't even react when the other pushed him again.

"What the hell are you talking about? What do I have anything to do with what happened that night?" he asked, confused and lost. And not liking how he felt. Like he was about to be told something very disagreeable.

"Well, it's grand time someone opens your eyes, Hemingway, because I'm done with your bullshit. You think you're something else, don't you? You're so obsessed with your little self you never stop to notice how everyone else feels around you. You only use people to your advantage. You don't care about your friends. As long as you're good, that's all you care about. You're the biggest asshole I ever saw. It makes me sick that Olivia is in love with you. What does she even see in you?"

As soon as the last words were out, Riley turned pale. He looked like he wanted to take the words back. There was a heavy silence where only their harsh breathing could be heard.

"What did you say?" asked Hayden, deadly quiet.

"Forget it," said Riley.

"You're lying," said Hayden, almost as if trying to convince himself. "Olivia doesn't love me. Not like that, anyway. She can't. We're best friends."

It was Riley's turn to scoff. "If only things worked like that. Look, I said things I shouldn't have said, things I promised I would never reveal. So, just go away. I really don't want to see your face. It makes me sick."

Hayden was stunned to silence. Riley took one last look at him and, rolling his eyes in disgust, walked away.

He must be dreaming. Olivia wasn't in love with him. Right? Best friends don't fall in love. He knew how illogical he was being now, but anything was better than to admit the truth. A truth he had suspected since that night.

Flashes of Olivia crying uncontrollably, her top discarded, as Riley had his arms around her danced in front of his eyes. When he had found them, he saw red. He had immediately assumed the asshole was trying to hurt Olivia and had lunged at him until Kane came to stop him. He was restrained by his best friend and only the image of his other best friend crying, huddled in a corner, hiding behind her shirt, made him stop.

He took off the shirt he was wearing on top of his tee-shirt and put it around her, shielding her from peoples' stares as they had gathered to see what had caused the ruckus, and the three of them left.

No mention was ever made of that night again.

But Olivia had murmured something in her sleep when Kane drove them home. She had whispered his name.

And a wedge appeared in their friendship. A crack in the wall of friendship that no matter how much Hayden had pretended did not exist kept growing until he became distant with Olivia.

He kept lying to himself and avoided any time alone

with Olivia, and he knew she knew.

Coward that he was, he kept dodging any conversation about that night she wanted to initiate.

He was a lousy friend. He took his head in his hands and gripped his hair.

Connors was lying. Hayden had seen with his own eyes what happened. He shuddered to think what would have happened if he hadn't come there on time.

Then, why did he feel like he was missing something?

He needed to talk to Olivia. It was high time he stopped being a coward.

CHAPTER THIRTY-SIX

Leah

Leah's head had been pounding since yesterday. She had taken so many Advil's but they weren't helping. She had also tried her best to avoid Hayden as much as possible in the corridors. Riley had asked her if she was okay, and she had lied that she felt a bit under the weather.

From his expression, she knew she wasn't fooling him, and he had heard about what happened at the soccer game.

But he hadn't pushed further and just sat with her. If he had noticed that she was avoiding Hayden, he didn't comment on it.

When she came home, she saw that her dad wasn't there. She put her school bag on her chair and went to sit on her bed.

She hadn't slept well since Saturday night. She didn't know when she started crying, but the tears started falling as she made her way home from the beach.

She was feeling guilty for saying those horrible things to him, but she was also so angry that he was hurting both himself and his mom with his unforgiving attitude.

She took her mom's picture and pressed it to her chest. She wished more than ever to have her back.

"Life is so unfair, Mom. Why do people hurt each other? Why do we have to suffer? Why does God separate children from their parents? Why did He take you away from me?" she whispered, tears falling on the frame.

She fell asleep, her tears staining the pillow.

When she woke up, the sun had already set. She felt groggy and disoriented and wondered why her dad had let her sleep all afternoon.

She went downstairs, but her dad was still not home. She called him, but it went straight to his voicemail. Frowning, she tried to call her grandad, but the phone kept ringing, and no one came to answer. She tried to stay calm, but she could feel the panic set in as she imagined the worst case of scenarios.

She tried to call Uncle Eric, but it went to his voicemail, too. She groaned in frustration. What was going on? Why was no one answering the phone?

Just then, the front door opened, and Leah ran out of the kitchen to see her dad come in.

"Dad! Where were you? I called you so many times!" she said, her voice high pitched from nerves.

His smile slipped as he took in her frantic state. "Sorry, pumpkin, my battery died. I didn't realize it until I got in the car," he apologized.

"I was so scared, Dad. I called you so many times."

"I'm sorry, pumpkin," he said again, taking her in his arms. He held her tight, and she started crying.

"I can't lose you. I won't be able to survive if I were to lose you, too," she sobbed.

"Oh, my baby, you won't lose me. I'm always here for you."

"I want our life back, Dad. I want our old house back. I want to be back in Montreal," she cried. "I want Mom back," she sobbed.

"Me too, pumpkin. I want that more than anything," whispered her dad, kissing the top of her head, his voice muffled by his own tears.

"Why wasn't I a better daughter when Mom was alive, Dad?"

"Don't say that, Leah. Why are you saying that?"

"I wish I had done more to make Mom happy while she was still alive," confessed Leah.

It felt almost liberating to admit her guilt.

She had been carrying too much hate since her mom died. Hating herself for causing her dad pain, hating herself for not being strong enough. Hating everyone for being happy. It hurt so much.

She didn't want to feel that despair again. She had worked too hard to get out of it.

She tried to take deeper breaths to avoid a panic attack, afraid to get lost in her head again.

"You are an amazing daughter, Leah. The best any parent could ask for. Your mom knew how much you were suffering. She kept telling me how much she was proud of you. My baby daughter, your mom wouldn't want you to live your life in guilt and regrets."

When Leah stayed quiet, her dad continued, "You know what your grandfather told me when I was grieving the loss of your mom? He told me that pain is the price we pay for love. Loving your mom was the most beautiful thing in my life even though it gave me the most pain. But you know what? I'll take that pain every day again and again, if that means I get to experience your mom's love."

He looked at Leah with his own face wet with tears, his eyes bright with love.

Her dad caressed her hair and kissed her forehead. "You're a wonderful child, my pumpkin. I just wish you would allow yourself to make mistakes. Life is a long journey when you're too hard on yourself."

She felt lighter as she wiped her tears. "I'm sorry for making you cry, Dad."

"Oh, my Leah, never apologize for showing your emotions," he said, embracing her, and she felt safe again.

She didn't know how long they stayed like that, but she felt at peace. Drained, but at peace.

CHAPTER THIRTY-SEVEN

Hayden

Hayden drove to Olivia's house in a daze, heart pounding and his mouth dry. She smiled when she saw him but frowned upon seeing his expression.

"Hayden, what are you doing here? Was soccer cancelled?" she asked.

"I need to talk to you, Liv," he said.

They sat on the sofa. He remembered all the rainy days they had spent indoors, watching movies, sitting on that same sofa. He sighed. Sometimes, he wished he was twelve again, his most important worry being the math test or when the next Marvel movie would come out.

He never felt as lonely as he felt now. He looked up at Olivia, and saw that she was watching him, her eyes full of concern. He felt even more horrible, if possible. He so didn't deserve her love; why did she choose him to fall in love with? Any guy would be fortunate to be her boyfriend, and so more deserving.

"I don't know how to say it. But I owe you an apology."

"For what?"

"Connors told me something today."

He saw her eyes became troubled. "Told you what?" she asked, her expression wary.

"He said that I caused you pain and that you were hurting because of me this summer," said Hayden, looking at his hands.

"He told you what happened at the party when I came to find him?" asked Olivia.

Hayden shook his head. "No, he didn't. He just said he spoke too much, and he wasn't supposed to say this. We got into an argument, and he got angry and said it in anger," said Hayden, wondering why he was justifying Connors suddenly.

"But he said that you had feelings for me?" asked Hayden, hesitantly. He was afraid to find the answer now that he had asked the question.

Olivia looked at her hands on her lap and sighed, looking defeated. "Hayden, it's been so long and it's not like I realized it immediately, you know? It took me a long time before I could understand it myself. So, don't blame yourself for not realizing it as soon as I fell in love with you when even I didn't know it yet."

Her laughter was choked, halfway laughter, halfway sob.

"And I'm not saying it because I want you to feel bad. How can I blame you for falling in love with you? It's not your fault. Before I knew it, I just did."

Hayden felt his eyes burn, hating himself for being the cause of his best friend's pain. Kane's face flashed in his mind, and he grimaced. He really was the crappiest best friend ever.

"I'm so sorry, Liv," he whispered.

"It's okay, Hayden. I knew you didn't like me like that, so I've learned to just live with it. And you know what? It doesn't hurt now, to not have you love me back."

"Liv, I love you. I love you a lot."

"I know, but not in the way I do, and it's okay," said Olivia, patting his hand.

"Why didn't you tell me? Why did you never try to let me know?"

She smiled. "I didn't tell you because I didn't want things to get awkward between us. Because I knew that you didn't love me back. Even if I was in love, I wasn't blind. And I also knew that had I told you, the guilt and loyalty for our friendship would not have allowed you to push me away. You would have pretended to return my feelings for my own sake. And don't try to deny it. I know you, Hayden. I've known you since you were two. You're one of the most selfless persons I know. And that's another reason in the super long list as to why I love you."

Although she had spoken softly, there was a glint in her eyes that told him that she was making fun of him. He smiled, even if he could feel his heart heavy with regret.

"Cheer up, Hayden! You aren't making it easier for me by being all gloomy and contrite."

He looked her in the eyes, and taking her hands, said, "You're the best friend I could ever ask for. And I know that you will find some great guy who will be the most fortunate person ever to have my best friend's love. And despite what you think of me, I don't deserve your love. I would never have been able to make you happy as you deserve to be. But there is one thing I'm asking of you. When you find that guy, please don't forget about your best friend. Who knows? I might become handy when you need someone to knock some sense into the guy or give him the beating of his life if he ever makes my best friend cry."

The redhead laughed, and he smiled back, but his smile dropped as he remembered a detail that had been bothering him.

"There's one thing I still don't understand. How come Connors knew about this?" he asked.

Olivia lowered her eyes, looking ashamed.

"When you found Riley and me in that room, he didn't do anything wrong that night. I was the one who came to him. And he actually stopped me from doing something stupid once he realized I was drunk. And then I started crying, telling him how miserable I was for being in love with you while you didn't love me," admitted Olivia, her voice small.

"Liv..." Hayden's voice was full of pain and self-blame.

"No, Hayden, it's not your fault. It was all me. I was the one who decided to act like a fool. When you found us, I was crying because I felt so wretched about my situation, and he was comforting me. But when you found us, and jumped to conclusions, I was too ashamed to correct you. Had he really been as bad as you think he was, he wouldn't have kept quiet that night. But he did. And he didn't tell anyone, even without me asking, when he had no reason to."

He grimaced. Turns out Connors was a decent bloke all this time and he was the one who needed to work on himself.

"Hayden, him being good doesn't make you the bad one. You're both good people," said Olivia, watching him with kind eyes.

"I made so many mistakes, Olivia, if only you knew," he said, sighing with regret.

As he confided to Olivia about his fight with Kane and Leah, Olivia patted his knee. "They'll forgive you, Hayden. They know you've been hurting. The situation with your mom isn't easy."

"Thank you for not judging me," said Hayden.

"Best friends don't judge. They just tell you the truth because they have your best interests at heart," said Olivia, and he knew it was her way of telling him that he should heed Kane's and Leah's advice.

And he knew that she was right. They were all right.

It was such a blow to realize that he had been in the wrong all this time.

"Hayden, I need to apologize, too," said Olivia, looking at her hands before looking up at him again.

"Why would you need to apologize?" asked Hayden, confused.

"I'm sorry I wasn't a good enough friend. I should have been more supportive of your relationship with Leah. My fear of losing you made me act like that," she said with a sad smile.

"I'm sorry I was so distant, Liv, I should have spoken with you earlier," said Hayden.

"I'm glad we're okay now," said Olivia, smiling.

"What happened to your eye?" she asked, looking at the bruise on his temple.

"I got into a fight with Tyler," sighed Hayden.

"Why?"

"He talked crap about my mom," said Hayden.

"The asshole," said Olivia with venom in her voice.

Hayden smiled. Trust Liv to always defend him. "But I was the one to be punished. I got suspended from soccer."

"What? But why didn't your coach suspend Tyler instead?" exclaimed Olivia.

"Because he told him that I punched him, which is true," answered Hayden.

"But he provoked you! I hope you told him that!"

"No, I wasn't going to be a snitch on top of being a jerk," said Hayden with a small shrug.

"But, Hayden, it's not fair!" said Olivia.

"Life isn't fair," said Hayden.

"Life is what we make it, Hayden," answered Olivia. For some reason, her words reminded him of Leah, and he realized he really missed her. He was still hurt by her words, but he knew she meant well. He wondered if she'd forgive him.

"I tell you what, go talk to Kane and Leah, apologize to them, and talk to your mom. Apologize to your mom and hear her out. It will do you both good," said Olivia.

"You're right," said Hayden.

Olivia smiled. "Of course, I'm always right," she replied as they made their way to the front door.

Hayden chuckled. "Thank you for everything, Olivia. You're really the best of friends," he said sincerely.

"Then, do as your best friend is telling you," she said with a wink.

She waved as he got into his car, and he smiled. He had his best friend back. It was an amazing feeling.

CHAPTER THIRTY-EIGHT

Leah

On Tuesday, the day passed in a blur and Leah had a hard time concentrating in class. English class had been excruciating as she could feel Hayden's presence behind her. As soon as the class was done, she had darted to the door. She had done her best to avoid him for the rest of the day after that. She didn't know if she was avoiding him out of guilt or anger or because she had felt hurt by his attitude, but she couldn't face him without feeling like she'd start crying.

She was on some tear-fest at this point.

When the last bell rang, she almost ran out of the building, relieved to escape the suffocating atmosphere. She felt guilty for not waiting for Riley, but she wanted to be alone.

Before she knew it, she had walked all the way to the beach. The cold breeze felt good against her tired eyes, playing in her hair.

She took a deep breath and felt slightly better.

The sun shone and the seagulls kept squawking in the horizon, looking for food.

She sat on steps made of stone that led down to the shore and watched the water sparkle under the sun. It was beautiful.

Why couldn't she be like the water? Calm and undiscriminating. No judgment.

She closed her eyes, letting her mind wander.

Memories passed through her mind quickly, like a movie on fast-forward speed. Never lingering long on any scene. And then it stopped on the one memory Leah hadn't allowed herself to relive for the last two years.

"Mom, are you scared?" she asked, her chin trembling. Tears singed her eyes and her throat as she lay beside her mom on the bed.

Her mom looked at her with love and patience. So much patience. "No, my love, I'm not scared of dying. I just want the pain to end." Her features had become gaunt, her body so thin, Leah was afraid to hurt her whenever she moved on the bed. "But I don't want to leave you and your dad. I also don't want to leave my father alone when Mom left him so soon. I wish I could see you graduate, get married, have kids. I am sad I will be denied of all those moments that most parents get to experience. Moments I expected to live when I gave birth to you and took you in my arms."

Leah's vision was blurred by her tears and her mom's beautiful face swam in her tears.

"Mom, I won't be able to live without you." She choked on her words. They were too painful. Like blazing knives piercing her throat and her heart. It hurt to even breathe.

"My love, I know how hard it is for you," said her mom, taking her face in her hands. A tear fell down her pale cheek. "But I also know that you're strong and you're brave. So much braver than you think. You will make it through."

Leah hugged her hard and cried. "I hate God for doing this to you," she sobbed. "Why doesn't He take someone else? Someone who doesn't deserve to live?"

Her mom smiled at her with that same gentle smile and Leah was amazed she wasn't angry at God. At the whole world.

"Leah, don't be angry at God. Don't be angry at anyone, least of all at yourself. We don't understand why things happen, but we must take each challenge and make the best of it. Yes, cancer is harsh, but it also made me cherish so many things I never took the time to consider before. Things I took for granted all my life. My health, my expectations, how short our lives are on this Earth, how many dreams I still have left that I will never get to experience. So, please, do me a favor, Leah. Live. For me. Live with all your heart. Follow your dreams and never give up. Love with all your heart. Don't be afraid to take chances and risks. Life is hard, but it is so worth it. Every single day of it. The bad and the good. The joys and the heartaches. The grief and the losses. These things make our lives meaningful. That's the price we have to pay to be able to know what happiness is. To be alive."

Leah's face was streaked with tears, her eyes and nose red from crying, her lips swollen, as she looked at the horizon. The sun was setting, the days getting shorter and colder.

All this time she had been angry that her love for her mom wasn't enough to take the sickness away. She had felt so powerless that she had failed to see what her mom was trying to show her: that it was enough to keep them connected, no matter what. For love was powerful like that, it transcended all barriers.

How she wanted to tell her mom that she understood now what she had been trying to tell her all this time. Love encompassed everything, erasing distance, forgetting separation.

Love kept loving no matter what. It didn't need to be near the person to love. It didn't need any reason at all.

She thought of Hayden and his mom. She wished she had told him about her regrets. How she would do anything to change those moments. How she should have spent the days making her mom happy instead of being so angry, so full of rage. How she wished she had prayed more. For one more day. One more memory. How she regretted being so blinded by her own grief, obsessed with her own pain, that she hadn't made the most of those final days.

Her hands were clenched. She opened her fingers. She felt the blood flow as her fingers relaxed.

She knew what she needed to do.

CHAPTER THIRTY-NINE

Hayden

Tuesday afternoon, Hayden drove to his grandparents' place after school.

His grandmother was sitting in her favorite chair in front of the window, a book on her lap as she seemed lost in her thoughts. She looked up and smiled with relief when she saw him. Hayden felt his guilt increase. He had refused to talk to her all weekend.

"Hayden," she said with warmth. "Don't you have soccer practice at this time?" she asked.

"Not today," said Hayden, not wanting to tell her about his suspension. He didn't want to disappoint her any further.

"Would you like something to eat? I made an apple pie," she said as she put her book on the coffee table.

"No, I'm good. Please sit, Grandma," said Hayden, sitting beside her on the couch. He took her hand in his. "You're not angry at me?" he asked her.

She sighed. "Hayden, I understand your pain. But you shouldn't have acted that way with your mom," she said.

"I know. I wanted to tell you how sorry I am." Shame made him lower his eyes.

She put a hand to his cheek. "It's not me you need to apologize to, Hayden," she said gently.

Hayden nodded. "I know. I will apologize to my mom as well," he said.

He dreaded seeing her. He felt like the biggest jerk on Earth. Would she even want to talk to him? Would she be able to forgive him?

As if his grandmother could hear his thoughts –or read his troubled expression–she squeezed his hand and smiled. "A mother will always forgive her child. A mother's love is unconditional," she reassured him and patted his hand.

"Yeah, but I would still understand if she would never want to see me again. After everything I told her."

"She understands your pain, too. She's your mother after all." Grandma squeezed his hand. Dark shadows under her eyes. She had been so worried about him while he had wallowed in self-pity and anger all this time. Shame squeezed his insides

"We were so worried for you," she continued. "Kane went to see you and he told us after you asked to be left alone."

Hayden felt his heart leap with gratitude. Trust Kane to

have his back, even when they had fought. He had thought Kane would never forgive him and seeing him ignore him completely at school had confirmed his fears. But maybe there was still hope.

"Yeah, I needed time alone," said Hayden. "Thank you for not telling Dad, either."

"Of course. I just told him that you lost the game," said his grandma with a smile.

"Yeah, I think he felt bad for not being there," said Hayden with a small chuckle. His grandma smiled and stroked his hair affectionately.

"Your dad wants you to be happy, Hayden. But, most importantly, you need to allow yourself to be happy. Don't hold on to anger, for you're only punishing yourself. I'm sorry, my love, I wasn't more considerate of your pain. I really thought that trying to reconcile you with your mom was the right path to heal—and I still do—but I didn't take the time to acknowledge your pain and your hurt."

Hayden stayed quiet, unsure of what to say. His grandma's words made him wonder if all this time his anger had been directed at himself.

He remembered all the times he felt consumed by guilt and self-loathing when he thought his mom died giving him birth. Seeing her alive had been a punch in the gut.

Why hadn't he been happy? Wasn't it what he had wanted all his life?

But, somehow, his anger had been too great. The feeling of betrayal had been unbearable.

He couldn't imagine himself carrying on like that for the rest of his life.

Maybe his grandma was right, and he needed to forgive himself. He needed to see he deserved to be happy.

"I was just so shocked. So hurt…" Hayden trailed off, not wanting to remember the pain.

"Hayden, nothing can ever justify the lie your dad told you, but his love for you made him weak. Please forgive him," said his grandma, taking his hand in hers.

He looked at their joined hands and remembered all the times she had rocked him in her arms.

"You can never get back the years you've lost growing up without your mom, but you can still have wonderful years ahead with her. Give her a chance, Hayden. For both of your sakes."

Hayden looked at her, feeling his chin tremble. He tried to take a breath, feeling ashamed of crying in front of his grandma. But she pulled him toward her, in her embrace, and he couldn't hold back his tears anymore.

He didn't know how long they stayed like that, him bawling like a child while his grandma comforted him, but he felt better. He felt lighter.

As if the weight of his pent-up emotions was gone.

He heard the door open and wiped his eyes hastily. He'd die of mortification if his grandpa saw him crying.

"Hayden, son, what a nice surprise," said his grandpa, coming into the living room.

"Hi, Grandpa, how are you?" asked Hayden, his voice scratchy. He cleared his throat.

"Are you sick?" asked his grandpa, frowning as he took in his red nose and eyes.

"Yeah, I think I better go home, I'm feeling a bit under the weather," said Hayden, grimacing.

"Make sure to rest so it doesn't get worse," said his grandpa with a smile.

Hayden nodded and after saying goodbye, left.

Outside, he looked at the piece of paper his grandma gave him and saw a phone number and address on it.

He knew what he needed to do.

There was an envelope with his name on it waiting for him at home.

The writing seemed familiar, but he couldn't place it. He went to his bedroom and was about to open the letter when his dad came home.

"Hayden, I'm home!"

Hayden went downstairs, the letter forgotten.

"Hi son, how was your day?" asked his dad.

"Fine."

"I'm going to change," his dad said.

Hayden set the table. He wondered if he should tell his dad about Friday night. Just thinking about it made him ashamed.

He took out the plates and the forks.

But, then again, his dad constantly told him that honesty was always the best policy, no matter what.

His dad returned for dinner, looking casual in his tracksuit.

"Dad, you almost look like a normal human, what's going on?" joked Hayden, who was not used to seeing his dad in casual clothes on a weekday.

"I decided to take tomorrow off to spend it with my son," replied his dad.

"It's a weekday. I have school," said Hayden.

"One day won't make a big difference. You're a smart boy, aren't you?" replied his dad with a smile.

Disconcerted, Hayden didn't know what to say.

"Your employees will have a heart attack tomorrow morning when they don't see you," said Hayden, only half-joking.

"My employees are the best, I'll have you know. Very efficient and autonomous. But, for tomorrow, I was thinking we can go hiking. What do you say? The fresh air will do us good."

Hayden shrugged. "If you want."

"You'll see, it will be fun," said his dad with a smile.

Hayden smiled for his sake, his resolve to tell the truth melting quicker than butter in a pan.

After dinner, he went to his bedroom and his eyes fell on the letter. He knew it wasn't his mother as it wasn't her handwriting. He had memorized her handwriting by heart. Her letters, too.

He glanced at his closet, knowing he'd wake up again in the middle of the night to go through the stack. No matter how many times he told himself to go back to sleep, he couldn't fall asleep until he had read at least one letter.

Then he would slowly drift to sleep, his brain full of her comforting words.

He sighed. Maybe Tyler was right, after all. He really was a screw-up. Here he was being a jerk to his mom, while at the same time reading her letters over and over at night.

He looked at the letter in his hand and, with a deep breath, opened it.

Dear Hayden,

I didn't know if you would want to talk to me after everything I told you last time, so I decided to write you a letter. I know, very old-fashioned of me. But I wanted to let you know how sorry I am for being so harsh with you. I just didn't want you to lose the opportunity to be happy with your mom. However, I realized only after that I was taking out my anger on you. An anger that was directed at myself to begin with. I didn't realize until that night when I wondered why I had been so angry at you that I was actually angry with myself.

Angry for wasting the last days I had with my mom being

angry at the world instead of enjoying the time with her. For not being grateful for those days that will not last, nor will ever come back.

Angry at myself for not being a better daughter. A more loving daughter. A daughter that should have spent the last days making her mom laugh instead of making her wipe away my tears and take away my pain by burying it inside her heart. By swallowing her own tears for my own sake. Me, the daughter who was too blinded by her own anger to see her mother's pain.

The daughter who was not strong enough and leaned on her mother for support until the last moment instead of offering the moral support she so needed.

The daughter who was fighting with everyone out of fear and hatred instead of showing love and care. The daughter who didn't have enough time to be a good enough daughter.

Who realized too late that the only thing that mattered, in the end, is being there for your loved ones. Loving them like it is their last day on Earth. Hugging them until you became one soul.

Until the love that was trapped inside of you could get free and envelop them with its power.

You have no idea how much I was jealous of you for having your mom back while I would never be able to have this chance. I thought you were being so selfish and ungrateful, and I was again so blinded by my anger, that I failed to see you were hurting and you were scared.

Now, I know. Now I see clearly. I will never be able to

go back in time and change the past for me, but I wanted to share with you my regrets so you don't have to go through them, too. So you can be spared and live your life happily. Because you deserve to be happy, Hayden.

You deserve to forgive and let go of the anger that is consuming you. For you and your mom. Because life is giving you a second chance. A chance that not everyone is lucky enough to have.

So, please don't waste your chance. Don't give up without even trying. Life is too short for being angry at things that won't matter in the end. Live and be happy while you can, Hayden.

As your friend who wishes you only well, I ask you to free yourself from the anger.

With love,
Leah

As he read the letter, he felt his eyes well up with tears. "Oh, Leah. If only you knew how sorry I am," he whispered.

He put her letter in his drawer where he also kept most of his mother's letters and wondered how he could repay Leah's kindness.

CHAPTER FORTY

Leah

Leah wondered if Hayden would talk to her at school that day. What if he simply ignored her? Had he even read the letter?

An image of him tearing her letter to pieces flashed in her mind and she winced.

When she had left it on his front steps yesterday, she had been so sure she was doing the right thing. Now, she wasn't so confident about her decision. *Ah, well, what's done is done. Regretting it now won't undo anything.* With any luck, she might not see him at all today.

Leah made her way to the library. She wanted to grab a book before the start of classes.

The library was deserted. Even Mr. Dumont, the librarian, wasn't there yet. But she thought she heard some voices. As she looked around the shelf, she saw Riley and Olivia talking to each other.

She wondered if she should let them know she was there or leave quietly. However, before she could decide, Olivia spoke, and Leah couldn't help but overhear what they were saying.

"Riley, I know I should have done it way sooner, but I didn't get the courage until now. I'm so sorry. But I wanted to let you know that I told Hayden the truth about that night at the party. I told him what you did for me," said the redhead.

She looked so contrite that Leah wondered more than ever what happened at the party.

"It's okay, Olivia, it wasn't your fault. If anything, Hemingway shouldn't have jumped to conclusions without asking first," said Riley.

"Hayden was really sorry he misjudged you," said Olivia. "He said he felt awful."

Riley scoffed. "Hemingway feeling bad about misjudging me? That'll be the day," he said.

"No, it's true. Hayden is a bit hot-headed, but he's really kind and he got scared for me, that's why he acted this way," said Olivia.

"Of course you'd say that," Riley replied, and although Leah couldn't see his expression, she could hear the bitterness in his voice.

"I know you and Hayden hate each other, but if you were to get to know each other, you'd realize that you're more similar than you think," said Olivia with a sad smile.

"I highly doubt that," Riley said.

"I also wanted to thank you, Riley. For not saying anything even when I didn't ask you to stay silent. You have no idea how guilty I feel for not telling the truth immediately," said Olivia, looking at the floor.

"Don't feel guilty. I totally understand your pain. If there's anything I can do for you, you just have to ask," said Riley, his voice sincere.

"That's very kind of you," said Olivia with a grateful smile, "but I won't be taking advantage of your kindness again."

"I'll do it again, without hesitation," said Riley.

Leah couldn't see his eyes as he was facing Olivia, but she was pretty sure he looked as earnest as he sounded.

"I better go to class," Olivia said finally. And just like that, she was gone.

Riley lowered his head, disheartened. She wanted to approach him and tell him everything would be okay. But she didn't get the chance as he followed Olivia and left the library.

She stayed where she was, processing everything she had just heard. She felt guilty, but she also wanted to do something to help Riley. Clearly, he liked Olivia. Did Olivia like him back? Was she even allowed to interfere?

She had always felt something was going between them two. She would be lying if she didn't admit that she was dying to know what happened.

Sighing, she made her way to class.

She shouldn't have eavesdropped on them. She felt the guilt pinch her insides, wondering how she would look Riley in the eyes without giving herself away.

"Hey, stranger, where have you been?" asked Riley, coming up behind Leah as she took out her schoolbag at the end of the day.

"Riley, you scared me!" exclaimed Leah. She hadn't seen him the whole day and now she didn't know how to act.

"Wanna go to Timmie's?" asked Riley, leaning on the locker near hers.

"Yeah, sure," said Leah. She had planned to tell him the truth and she knew the sooner, the better. She knew she wouldn't feel comfortable hiding the truth from him. Not when it was so personal.

As they made their way to the Tim Horton's near their school, Leah wondered how to start the conversation.

"You're very quiet," said Riley. "Are you okay?"

"Riley, I wanted to tell you something," she said, stopping in her tracks.

"Why do you look so guilty, Leah?" he chuckled, taking in her expression.

"Because I eavesdropped on you and Olivia."

His smile left his face. "You did what?" he asked, looking startled.

"I'm really sorry, I didn't mean to, it's just that I was in the library and then I heard you, and before I could come out and let you know I was there, you were already talking and I felt so bad for intruding, I just stayed quiet," she explained.

Even to her own ears, the explanation sounded pitiful.

"Sorry," she said again, looking at her feet.

"It's okay," said Riley, and when she looked up, she was relieved to see he really meant it. He didn't seem angry, just resigned.

"How much have you heard exactly?" he asked with a small frown, furrowing his eyebrows.

"Enough to understand that something bad happened last summer between you, Olivia and Hayden," she admitted. "I kinda figured it out on my own to be honest. Like I could see how you two were acting around each other."

He looked uncomfortable as he scratched his neck. "I didn't know I was that obvious."

"Do you like Olivia?" she asked.

He looked almost startled. But not enough to fool her. He seemed like he was about to protest but her raised eyebrow and knowing expression made it clear she wasn't going to accept anything other than the truth.

He sighed. "I guess, yeah, I did. I did like her at some point, but it never worked out, so I moved on," he admitted, looking beyond her, at the red coffee shop with its reddish bricks and bright red sign.

They weren't the only students who were going there. The spot was a popular place to go to after classes for all the students.

"Why didn't it work out? Because of Hayden?" she

asked, remembering their conversation at the cafeteria at the beginning of the year. It seemed like years ago.

"Yeah, you can say that," he replied. "To be honest, I knew from the beginning that it would never work."

"Why?"

Riley looked her straight in the eyes. "You really want to know?" he asked softly.

She nodded, feeling like she already knew the answer.

"Because she always liked Hemingway," he answered, gauging her reaction.

She didn't blink. She had known all along. "I thought as much," she said, with a small nod.

He looked surprised. "You did? Well, Leah, what can I say? You never cease to astonish me. How did you know?"

"I am very observant," she said.

"That I noticed," said Riley with a small smile. "Hey, if your curiosity has been properly satisfied, let's go inside before I literally freeze to death."

The day was quite windy.

"It's not even that cold," said Leah, rolling her eyes.

"Look who's talking. You are wearing like ten layers at least, and that scarf of yours alone seems warmer than my whole jacket," said Riley.

"Being smart, I dress warmly because that's what people do in the fall. They don't wear tiny jackets to look cool and impress others," she said teasingly.

"Looks are everything," he answered with a wink, his cheeks and nose already getting pink.

She shook her head in exasperation. "Urgh, you're so much like Hayden," she said. Her eyes widened in horror as she realized what she had just said.

He laughed at her expression. "It's okay, Leah, I won't combust if you compare me to Hemingway. Maybe the fact that we're so similar is the reason why we can't get along, who knows?" he said, shrugging.

"Probably," she said as they went inside, glad for the warmth.

After getting their hot drinks, they went to sit by the table near the big, panel windows.

Leah got a hot chocolate while Riley got a French vanilla.

She put her hands around the warm cup and smiled as she felt the warmth spread from her fingertips to the rest of her hands.

"So, are you going to tell me?" asked Riley.

"Tell you what?" asked Leah, confused.

"What happened between you and Hemingway," replied Riley.

"Oh that. Nothing really. We just kinda had a fight, I guess," she mumbled.

"You guess?" He sounded incredulous. "How can you guess? You either fought or you didn't, it's that simple."

She sighed. "It's complicated."

"Ah I see. Feelings are always complicated," Riley replied sagely.

She rolled her eyes. "It's not like that. We fought about something else. I can't tell you as it's personal. It concerns

Hayden and his family."

"I see. Well, do you want to make up with him?"

"I don't know," she said finally because she had realized that she truly didn't.

"You really don't, or you don't want to know the answer? There's a difference," said Riley.

"Oh, stop it, with your philosophical quotes. Why don't we talk about you and Olivia instead?" she smiled sweetly.

"There's nothing to talk about," he said, his expression serious.

"You really think so or you want to think so? There's a difference," replied Leah smartly.

"There is a difference. Olivia and I are friends, you and Hayden are–"

"Friends, too," said Leah, interrupting him.

"No. You and I are friends. You and him, I don't know what you are, but you're not friends," said Riley.

Leah stayed silent, unsure of what to say.

"You're more than friends," he added kindly.

Leah looked up at him. "Not anymore, I think," she said, playing with the lid of her cup, hoping she looked more nonchalant than she felt.

"Why not?" inquired Riley.

"I was really harsh with him. I told him things I regret now," admitted Leah, dejected.

"Knowing you, I'm sure you meant well and knowing Hemingway, I'm sure he deserved everything you told him," said Riley.

Leah wanted to smile. "Maybe, I don't know. Or maybe I should have been more understanding. He's suffering, you know?"

Riley sighed. "I wonder for which sins I am being punished that I have to be friends with people who decided that it is their duty to defend Hemingway's honor at every opportunity," he said, sounding like he was in pain.

Leah laughed. "Don't overdo it. Defending him once doesn't make us his guardians."

Riley smiled. "Hemingway is a jerk, in my humble opinion. But I guess he might not be so bad if he has two amazing people attesting to his wonderful personality." He had a twinkle in his eyes.

Leah smiled back. "Aha, so you're admitting we're right to say good things about Hayden," she said.

"No, more that you're too good for him," said Riley.

Leah looked away.

"But that doesn't mean I won't be supportive of you," he added.

"You're too good for me, Riley. Why did you decide to befriend me again?" she asked, only half-joking.

"You looked like you needed a good friend. And you seemed like a good friend yourself," Riley said. He grinned.

Leah smiled back and took a sip of her hot drink. She was thankful for her friendship with Riley.

"Riley, why don't you try telling Olivia how you feel?" Leah asked as they drove back home.

"What is that going to change?"

"Honesty is the best policy. You never know what she'll do," said Leah.

"No, I don't want to make her uncomfortable. Especially when I know how she feels," said Riley.

"Well, feelings change. People change, Riley," said Leah.

"We're here," said Riley.

"What?" asked Leah, startled.

"We're at your place." He pointed to her house.

"Wow, already. That was fast."

"What can I say, I have that effect on people," he replied with a smug grin.

"Oh God, I need to get out before I get suffocated by your ego." She laughed as she got out of the car. Her laughter subsided as she had a feeling of déjà-vu. She remembered the conversation she had with Hayden when he had dropped her off, and her heart felt heavy again as she thought of their fight.

"Good night, Leah," said Riley through the window.

"Good night, Riley, drive safe." She waved as he drove away.

As she walked the paved alley to her house, she thought of Hayden.

She wondered how they would complete their English project together. The deadline was fast approaching.

I guess I'll find out when I see him in class.

CHAPTER FORTY-ONE

Hayden

On Wednesday morning, Hayden and his dad drove to their favorite hiking spot. Autumn meant the trees were red and orange while the fir trees remained loyally green. Hayden loved the explosion of colors in autumn, and the day was beautiful and sunny.

"So, what really happened to your eye?" asked his dad as they walked side by side, their hiking boots crunching the dry leaves.

Hayden sighed. "Just a stupid fight over something silly. I had a bit of an argument with a teammate."

"Why?"

"He was talking crap," said Hayden, evading details.

His dad looked disappointed.

"I know, I'm sorry I lost my temper. I won't do it again, I promise," said Hayden, feeling guilty.

"Hayden, you need to let go of the anger," said his dad and Hayden almost faltered in his steps. Leah had written the same thing. But his father didn't seem to expect an answer as he walked ahead, sometimes stopping to look at some trees or plants.

"It was a good idea to come here. I missed this place," admitted Hayden.

"I told you it'd be fun."

Hayden had many good memories of this forest, even if the trails seemed smaller and narrower these days. It no longer felt scary like it did when he was small, and he would run after his dad to make sure he didn't get lost in the dark woods.

After what felt like an hour, his dad asked that they stop to rest.

"Already?" asked Hayden with a playful smirk. Inside, he was glad for the break. His legs were on fire. He shrugged off his backpack. He took one water bottle and gave a second one to his dad who accepted it with a grateful nod.

"Don't be a smart aleck," said his dad. "I'm not getting younger, you know."

Hayden stayed quiet. He didn't like it when his dad reminded him that he was getting older.

"You just need to exercise more. You're always in your office," said Hayden.

"Yeah, maybe I should join you on your morning jogs?" asked his dad with a raised eyebrow and a smile.

"Sure," said Hayden.

"I saw Aunt Kim the other day while getting groceries," said his dad, and although he said it spontaneously, Hayden knew him well enough to know he had been thinking about it for a while.

"Yeah?" said Hayden, trying to sound nonchalant.

"Yes, she told me she hadn't seen you in a while and that Kane had been quite moody lately."

"We've been very busy with, you know, school and stuff," replied Hayden. He winced inside at the lame excuse.

"Never stopped you before."

Hayden sighed. "We kinda had a fall out," he said, looking at his boots as he gave a small kick at the dirt, making the twigs fly.

"You've had fights before."

"It's different this time," said Hayden. He didn't want to burden his dad with his issues.

"How?" asked his dad, ever persistent.

"We said a lot of stuff, and it was hurtful."

His dad waited for him to continue.

"I don't know, I guess it was my fault. I said things I shouldn't have."

"When did it happen?" asked his dad.

"After the soccer game," answered Hayden. He hesitated before continuing. "Grandma didn't tell you, but she brought Mom to the soccer game and..." Hayden trailed off, feeling the flame of shame in the pit of his stomach as he remembered his behavior. How he wished to take it all back now. How many heartaches he could have spared.

"And?"

"I acted like a jerk. I was horrible to Mom," admitted Hayden, closing his eyes.

His dad was silent for so long, Hayden wondered if he had heard.

"Hayden," said his dad, finally breaking the long silence. "I didn't try to talk to you about your mom because I wanted to respect your wish. I didn't want to hurt you more and I wanted to give you time to process the situation on your own, so that when you felt ready, you'd come and find me. But you need to know, your mom always loved you."

"Then why did she leave me? Why did she leave us?"

"I am to blame for her leaving," sighed his dad, his eyes full of regret.

"What?' said Hayden, taken aback.

"We had a huge fight after that horrible incident in the bathtub. When we came back from the hospital, I accused her of so many horrible things. I told her she was unfit to be a mother, and that I regretted marrying her, and that she was a danger to her family and that it would be better if she left. I was so tired. I was angry and scared. I felt incompetent and useless. My family was falling apart, and I couldn't do anything to stop it. I took out all my insecurities and my anger, my resentment, on her. Aviannah took it to heart." Hayden's dad put his hand to his heart as if it was his own heart hurting.

"I went to stay with you at your grandparents' house. When I came back a couple of days later, she had already left. I found a note where she apologized for everything, asking me not to tell you about anything because she didn't want to be a cause of pain to you. At first, you were always asking for your mom, and then, slowly, as days went by, you stopped asking and forgot her altogether. I removed all the pictures and I let you assume she died in childbirth. I thought this version would be easier for you than the truth. Had I known how much you were feeling guilt and anguish for believing you were responsible for her death, I would have told you the truth much sooner. I'm sorry, Hayden. Forgive me my cowardice, my son," said his dad, his eyes wet, his voice breaking at his last words.

Hayden felt the burning sensation of tears in his throat, and he wanted to say something. But his voice wasn't working. It was swallowed by grief.

His dad had a pained look in his eyes, all the guilt and hurt of the last years finally resurfacing. "I was so angry when I found out she had left," continued his dad. "Angry that she had listened to my words. That she had given up on us. I missed her so much, but I let pride get in the way. Days became weeks, weeks became months and months became years. I wish I had fought harder for us, you know? But my pride wouldn't let me. And I was so afraid of the prejudice and the judgments of people knowing the truth. Moms don't leave their sons, right? So, I lied, I pretended she was dead. It's better to be dead than an absent mom, I told myself."

His Dad put his face in his hands, and Hayden could hear his strangled sobs. "My hate made me so ugly. So horrible. I was so terrified. I didn't know what to do. You didn't come with a manual. I was overwhelmed. And I forgot your mom was too."

Hayden stayed silent, trying to breathe. The pain was agonizing. He bit the inside of his cheek to distract himself from his throbbing heart.

"I was angry that my love turned out to be not enough. I failed to realize that you can't make a person happy. You can make something good for them, but it won't replace happiness. In the end, my love for Aviannah was not enough to save her or our marriage. And it made me so mad. I failed to understand that pressuring your mom to get better, forcing her to snap out of her depression, was making things worse. I was not helping her at all. But loving means helping, not forcing," said his dad, sighing, as if the words were too heavy for his chest.

"I was so angry at her for not trying when I was trying so hard. But I got it all wrong. Only she could save herself. Instead of forcing her to get better, I should have tried to be more patient and understanding. Maybe it would have helped. Maybe it would have changed the outcome. I don't know. We'll never know now, I guess. But I do know that you should not be angry at your mom for not staying. She had to deal with her own demons. It doesn't mean she didn't love you. On the contrary, she did it out of love for you. She got better for you, Hayden. That's love."

His dad's expression was apologetic, yet full of love. Hayden felt like the ground had opened under his feet and he wondered how he'd be able to stand up.

"I realized too late that we all have different ways of showing our love. And dealing with our pain," said his dad, rubbing his face. "Your mom thought she was doing what was best for you. Her leaving doesn't mean she loves you any less. If anything, she sacrificed everything, her own happiness for your happiness. For our happiness. Because I convinced her of that lie."

Hayden heard the birds chirping and he felt the sun's rays through the branches of the trees, but the forest had lost its charm. He felt cold, tired and lonely.

So lonely.

The silence dragged on. Only the birds continued to sing, unaware, unapologetic.

"You won't say anything?" asked his dad, looking him in the eye. Waiting for his judgment.

"There's nothing to say," said Hayden curtly as he got up.

His dad seemed to want to say something but changed his mind as he pointed to the path that led to the exit. The path was even more sinuous and narrow in that part.

"Be careful not to slip," said his dad, giving him a glance over his shoulder.

Hayden focused on each step. On each breath.

"Argh!" his dad screamed as his foot slipped and he fell.

Before Hayden could understand what happened, his dad went tumbling down the slide.

"Dad? Dad, you okay?" yelled Hayden as he ran toward him, careful to not slip. His heart was pounding madly as he saw his dad land on the ground.

"Dad?" Hayden's voice was shaking as he tried to keep calm.

His dad grunted as he tried to sit. "Wasn't expecting that fall," he said, wincing with pain as he grabbed his right leg.

"You okay, Dad?" asked Hayden, feeling relieved to hear his dad talk normally.

"Yeah, I'm fine, just help me get up. I think I sprained my ankle. Hurts like hell," he hissed as Hayden grabbed his arm to put it around his shoulders.

"Be careful. Lean on me," said Hayden, trying to support his dad's weight. He was lighter than he had expected.

Had his dad lost weight? Hayden thought of all the times in the past months when his dad only had coffee for breakfast, not bothering to eat anything else. No wonder he was so light. Hayden felt guilty he had not been more supportive since his mother came back. His dad was clearly suffering. Suffering in silence. For his sake.

Hayden felt a wave of self-hate. He couldn't even be a good son for his dad. They reached the car, and he helped his father get in the passenger's seat.

"I'm taking you to the hospital, to make sure you didn't get a concussion," said Hayden as he got behind the wheel.

"It's not necessary, Hayden, I'll be fine after a couple of days. I just need to bandage my foot."

"No, you need to see a doctor," Hayden insisted.

His dad sighed. "You're more stubborn than your mom,

you know."

Hayden felt something sharp pinch inside of him.

His father sighed once more. "Hayden, you can't simply not talk about your mom forever."

"Why not?" he asked, hating how petulant he sounded. He tried to grip the wheel tighter to prevent them from shaking.

"Because she's your mom."

Hayden bit his lip, trying to keep the words inside, but they left anyway.

"Why did you lie to me all those years? Why did you never try to tell me the truth?"

"I didn't know how to tell you. What to tell you. I couldn't bear to see your pain," said his dad.

Hayden took the next exit that led to the hospital, his eyes trained on the road. He needed to focus. His fingers tightened around the wheel.

"Hayden, I'm sorry I didn't tell you sooner. I'm sorry you had to find out the hard way."

Hayden tapped his foot impatiently as he waited for his dad in the waiting room. The hospital's walls were still that ugly color that was neither green nor blue, a sad mix of both that would make even the cheeriest person depressed.

He remembered coming here when he broke his arm when he was twelve, after falling from a tree. His dad had been so worried yet remained calm. When they had put his arm into a plaster, the doctor told his dad to not worry.

"Your son has seen worse. This will heal quickly," he had added with a smile toward Hayden.

Hayden was too dazed by the painkillers to pay much attention to the doctor's words, but now they made perfect sense. He had been there before. The doctor had saved him when he was a toddler.

Once they were home, Hayden helped his dad to the sofa. "I'm gonna make dinner," he said.

"There's frozen pizza in the fridge. You can put it in the oven," said his dad as he made himself comfortable on the couch.

Hayden nodded. "Do you want anything?"

"Tea would be wonderful, thank you," answered his dad with a tired smile.

When he came back into the living room with a plate of pizza slices and tea, he saw that his dad had already fallen asleep. The pain medication worked its magic.

Hayden covered him with the blanket, deciding to let him sleep for a couple of hours before waking him up for bed.

"I'm sorry you had to go through so much pain alone, Dad," he whispered. He thought of his mom and his heart ached. What must she have endured all those years?

He put his arms around his legs and put his face on his knees, trying to keep himself from shaking. Brave hearts are loving hearts, his grandma had told him when he was small. He knew now how true it was. But he was realizing now that a loving heart also needs to be a forgiving one.

CHAPTER FORTY-TWO

Leah

Saturday morning, as Leah made herself a cheese sandwich and scrambled eggs, her dad came into the kitchen.

"This was on the front steps this morning." He placed a small, blue gift bag on the table.

"What is it?"

"I don't know, I didn't check. But your name is on it," said her dad, eyebrows raised.

When her dad left, Leah took the elegant, long box out of the bag. Inside was a delicate necklace with a golden sun pendant. Who could have given her such a beautiful gift? What for?

The card depicted a splendid sunrise. Her eyes welled up at the beautiful message inside.

Thank you for your letter, Leah. Thank you for sharing

your regrets and for caring for my happiness. You have no idea how much your words touched me. I wanted to give you this necklace as a thank you, so you can feel your mom close to your heart when watching sunrises and every day.

Hayden.

Leah wiped away the tear that slipped down her cheek and smiled. She was glad Hayden had read the letter, and maybe he even found it in himself to forgive his mom. Leah hoped he did. For both their sakes.

"Hey, Mom," said Leah softly as she stood in front of her grave, the marble gleaming under the cold sunshine. It was only the beginning of November, but already, winter could be felt in the air. The weather forecast had announced that snow would be early this year.

"I brought you these flowers," she said as she deposited the pink gladiolus on the stone. "They didn't have peonies."

She put her hands in the pockets of her coat.

"Yesterday, Dad and I were looking at our photo albums. We laughed so much at some of the memories. Remember that time when Dad tried to bake a cake for Mothers' Day, and he mistook the fine salt for sugar? Or the time I wanted to do the laundry and turned all of Dad's clothes pink?"

Leah smiled as she remembered her dad's incredulous expression when he took out his beige pants that had turned bright pink and his shirts.

She didn't tell her mom that they had also cried. In all of the pictures, her mom was always smiling or laughing, looking like she had just heard a funny joke or a nice surprise.

Leah envied how her mom was so optimistic, always finding the positive in every situation, no matter how crappy or difficult it was. Life was a game for her mom. A game meant to be enjoyed and played to the fullest.

"I got a nice gift today," said Leah, taking out the necklace box from her bag. "It's a necklace with a sun pendant," she said, taking the jewelry in her hands. The necklace shone bright in the sunlight.

Leah hesitated before putting the necklace on. She clasped the necklace around her neck and freed her hair, unzipping her coat slightly to put the necklace inside.

She touched the pendant as it rested nicely on her sweater.

"You know, Mom, I read a quote by Rumi recently. Maybe you've heard it. I know that you like Rumi's poems a lot. But this one really spoke to me. It said 'The Wound is the place where Light enters you.' Beautiful, isn't it? When I read the words, it was as if everything made sense."

Leah felt the words deeply. Like a switch was turned on in a dark room and she could finally see what she was not able to see before. As if the darkness inside her had dissipated.

She understood her love for her mom made her life meaningful, and the loss she felt was filled by the gratitude she felt for having someone that she loved so much that loved her back.

"Grandpa's right. Pain is the price we pay for love, and if we look at how much we get in return, it is a small price to pay," said Leah.

For the first time, remembering her mom didn't hurt as much. Like she had found a warm place in her heart to stay in forever.

She could smell her mom in the air. She could smell her love around her, warm like the sun caressing her face. A bird was singing in the branches and Leah looked up to see a blue jay in the branches. She also saw that the branches had become sparser, the yellow and red leaves now making a rich, colorful carpet under her soles.

The bird started singing louder.

Leah smiled. "Can you hear its song, Mom? It's singing for us."

The bird chirped joyfully as if acquiescing.

Her mom used to say that blue jays were like she and her father, they stayed together no matter what. They mate for life and don't let go of each other.

"Dad's better, too."

He might think he had her fooled, but she could always feel his sadness. Heavy and suffocating.

But these days, he had started breathing more easily. As if he, too, could feel his wife's presence through the veil of pain.

She looked at her mom's name, the flowers on the light marble.

"I'll come by again next week. Bye, Mom," she said with a smile before going out of the graveyard.

As she walked home, she felt light. At peace. With herself and the world.

CHAPTER FORTY-THREE

HAYDEN

As Hayden stopped in front of Kane's house, he felt nervous. Would Kane even want to see him? Hayden took a deep breath and rang the doorbell. Kane's little brother, Kai, opened it.

"Hey, Kai, what's up? Is Kane home?"

"He's in his bedroom," said Kai.

Hayden went up the familiar stairs and turned left to get to his best friend's bedroom.

The door was closed, and Hayden found himself hesitating as he was about to knock. It was funny how before he would simply barge in, not even bothering to knock, and now he couldn't even bring himself to tap.

He rapped on the door.

"Yeah?" said Kane.

"It's me," said Hayden, immediately hating how awkward he sounded.

He heard some noise and then the door opened, revealing Kane in gray sweatpants and a sweater. For a second, Hayden wondered if he was going to close the door on his face. Kane seemed to be debating the same thing, but after a few silent seconds, he sighed and pushed the door open wider.

"Come in," he said as he went back to his bed.

Hayden followed him and noticed how messy the room was.

"It's not like you to have your room so messy," commented Hayden before he could stop himself.

Kane shrugged. "I'm sure you didn't come here to pass judgment on my room," he said with almost a bored tone and not looking at Hayden.

That was a bad sign. Kane always looked everyone in the eye. Because he was Kane, and he was genuine and he always cared about everyone else.

Unlike Hayden.

Deciding now was not the time to beat around the bush, Hayden went straight to the point.

"Kane, I'm sorry, man, I was an ass."

Kane nodded. "Yup and a jerk."

"Totally, a bastardly jerk," agreed Hayden.

"A selfish idiot, too, if I might add," said Kane with a serious face and a raised eyebrow.

"The biggest there is," said Hayden, nodding, his hands in his pockets.

"A moron jackass," said Kane, still not looking at him.

Hayden winced. He deserved that. "I know," he said with a small voice, looking at his feet. Was that Kane's way of saying he wouldn't forgive him? Was this really the end of their friendship? He stood in his spot, feeling lost.

When Hayden decided Kane would simply continue to ignore him until he left, Kane spoke up. "Just so we're clear, my life is not perfect. You're telling me my life is perfect. Like I have no care in the world. My parents have their share of fights, too, you know? Sometimes, it's so bad, I wonder if they'll announce to us that they're going to divorce. But, then, they make up. And everything is fine. Until the next fight. So, no, my house isn't perfect, okay? And don't ever make me feel guilty for having two parents. I always tried to be supportive of you. Always tried to let you know you can tell me everything. When did I ever judge you for anything?"

Hayden had never seen Kane so incensed. He hadn't realized how much his words and attitude had hurt him. Leah was right, he had been really self-absorbed.

"I'm sorry, Kane. I'm sorry I was so selfish and blind." He hoped his friend could hear the earnestness in his voice.

"Even if you're the biggest imbecile I know, you're still my best friend," said Kane.

Hayden looked up and saw that he was smiling at him.

"And I won't change that for nothing in the world,"

finished Kane.

Hayden felt his eyes sting, but he refused to cry lest Kane call him a pansy. "Thanks, man, that went straight to my heart," he said, laughing, relief flooding his chest and making him feel light. Lighter than he had been in a long time.

"Are you gonna stand in the middle of the room all day?" asked Kane, extending the video game console.

Hayden took the green beanie bag that he always used to sit on and brought it close to Kane. Kane was playing Assassin's Creed, their favorite game.

It felt so nice, like the good old times. Without any words needed.

"Hayden," said Kane, his eyes focused on the video game.

"Hmm?" said Hayden, trying not to let the opponent win.

"I'm sorry, too. I should have been more patient instead of getting angry. I knew you were hurt, but I was blinded by my own anger," said Kane.

Hayden knew exactly how Kane felt, for he has been feeling that way since his mom came back. "It's okay, Kane, you don't have to apologize for that," he said.

"I was just so shocked and hurt that you didn't trust me enough to share such an important thing with me," Kane said, glancing at him, his eyes remorseful.

"I tried, trust me. But every time I tried to speak up, I didn't know what to say," Hayden said.

"Did you try to talk to your mom?" asked Kane.

"Not yet." Hayden sighed.

"I think you should go see her," said Kane, his expression serious.

"I know. I just–I don't know what to tell her."

"Maybe start by listening to her, and then, you'll take it from there," said Kane.

"Yeah, I should do that."

Kane's face lit up with his cheeky smile, and Hayden remembered how he had smiled exactly like that when they became friends, all those years ago.

"I won," said Kane, his dark eyes laughing.

"What?" exclaimed Hayden, looking at the screen. "Hey, you did that on purpose to distract me," he complained.

"Not my fault you can't multitask," tsked Kane, mock disapproval on his face. "I can't help it if I can have an intelligent conversation and beat you at the same time," he added with a smug smirk.

"I let you win today to make you feel better. Be prepared to lose next time," said Hayden.

"If that makes you feel better," replied Kane, chuckling.

Hayden knew he had a foolish grin on his face, but he didn't care. It felt good to be on good terms with his best friend again.

As he drove home that night, his stomach still full from Aunt Kim's dinner, he was so grateful Kane had forgiven him so easily, and he realized just how lucky he was to have such supportive and loving people in his life who were ready to give him a second chance when he messed up.

He knew now what he needed to do to heal. He just hoped it wasn't too late.

CHAPTER FORTY-FOUR

Leah

Leah saw Riley first. She waved and smiled when his eyes met hers. He approached the table where she was sitting.

"Hello," he smiled as he took the seat in front of her. "I love the interior," he commented.

She had invited him to the Gourmand café. "Wait till you try their cakes. You'll fall in love," grinned Leah.

"Wow, they have so many choices. Do you have a favorite?" he asked.

"They're all good, but it depends whether you're feeling up for a cake or a pie."

"What are you getting?" he asked.

"Caramel fudge," she said immediately. Some days, you just know what you need.

"Yum. I think I'm gonna try the red velvet," said Riley.

As they waited for their orders, Leah took off her coat and scarf.

"Nice necklace," said Riley.

She put a hand to her neck and realized Hayden's necklace had come out from under her sweater. "It's a gift from Hayden," she added, deciding that she didn't want to hide from Riley.

"It's beautiful," he said. "Did you talk to him?"

"No, not really," she said.

Riley laughed. "Why can't it ever be a simple yes or no answer with you, Leah?"

"We didn't talk directly," she explained. "I wrote him a letter and he left this today in front of my house this morning."

"How romantic," Riley smirked.

Leah rolled her eyes. "What's wrong with keeping up with the old tradition and using paper for what it was meant?" she asked.

"Nothing wrong with that. If you're in the 80's," said Riley, grinning.

Their orders came then, preventing Leah from replying something sarcastic. They attacked their desserts, too busy to enjoy their cakes to talk.

Leah wondered how to tell him what happened Friday when she went into the bathroom and had bumped into Olivia after school ended.

Unable to keep her mouth shut, Leah had asked Olivia if she had heard from Hayden. He hadn't been in school since Wednesday, but she didn't want to intrude on him. Since she left the letter for him, she hadn't received any response.

"He's okay, he's taking care of his dad who sprained his ankle," said Olivia.

Leah felt relieved and realized Olivia was watching her.

"I don't know if I should say anything, and I don't want to interfere, but I just wanted to let you know that Hayden is really sorry for the fight he had with you. I know he made mistakes, but he really didn't mean to hurt you, that I know for sure," said Olivia with a kind smile.

Leah thought about Riley telling her that Olivia loved Hayden. "Thank you for telling me this, Olivia, it means a lot. I thought he would never want to talk to me after everything I told him," Leah said.

"No, he knows he was in the wrong, too, and you only meant him well," said Olivia. She seemed to hesitate before adding, "He likes you very much, I hope you know that."

Leah wasn't blind, she knew there was something special between Hayden and her, but hearing Olivia confirm it made it strangely real for some reason. Like a secret out.

"Are you angry with me?" asked Leah before she could stop herself.

"Why would I be angry?" asked Olivia, surprised.

"Because… don't you like him, too?" Leah had a hard time meeting her eyes, feeling guilty.

"Yes, I do. I like him a lot. But he's first and foremost my best friend, and I only want the best for my best friend.

Whatever makes him happy, I will make sure he gets it. And you make him happy, Leah," said Olivia, her beautiful smile generous.

"I'm sorry, I didn't want to offend you with my question," said Leah, feeling ashamed.

"Don't be, you didn't say anything wrong or untrue. I can see that he's happy around you, and I hope you can forgive him," said Olivia.

"I realized that I was too harsh with him," she admitted.

Olivia smiled and Leah wondered if she had the right to tell her about Riley.

As the redhead made to leave, Leah spoke up, "Olivia, I have a confession to make. I overheard you and Riley in the library on Wednesday. I'm sorry I didn't interrupt you, but I felt so awkward, and I knew it was important, so I just stayed quiet," said Leah.

Olivia's surprised reaction changed to a sad smile. "It's okay, I guess it was time for my secret to be out."

"Riley didn't tell me anything at all, I swear," said Leah, not wanting to cause her friend trouble.

"That's Riley for you, always helping you even without you asking. Any girl would be lucky to be with him," said Olivia with a little shake of her head, a small smile on her lips.

"Yes, Riley is a very good friend indeed, but I think he will go an extra mile for you," said Leah, looking her straight in the eyes.

Olivia's eyes widened and she became pale. "What?"

she whispered. However, Leah could see that Olivia had known the truth all along.

"I know Riley will be angry with me for telling you this, but, like you, I want my friend to be happy, and I think he'll be happy with you," said Leah.

Olivia cradled herself, as if she suddenly felt cold. "I can't..." she mumbled. "I feel so guilty whenever I look at him, I can't stand myself when I remember how I acted with him," said Olivia.

Leah frowned, wondering if it was guilt that was making Olivia push Riley away. "I think you need to forgive yourself."

Olivia's beautiful green eyes were full of tears. "I'm trying, but it's hard. I keep remembering every time how cowardly I acted that night, and I feel so angry with myself," she said.

"I think you need to realize that you did nothing wrong, and you deserve to be happy, Olivia," said Leah.

Her heart ached as she observed the hurt in the red-head's eyes. Before she could stop herself, she put her arms around Olivia. The other girl embraced her, sobbing on her shoulder.

"Leah?"

Leah startled, realizing that Riley was talking to her while she had zoned out.

"Sorry, what did you say?"

"I was asking what you were thinking about?" asked Riley, raising his eyebrow.

"About Olivia, actually," said Leah, deciding to be direct.

Riley's amused expression turned confused. "Olivia?"

"Yes, I've been wanting to tell you that she and I saw each other on Friday afternoon, and we talked," said Leah.

"About?" asked Riley. His attention was focused on her so intensely Leah wanted to smile.

"About you," she said softly.

Riley looked unsure.

"She felt really guilty about what happened between you and that's why she's been so distant with you," said Leah, watching his reaction.

He folded his hands and put them in front of his lips, frowning.

"You won't say anything?" asked Leah.

"What do you want me to say?" asked Riley, sounding defensive.

"Riley, I know how you feel about Olivia," said Leah gently.

He looked at her, his eyes sharp. "I told you I've moved on," he said, his tone irritated.

Leah shook her head. "Not true. And you know that I'm right."

"What do you want me to do? I'm trying to move on, okay? Do you think I like feeling like that, knowing I have no chance?" exclaimed Riley.

Leah knew he was trying to hide his pain behind his anger. "I think you need to talk to Olivia."

"What?"

"She asked me if you'd be willing to meet her in the park in half an hour," said Leah, watching the time on her clock.

She had timed her move right. They had just enough time to reach the park. If Riley agreed, that is.

"What do you mean, she asked you? What's going on, Leah?"

"Just give the two of you a chance to talk honestly, that's all," replied Leah.

When they reached the park, Leah saw that Olivia was already waiting for them, sitting on a bench, looking in the other direction.

"She's here," said Riley, sounding like he didn't believe what he was seeing.

"Yes," said Leah with a smile. "Now go talk to her," she said, pushing him gently.

Riley looked scared. "I don't know what to say," he said.

"Just say what you've been wanting to say, that's all."

Riley nodded. "Thank you for doing this for me, Leah."

"You're my friend, no need to thank me. Now go before she gets tired of waiting," she said, grinning.

As she watched Riley approach Olivia, she saw the redhead turn around, as if sensing his presence and the smile that bloomed on her face made Leah smile.

As she walked home, she felt content all the way.

As Leah set the table for dinner in the evening, she felt happy. She didn't remember feeling like this since her mom passed away.

She took out the apple pie she had baked from the oven and smiled. It smelled delicious and the crust was beautifully golden. Just like her mom used to make it.

She left it on the stove to let it cool off and went to heat the broccoli and cheddar cheese cream soup. It was a perfect evening for a warm, filling soup.

The front door opened, and her dad came into the kitchen.

"Hmm, what smells so heavenly in here?" he asked.

"Apple pie. It's cooling off, but I can cut you a slice now," replied Leah.

"I'll take a piece later on," he said. "How was your day, pumpkin?"

"Good, yours? Do you want some soup?"

"No, thank you. I already ate. Kristina made chicken patties," he said as he put a Tupperware container on the table.

"Aw, that's so nice of her. I've been craving her patties since forever," smiled Leah, opening the lid of the container and taking out a baked patty. "Hmm delicious," she said, taking a bite. "I'm gonna text her to thank her later.

How's everyone? Jamie?"

"They're good. Jamie was upset you didn't come," he said. "We're planning to visit Grandpa tomorrow. I hope you're free?"

She nodded.

"I'm going to work a bit and then go to bed," said her dad, making to leave to go to his office.

"Dad?" said Leah.

"Yes?"

"Do you want to come watch the sunrise with me tomorrow?" she asked.

His eyes widened in surprise. This was something she had always done with her mom. Even after her mom passed away, the rare times she would go watch the sunrises, she preferred her own company. To keep everything intact. To cling to the past as long as she could. Until Hayden came with her, and she realized that it was good to not be alone.

Now she knew that moving on didn't mean she was forgetting her mom. It wasn't a betrayal. It was healing and accepting to create new memories. To continue to carry on and live on.

That's what her mom would have wanted her to do.

"Of course, pumpkin, I would love that," said her dad after a short moment of silence.

"Great, you'll love it," said Leah with a smile.

Her dad nodded and went out, looking happy. She realized she had forgotten her soup in the microwave, but before she could get it, her dad reappeared in the doorframe.

"Thank you for inviting me, pumpkin," he said, his eyes radiant.

"Thank you for agreeing," she replied with a smile of gratitude.

CHAPTER FORTY-FIVE

Hayden

Hayden's heart was beating painfully slow, as if his whole being was beating in unison. His mouth was dry. Constricted.

He looked at his shaking hands on the car wheel and tightened them around the leather.

You can do this, Hayden. You have to. You can't lose this opportunity.

His grandmother's smile flashed in his mind as he asked for her address, and she had patted his cheek lovingly.

"I'm so proud of you, my boy," she had said, her eyes full of light.

Hayden looked at the small house where he had stopped. It was quaint with yellow shutters on the windows. How would she react? Would she still want to hear him out? Was she even home?

He took a deep breath and, turning off the car engine, got out.

Each step was torture, but suddenly, there he was, knocking on her door.

He heard footsteps and the door opened to reveal his mother in a purple cardigan, her long hair in a ponytail.

Hayden could see himself in her and his heart ached. "Hi, Mom," he said, feeling his lungs burn with anxiety and fear.

"Hayden," she said, her expression of astonishment making her look vulnerable.

As Hayden stood there, his mind blank, the speech he had prepared forgotten, he realized that none of that mattered.

Only this moment mattered. Only their reunion.

"I already lost you once, Mom, I don't want to lose you again," he whispered, his hands on his sides, not bothering to hide his tears.

"Oh Hayden," said his mom, taking a step toward him and opening her arms.

Before he knew it, he was hugging her, and they were drowning in their tears, and he had the feeling he could never let go.

"I'm so sorry, Mom, so, so, so sorry. I never meant to hurt you. I was just so scared," he confessed through his tears.

He could feel his mom's sobs and he embraced her

harder, wishing to take away her pain.

“Oh, Hayden, if only you knew how long I’ve been waiting for this day. For being able to hold you in my arms and hear you call me Mom,” said his mom, her tears mingled with light laughter.

She was smiling at him, her eyes glistening, and Hayden wondered how he couldn’t see her love for him. How could he have been so blind?

They were sitting in the living room, their cups of tea on the coffee table.

“Are you sure you’re not hungry?” asked his mom. “I can make you something very quick.”

“No, Mom, I’m good, thank you. I’m really not hungry,” said Hayden. He was amazed at how comfortable he felt being around her.

She leaned back against the sofa, observing him. “You must be thinking how could I leave and abandon my own child? You cannot imagine how much I have come to regret my decision. I thought I was doing the right thing. The selfless thing. I was trying so hard to give you a good life. I didn’t think I deserved to be your mom when I couldn’t be a good mom,” she said, her voice breaking.

She was wringing her hands and Hayden put a hand on hers. “It’s okay, Mom. Dad told me everything.”

“He did?” she asked, surprised.

“Yes, he explained what happened. Your fights, how unwell you were, the bathtub incident and how he yelled at you, saying all those horrible things."

"I still wish I hadn't left," she said.

"Me too," he admitted before he could stop himself.

She looked at him with a desolate look on her face. "I'm so sorry, Hayden."

He nodded. "Please, don't apologize. I should be the one asking for your forgiveness. I was so angry, and I acted horribly with you. I'm really sorry, Mom."

"Hayden, even if it hurt, I understood your reaction. I could see your pain behind the anger, and it made me regret my decision even more," said his mom, her eyes shining with understanding.

"Why did you decide to come back? I mean, what made you go back on your decision?"

"Because I forgave myself and I realized that I deserved to be happy. That I deserved to be with my son," she said, a wobbly smile on her lips.

Hayden looked at her and put his arms around her. "Thank you for coming back," he whispered.

A couple of hours later, they were sitting in the same park they used to come to when he was small.

Remembering the old lady, Hayden told her mom about the strange encounter and how he had assumed the woman had mistaken him for someone else.

"I think I know who you're talking about. Mrs. Sauvé was a close friend of your grandmother. We used to come here often when you were a baby, and we would walk around the park with you in your stroller."

"I wish I could remember it," admitted Hayden.

His mom smiled. "You loved this park. You would always cry whenever we would leave early."

"Do you have pictures of my grandmother? Your mother?" asked Hayden, hesitant.

Her smile dropped. He wondered if he had hurt her with the request. Maybe it was still too painful for her.

"Of course," she said, recovering. "I would love to show you pictures of my mom. She loved you so much. You were the apple of her eyes."

Hayden took his mother's hand. "I'm sorry she passed away so soon. I'm sorry you had to go through such pain," he said.

His mom's eyes shone with unshed tears, and she smiled.

"I'm glad you're here, Hayden," she said.

Soon, the sun started setting and it was getting chillier.

"I guess we better go home before it gets too dark," said his mom, looking at the time.

They got up and made their way out of the park. Hayden had parked his car not far, on the other side of the street.

As the light turned green and they started crossing the street, they heard the sound of honking. The car seemed to come out of nowhere.

"Hayden, look out!" Before he could understand what was happening, his mom pushed him out of the way and he fell on the side, a few feet away.

He heard the screeching of tires and the impact as the vehicle hit his mom and she flew forward, skidding on the asphalt.

Dazed, he turned around and saw his mom sprawled on the road.

No! No! No! His heart pounding, Hayden got up and ran to her. “Mom!” he screamed as he ran faster and fell beside her, taking her in his arms. “Mom? Mom!” sobbed Hayden in panic.

“Hayden?” she whispered, her eyes unfocused, her forehead bleeding. She closed her eyes.

“Mom! Please wake up!”

A man approached them rapidly.

“I’m so sorry! I didn’t see her!” he said, white as a sheet.

“Call an ambulance!” Hayden yelled.

“Yes, yes,” the man said, looking for his phone in his pockets and running to his car when he realized it wasn’t on him.

“Oh Mom, please, don’t leave me,” said Hayden, holding her, sobbing. Her forehead was bleeding and gently, he put pressure on the wound to stop the bleeding.

“They’re coming,” said the other man.

Hayden hugged his mom tighter. “Help is coming, Mom, you’ll be alright,” he whispered.

In the distance, he could hear the sirens of the ambulance.

“I won’t let you go, Mom. Not anymore,” he promised in her ear as she lay unconscious in his arms.

Oh God, please let me wake up from this nightmare. Please don't let her die. Not when I finally got her back.

He clasped his hands together, putting them against his mouth to keep from screaming.

How could he ever make it up to her?

Feeling powerless, Hayden started praying. Clumsily. Fervently.

Please, God, don't take my mom. She has suffered too much already. I should have been hit by the car. I deserve that punishment. Please, God, please, don't take her away from me. Not when I have realized how much she means to me. How much I love her. How much I have missed her. I will do anything. I will ask for forgiveness every day. I will never ask for anything again. Please just let my mom be okay. That's all I'll ever ask of you, God.

"Hayden!" His father was running down the hallway toward him. "What did the doctors say?"

Hayden had never seen him so disheveled or worried. "I don't know," said Hayden listlessly, getting up. "I've been waiting here, but no one has come yet."

His father went to inquire at the receptionist.

Hayden let himself fall back into the blue chair with leather cover and metallic handles. They were cold and clammy. Or maybe it was his hands. He hated hospitals.

The sterile colors and the cold atmosphere. It smelled of despair. He couldn't stand the smell. He felt suffocated.

Hayden went to the bathroom. He looked at his reflection and hated the face he saw there. He could only see the pettiness, the selfishness, the bitterness, the ugliness of his soul.

"It's all your fault," he whispered hatefully. "You hear me? It's. Your. Fault."

The sight in the reflection was unbearable. Before he knew what he was doing, he punched the mirror. Hard.

The glass shattered under the impact and the shards went flying.

An explosion of pain shot through his left hand. His knuckles were raw and bloody. His hand throbbed, but it was as if he was looking at someone else's hand.

He felt numb. He was glad for the pain. His brain seemed to have switched off and went into shock mode to deal with the pain.

"Oh God, Hayden, what did you do?" said his father, opening the door of the bathroom and taking in his bleeding hand. "We need to get a doctor."

"I'm fine," said Hayden as he tried to pull away his hand, but he suddenly felt weak and dizzy. He took one step forward, and everything went dark around him.

CHAPTER FORTY-SIX

Leah

As Leah walked on the beach with her dad, she felt peaceful and happy. She took a deep breath of the fresh air, smiling, feeling the breeze on her face. She put her scarf around herself tighter. It was cold and still dark.

"Wow, I never saw a beach so empty," said her dad with a smile, watching the water.

"That's because you never came before sunrise," said Leah, chuckling.

"True, it's nice. Cold, but really nice."

The seagulls were flying above, squawking. Her dad bent down to pick up a seashell.

"That's a pretty seashell, don't you think?" he asked, giving it to her.

Leah looked at the pink, smooth seashell. "It is," she

agreed. The sandy beach had many small seashells of different shapes and sizes, varying between white, pink and gray.

"Oh, look, the sunrise," said her dad suddenly, looking at the horizon. Leah followed his gaze and smiled.

"Told you you'd like it," she said, watching her dad's reaction.

"Wow, it's quite a sight, isn't it?" he said. "Makes you feel small and insignificant."

"Mom used to always quote *Les Misérables*, saying, 'Even the darkest night will end, and the sun will rise,'" said Leah, watching the splendor of the sun illuminating the gray morning, casting away the dark shadows.

"She loved Victor Hugo," said her dad, a wistful smile on his lips, his eyes sad.

Leah put her arm around her dad's and leaned on him so he could feel her presence. *I'll always be with you, Dad.*

"She also loved to quote Robert Frost," she said, smiling at the fond memories. 'In three words I can sum up everything I've learned about life: It goes on.'"

Father and daughter looked at each other as they finished the sentence together and, hugged each other, seeking comfort from each other's presence.

Leah watched the sun make the water shine and knew that everything would be okay.

"Grandpa, do you still have Halloween candies left?" asked Jamie as they all sat at the dinner table at her grandfather's place.

"I might have a few left, ma chouette," said her grandpa with a smile. "But only if you finish your meal."

"Yes! I will!" exclaimed Jamie excitedly. "Tadi, do you know I was TinkerBell for Halloween and Jaiden was Silvermist?" asked Jamie, looking at Leah with a wide grin.

"Yes, your mom told me," said Leah, returning her smile. "I'm sure you looked ravishing, the both of you."

Jamie nodded. "Can you show Tadi the pictures, Mommy?" she asked, looking at her mom.

"Of course, my love. Once we're done dinner, you can show her yourself," replied Aunt Kristina.

As Leah sat on the patio, looking at the beautiful moon, her grandfather came to sit beside her.

"How have you been?" he asked her, his gaze affectionate. "It seems we didn't get the chance to talk much lately."

She smiled. "I'm good, how about yourself?"

"Never been better," said her grandfather with a big smile. "How's the jeune homme? What was his name again?"

"Hayden. He's good," said Leah.

"When is he going to visit? I quite liked him," said her grandfather, watching her.

"I don't know, we haven't talked much these days," she said, looking at her feet.

"Why is that?"

"We had an argument," said Leah. She knew her grandfather would be able to tell if she tried to lie.

"Ah, young love, complicated, isn't it?" said her grandfather, his smile kind.

Leah rolled her eyes. "It's not like that, Grand-père. Let's just say we disagreed about a certain situation concerning his mom."

"His mom?" asked her grandfather.

"It's a long story, and I'm not sure I'm even allowed to tell you about it. I don't know if Hayden would want it."

Her grandfather nodded. "Family problems can be complicated, that's for sure. And people we love can be unreasonable or hard to deal with. Obviously, I don't know what happened with Hayden and his family, but family ties are much harder to break. We don't get to choose it, but we also can't simply break it, you know? The bond between a parent and their child, it's a special one. It's not perfect, but I think it's one of the strongest there is. It was meant to stand the test of time and the trials and tribulations each relationship has. Anyways, I hope Hayden and his mom can overcome their problems."

"Me too, Grandpa," said Leah, putting her head on his shoulder as they watched the moon shine through the trees.

"Did I tell you that you're the best grandpa there is?" she added after a short moment of silence.

"And did I tell you that you're the best granddaughter there is?" he said with a chuckle.

"Shhh, don't let Jamie hear you or she'll have a fit," said Leah, laughing.

"She's also my favorite," said her grandpa, his laughter rocking his shoulders.

"Hey, didn't you say I was your favorite?" said Leah, poking him.

"I said you're the best," he replied.

"So? Isn't that the same?"

"You're both special to me in your own ways, for no relationship is alike."

Before she could reply, Jamie came through the door. "There you are! I was looking for you!" she exclaimed, coming to sit between her and grandpa on the swings.

Leah smiled and put her arms around her. Family was special, indeed.

CHAPTER FORTY-SEVEN

HAYDEN

Little Hayden looked at his chubby hands. He was tired from crying. He wanted his mommy. Where was she? Why wasn't she giving him his hugs and kisses? Reading him good night stories?

The door to his bedroom opened and his dad came in. He sat on the bed. "Hey, buddy, why aren't you sleeping?" asked his dad, looking at him with a sad smile. Hayden wondered why his daddy looked like he had been crying.

"I want mommy," he said, trying hard not to cry. He didn't feel like a big boy. He didn't want to be a big boy. He wanted to be mommy's baby again.

His dad looked at him in silence and took him in his arms.

"From now on, it's you and me, okay, little man? We need to have each other's back," said his dad.

Hayden didn't understand what was going on and he was scared, but his dad looked sad, and he didn't want to upset him. "Okay, daddy."

His dad hugged him and held him tight.

Somehow, Hayden felt like he was the one comforting his dad and not the opposite, not how it should be. He felt scared. His dad sat beside him and put an arm around him. The light of the night lamp was casting shadows on his dad and the walls. Hayden got closer to his father, but he was still scared. Despite his dad's arm around him, he felt alone. He wanted to ask when his mommy would be back, but he couldn't ask. Something was burning in his little chest, and he wanted the sensation to go away. It didn't let him speak.

Somehow, he realized that, from now on, it was only he and his dad in his world. His mom's face floated in front of him, and he closed his eyes, letting his hot tears fall to resist the temptation of running to her.

Until she became like a dream. A dream he couldn't remember.

Hayden felt movement around him and opened his eyes, only to be blinded by light. He groaned. Where was he? The bed didn't feel like his bed. He tried to move, but his dad's face appeared in front of him.

"No, Hayden, don't move. The nurse said not to get up until the IV is done," he said.

Hayden looked on his side and saw an IV tube attached to his arm.

"Hey, Dad," said Hayden, his throat parched.

"Where's Mom? Is she okay?" he asked, feeling the fear tighten his chest, constricting his throat.

"Yes, son, yes, she's fine. She's resting. The doctor said she suffered a concussion and a dislocated shoulder, but she'll be discharged soon," said his dad, his voice reassuring.

Hayden fell back on the pillow, feeling lightheaded and relieved. "Thank God, I was so scared," he breathed out.

"I know, son, I know," said his dad, sitting beside him.

"I'm sorry for scaring you," said Hayden, remembering his dad's expression when he found him in the bathroom earlier.

His left hand was throbbing dully, and he was glad for the painkillers for keeping the pain at bay.

"Hayden, I think I understand why you did that, but I can't have you thinking that it's your fault," said his dad.

"Mom pushed me out of the way, Dad," said Hayden, his face pinched in pain at the memory.

"Yes, Hayden, she did it because she's your mom, and she loves you," said his dad, putting a hand on his arm, careful to not touch his hand.

"I know, but I should have taken the hit, I'm stronger. I wish she hadn't gotten hurt trying to save me," he said.

His Dad looked at him, eyes sunk with exhaustion.

"You know, Dad, I was so angry, at first, when I learned the truth. But I still wanted to forgive her. Because I wanted to have her back in my life. I always wanted my mom in my life. But every time I thought of forgiving her, I thought I was doing wrong by you, I felt like I was betraying you," said Hayden, watching the ceiling, feeling tears trickle down his temples.

"Hayden, I only want your happiness. I only want what's best for you, you know that, right? Your mom and I, we only want your happiness, that's all that matters to us," said his dad, his voice tight with emotion.

Hayden turned to look at his dad who was watching him with compassion and pain in his eyes.

"I know, Dad. My anger made me blind." His eyes burned, and he turned away, not wanting to cry in front of his dad anymore.

"I know, Hayden, and I'm so sorry for that. I'm sorry for not telling you the truth and allowing the anger to take place in your heart."

Hayden heard his dad sigh and he turned to look at him. Before he could say anything, the door opened and in walked his grandparents.

"Hayden, my love, how are you feeling?" asked his grandma, approaching his bed and putting her hand on his forehead.

"I'm fine, Grandma," said Hayden, trying to smile for her sake.

"You gave us quite a scare, my boy," said his grandfather, and despite his stern expression, Hayden could hear the relief in his voice.

"Sorry," he said, the response automatically coming from his mouth.

It had always been like that with his grandfather. Both he and his dad always apologized while his grandfather always reprimanded them for not thinking or acting better.

"Do you want something?" asked his grandma, arranging his bedsheets.

"Something to drink would be nice," said Hayden.

His dad got up. "I'll go get you something," he said.

His grandfather followed his dad, leaving them alone.

His grandma sat on the bed and took his hand, careful to not apply pressure on the bandage. "Oh Hayden, I was so worried," she said, looking at him. Her eyes shone brightly, and her mouth was tight.

"I'm sorry, I didn't want you to worry, I just… I don't know what's gotten into me," said Hayden. He tried to sit up higher.

"Be careful," said his grandma, making sure the IV didn't fall while arranging his pillows behind his back.

"Did you see Mom?" he asked.

"Yes, she's resting," said his grandma.

"It was my fault. She pushed me so the car didn't hit me," he confessed, the guilt burning his chest.

"It's not your fault, Hayden. It was the driver's fault, if anything, and your mom did what any mother would do," replied his grandma, patting his knee.

"Well, I didn't deserve her protection. I was so horrible to her. I couldn't even be a good son," said Hayden, the words feeling like broken glass in his throat.

"Hayden, don't say that. Your mom understood your

pain," said his grandma.

Hayden glanced at her before looking down at his lap. There was a painful pressure behind his eyes and his throat felt scalding hot.

"Sometimes, I think I don't know how to love. I don't know how to make the people I love happy. I just end up disappointing them," whispered Hayden, swallowing through the pain of the words.

"No, Hayden, it's because you love so much that you hurt so much," said his grandma, putting a hand on his face and making him look at her.

Hayden felt a tear escape and his vision became blurry.

"I wish I could take back everything I did. Every hurtful word, everything," said Hayden, his voice strangled.

"We can't change our actions, my love, but we can always make things better," said his grandma with a smile.

"I don't deserve her love," said Hayden.

"Of course you do. She's your mother. She did everything out of her love for you." His grandma looked at him kindly.

Hayden felt his chin tremble and embraced his grandma, hiding the tears in the nook of her shoulder. "Thank you for always being there for me, Grandma," he whispered.

"Always, Hayden. Always," she whispered back, holding him tighter.

When Hayden approached her bed, he saw his mom was sleeping. She had a bandage on her head and right shoulder and tubes were going out of her left forearm. The monitors on the other side of the bed were beeping steadily.

He felt his heart beat painfully as gratitude coursed through him, to see his mom alive and well. He sent a thousand prayers to express how much he was grateful to God for giving him another chance and keeping his mom safe.

As if she could feel his presence, his mom's eyes fluttered before opening slowly. She looked tired and pale, but she smiled upon seeing him.

He sat in the chair and grabbed her hand gently. "Hayden," she said, her voice barely a whisper.

"I was so scared," said Hayden as he put his face beside her hand. Too ashamed to look her in the face, the guilt burning his throat. He felt her hand on his hair and looked up.

"I'm fine, I'm glad you were not hurt," she said with a tired smile. He could see that she was already drifting back to sleep.

He kissed her hand and stayed beside her for a long time, basking in the warm feeling of being a son near his mother. Of having his mom back in his life. His grandmother was right. Life was too short for resentment and anger. Now, he could breathe freely. The painful tightening of his chest was no longer present, and he could take full breaths. He could taste the joy of life.

Thank you for not giving up on me, Mom. For giving us another chance at happiness.

The next morning, Hayden made his way toward his mom's hospital room. He went home the evening before, promising his mom to be back first thing in the morning as they were going to discharge her.

When he woke up, his dad had already left, and Hayden wondered if he had gone to work. He had texted him but didn't receive any reply.

As he approached the room, he saw that the door was slightly open, and as he was about to go in, he heard his dad's voice, making him freeze on the spot.

"I wish I could take back the years and amend for my mistakes," said his dad, his voice sorrowful.

His mom stayed silent, and Hayden wondered if he should let his presence known. He felt prickles of shame in his back at listening to his parents, but he couldn't bring himself to enter the room. He needed to hear his mom's reply.

He gripped the handle tighter, trying to breathe slowly. His heart was pounding painfully.

The silence in the room was broken by his mom's deep sigh.

"Liam, if only you knew how many nights I spent thinking what I should have done differently. But life doesn't work like that. We just need to carry on, trying our best to make better decisions in the future," she said, her voice tired.

He could almost picture her sitting on the bed, her eyes closed, her features drawn by exhaustion. His heart squeezed.

"I never stopped thinking about you, you know," said his dad, his voice strangled.

"I always thought about Hayden and you," replied his mom, her voice getting stronger. "Thoughts of Hayden pulled me through the worst of my depression. Whenever I felt darkness swallow me whole, Hayden was the light to guide me back."

Hayden swallowed hard, biting the insides of his cheeks to keep from crying. He wondered when the guilt would stop feeling so raw.

"But you would never understand because you didn't have to live without Hayden," added his mom, her voice unflinching.

"I'm so sorry," said his dad, his voice breaking. "I never stopped missing you, but I didn't know what to do."

His mom stayed silent.

"Can you find it in yourself to forgive me?" asked his dad, his voice sounding fearful.

Hayden held his breath, his knuckles turning white as he held onto the door.

"Liam, I already forgave you a long time ago. That's how I was able to go on. Because I found the strength inside of myself to forgive both you and me, I was able to realize that I deserved to see my son," his mom said.

"Of course, he's your son," said his dad.

"I also wanted to thank you," added his mom.

"What for?" asked his dad.

"For showing that I can be strong by myself, and I don't need anyone to pull me through the difficulties."

Silence fell and Hayden retreated from the door. He had heard enough.

He walked down the corridor and leaned against the wall, closing his eyes, feeling the sting of tears behind his eyelids.

"I'm so sorry, Mom," he whispered to the empty corridor.

He opened his eyes, wiping his eyes almost angrily.

He would make it up to her. He would make up for all those lost years by showing her so much love, she would never hurt again.

I promise you, Mom, from now on, I'll always be there for you. No matter what.

"Wait, let me help you," said Hayden as his mom tried to put on her coat.

"Thank you, Hayden," his mom said, smiling, putting her hair out of the way with her good hand.

He put the coat around her, careful to not touch her bandaged arm and helped her to sit.

She was still weak, but the doctor said she was free to go home.

His grandma packed the rest of his mother's belongings and held the door open so he could wheel her out.

The nurse had been kind enough to provide a wheelchair so his mom didn't have to walk all the way to the parking lot.

His Grandma was going to stay over at his mom's place for the next few days to help her, and while he was planning on visiting daily, he felt reassured knowing she wouldn't be alone.

After dropping his grandma and mom at her place, he went home.

His dad had left the hospital after his conversation with his mom, and he hadn't gotten the chance to talk to him since.

"Liam, stop acting like a child. Haven't you learned your lesson?!"

His grandfather's voice boomed from the office and Hayden felt his pulse quicken as he strode inside.

"Dad, you're saying it as if Aviannah did it on purpose.

You know very well what she was going through," said his dad.

As Hayden stepped in the room, he saw that his dad was pacing the room while his grandfather sat on the leather chair, watching his son with disapproval.

"That woman doesn't deserve your forgiveness," said his grandpa, his voice icy.

"Stop, Grandpa. Stop it. What did Mom do to you to deserve such hate?"

His grandfather turned around, his surprise evident on his face before his expression turned cold.

"What did she do? Did you forget she left you?" he asked.

"You wouldn't understand because you don't know how hard it was for her, but she did it out of love."

"Hayden, this woman abandoned you, and you're talking about love?" His grandfather scoffed, his nostrils flaring in anger.

"She was sick, and you know it. And yet, you're always against her. Always treating her like she's some callous person who left us on purpose."

Hayden looked at his grandfather, trying to remain calm.

"She thought her leaving was for the best, Grandpa. Not because she was egotistical. It took me a long time to understand her sacrifice, and I won't let you badmouth her anymore. She's my mom, whether you like it or not."

He clenched his fists, trying to take deep breaths. He felt a pounding in his left temple and knew he'd have a splitting headache soon.

His grandfather looked at him coldly and his dad looked so tired and defeated, Hayden wanted to shield him from all the bad things he had to endure.

He took another deep breath.

"Look, Grandpa, I didn't mean to shout at you. But please, stop making mom the bad one here. She's not the only one to blame and she shouldn't bear the guilt alone. She deserves to be happy. We all deserve to be happy."

His grandfather stayed silent, and Hayden thought he was going to leave without a word.

But he sighed and put his hands to his face. He seemed old and spent.

"Hayden, son, I understand your wanting to protect your mother, she's your mother after all, like you said. But it's not as black and white as you make it out to be."

"I never said that. I said we all deserve to forgive and move on, don't you think, Grandpa? Let it be behind us so we can all heal."

His grandfather looked at him, an unreadable expression on his face, before nodding and approaching him.

He took him by the shoulder and looked him in the eye.

"All I ever wanted, Hayden, was your happiness. Please believe me. All I care about is protecting my family."

"I know, Grandpa."

His grandfather sighed and hugged him tight before releasing him just as quickly.

"I better let you rest, then," he said.

He glanced at his son and, without another word, left the room.

"Hayden," said his dad, approaching him. He seemed to be on the verge of tears and Hayden hurt seeing him like that.

"Dad, please don't think I'm blaming you," said Hayden, seeing his father's eyes.

His dad shook his head and his face crumpled. Hayden put his arms around him, hugging him and he held him tight as he felt sobs wreak havoc on his body.

He didn't know how long they stayed like that, crying and holding each other, but it felt good.

He was so grateful to have his mom back in his life and that he found his way back to his dad.

CHAPTER FORTY-EIGHT

Hayden & Leah

As Hayden walked toward the school, he felt different. When he approached his locker, he saw that Kane was already waiting for him. "How are you?"

"I'm good, yourself?" asked Hayden, trying to open his lock, but his bandage was making it difficult to turn the knob.

"Let me," said Kane, taking the lock out of his hands and quickly inputting the combination.

"Thanks," said Hayden, scratching his neck. He felt like a baby that needed babysitting.

"Hey, guys," said Olivia, coming up behind them.

"Hi, Liv," said Hayden.

"How are you feeling?" asked Olivia, worry in her eyes as she took a look at him.

Since Kane and Olivia had learned what happened, they'd been visiting every day.

Hayden smiled. "Good, but I wouldn't mind another few days off," he said.

Kane smirked, punching him lightly on the shoulder. "Slacker, I don't think you can afford to take any more days. The teachers are going to have a fit," he said, laughing.

Hayden took his textbooks, and they made their way to their class. Hayden looked down the corridor, but Leah was nowhere in sight. He felt Olivia watch him, and he smiled. She smiled back, her smile real.

"Don't worry, I'm sure she'll be in later," she said, guessing who he was looking for.

It felt good to have things back to normal between them.

Kane smirked. "Oh, I see what has you all preoccupied and here I thought you were actually worried about your schoolwork."

"Why should I be worried about that when I have my bestie who will help me out?" replied Hayden with a smirk of his own.

"Don't be so cocky or I'll just decide I won't help you at all," said Kane, rolling his eyes.

"It's okay, I have my other bestie to help me," grinned Hayden, winking at Olivia, who rolled her eyes and smiled.

"Fickle," coughed Kane before Hayden punched him on the shoulder.

"Looking out for my best interests," replied Hayden.

They laughed as they went into their class, and Hayden never felt better. It was good to have his friends back.

The day went by quickly, and at the end of the day, Hayden went to see his coach in his office.

His coach was filling some papers, sitting at his desk.

"Hi, Coach," Hayden said, pulling his backpack higher on his shoulder.

"Hayden," said his coach, looking surprised, but happy to see him. "How have you been, son?" he asked him. Seeing his expression, Hayden could see that his coach knew what had happened. His dad had called his school, after all.

Hayden nodded. "Much better now, thanks," he answered. He decided there was no point beating around the bush.

"I was wondering if I can come back to the team?" he asked, trying to keep eye contact with his coach as he squirmed inside. He had already imagined the refusal ten times while making his way to the gym.

"Come back?" repeated his coach, his expression unreadable.

"Yes, I want to play on the team again," he said. "If I can, that is," he added.

His coach stayed silent.

Ah well, at least I tried, thought Hayden, preparing to accept the rejection.

"When did you ever leave?" asked his coach.

Hayden looked up at him in surprise. His coach had a small smile on the corner of his lips.

"I'm sorry I acted like an ass," said Hayden. "I won't let the team down again," he said, relief coursing through him.

"I know, son. I'll see you tomorrow at practice," said his coach, smiling.

"Thank you, Coach," said Hayden, still not believing it had been so easy.

His coach gave him a playful wink and Hayden walked away.

He felt like everything was falling back into place and it was an amazing feeling.

As Hayden reached the parking lot, he saw Riley ahead of him, toward his car.

"Hey, Riley," he called out after him.

Riley turned around and raised his eyebrows, watching him quizzically. Hayden realized it had been a long time since he called him by his first name.

"Hemingway," he said, his expression cautious.

Hayden wondered how he was going to say what he wanted to say. When he had seen him, he had called him impulsively and now he didn't even know what to say.

"Look, I wanted to tell you that Olivia told me the truth. About that night at the party. She explained what you did for her, and I wanted to thank you. And I wanted to apologize, too. I'm sorry I was such a jerk, and I assumed the worst about you. I was blind."

Riley didn't say anything at first, almost as if he was trying to judge if he was being sincere. Hayden's earnest expression must have convinced him he was being genuine, for he nodded. "It's okay, Hemingway, no hard feelings. It's all good. Let bygones be bygones," he added with almost a smile.

"Thanks, man," said Hayden, extending his hand for a handshake.

Riley looked at his outstretched arm and Hayden thought he wouldn't take it. But after a slight hesitation, he slowly took his hand and shook it.

"See you, then," said Hayden.

Riley nodded and left.

Hayden turned to walk away and was surprised at how light he felt. At how good he felt.

Leah

As Leah made her way to the beach, she saw that Hayden was already there. He was looking at the horizon and seemed absorbed in his thoughts. She put on her hoodie as she approached him, the cold wind making her shiver.

"Hey," she said softly.

"Hey," he said, turning to look at her with a small smile.

"I hope your mom is feeling better," she said.

"She is," he said, his expression serious as he watched her face.

"Thanks for coming, Leah," he added. "It really means a lot."

She nodded, unsure of what would be an appropriate answer. The sun reflected on the water, making it sparkly. Like a thousand diamonds spread on the surface. She looked at the sand, a habit now, and saw a small, beautiful seashell. She bent to pick it up, conscious Hayden was watching her silently.

"Do you want to walk?" she asked.

He nodded and followed her lead, putting on his hoodie as well. The wind was particularly strong on the beach. She watched their footsteps leave footprints in the wet sand—it had rained in the morning—and wondered if he was waiting for her to say something.

"I wanted to thank you," he said at last.

"For what?" she asked.

"For making me open my eyes and realize the truth. For telling me what I should have known all along. About my mom. About my selfishness and my ungratefulness. I realized how much of a horrible jerk I was being when I almost lost my mom."

"I'm glad she's okay now. That you're both okay and that you have reconciled," said Leah.

She didn't know Hayden's mom a lot, but she seemed like such a kind person, and she had such a sad past, she felt it was unfair for her to suffer even more.

"Me too," he nodded, his expression serious.

She smiled. "I'm really happy for you, Hayden. You and your mom deserve to be happy."

"I just wish I hadn't caused her so much hurt, you know."

"We all make mistakes. That's why forgiveness exists."

It was his turn to smile before his expression turned serious. "I also wanted to apologize," he said, looking her straight in the eyes.

"You don't have anything to apologize for. If anything, I should have been more understanding of your pain."

He shook his head. "Don't say that. You did a lot. You tried to help me. It was I who refused to see the truth. To admit I was wrong. It was easier that way."

"Sometimes, we do things out of fear of being hurt. We act irrationally because we are afraid. I guess that's what it means to be human," she said with a small smile.

He nodded. "Leah, I thought a lot about what you said in your letter, and I just wanted to tell you that I'm sure your mom could see how much you were hurting, and she understood your reaction. It came from your love for her and from your fear of losing her. She knew you were in pain."

Leah tried to smile. She knew that Hayden was right, but it didn't make it easier.

However, even if the pain never lessened, she had gotten stronger. She knew now that it was something that she would have to live with all her life and instead of letting it destroy her, she would use it as a testimony to her strength.

They turned to look at the magnificent sunset.

"It reminds me of a quote from one of my grandma's quotes on the walls of her living room," Hayden said. "I remember thinking it was a nice quote. I reread it a few days ago and now I can fully appreciate what the author—I think it was Tagore—meant when he said: 'Clouds come floating into my life, no longer to carry rain or usher storm, but to add color to my sunset sky.'"

"It's beautiful. I love it," said Leah, smiling at the setting sun.

He smiled. "I know, right? Never knew words could be so healing."

She realized how much he had changed. He looked peaceful and open. Gone was the moodiness, the anger. She smiled, happy to see him this way.

She looked on the horizon and saw the sun setting, bathing the sky in hues of purple and blue with streaks of bright orange.

"I better go home. I still have a lot of homework to do," she said.

"Yeah, me too," said Hayden. "I have so much catching up to do." He grimaced.

"Don't worry, I can help you," said Leah with a genuine smile. "At least in English since our project is due very soon."

He laughed, "You'll make me work harder, if anything."

She laughed, "Well, at least, you'll get a perfect grade."

He laughed, his eyes twinkling. "Then, I should only be grateful, in that case."

"You should," said Leah, grinning.

"I'll drop you home," he said as they made their way home, the sun disappearing behind them.

Bahora Saitova

grew up in Montreal, Quebec and graduated from McGill University. Since she was little, she had two obsessions: chocolate and words. She learned that words give your existence meaning and chocolate gives your life flavor, so she makes sure she's surrounded by both at all times. If she's not writing with a cup of tea at her desk, then, she can be found reading, watching movie adaptations, planning her next trip or daydreaming about fictional characters. She is currently working on her second novel.

Instagram: Bahora_Saitova

Twitter: @BahoraSaitova

www.ingramcontent.com/pod-product-compliance
Lightning Source LLC
Chambersburg PA
CBHW020523310726
48979CB00014B/2180/J

* 9 7 8 1 7 7 7 8 9 7 4 2 0 *